# PHANTOM REALITY

# PHANTOM REALITY

*The Phantom Series Book* I

## LAURA C. REDEN

# CONTENTS


| | |
|---|---|
| Prologue | 1 |
| Chapter 1 | 3 |
| Chapter 2 | 20 |
| Chapter 3 | 36 |
| Chapter 4 | 53 |
| Chapter 5 | 69 |
| Chapter 6 | 83 |
| Chapter 7 | 97 |
| Chapter 8 | 110 |
| Chapter 9 | 125 |
| Chapter 10 | 140 |
| Chapter 11 | 154 |
| Chapter 12 | 170 |
| Chapter 13 | 182 |
| Chapter 14 | 192 |
| Chapter 15 | 206 |
| Chapter 16 | 219 |
| Chapter 17 | 234 |
| Chapter 18 | 246 |
| Chapter 19 | 259 |
| Chapter 20 | 272 |
| Chapter 21 | 284 |
| Chapter 22 | 297 |
| Chapter 23 | 311 |
| Chapter 24 | 326 |

Thank you                                    343
About the Author                             345
Notes for Book Club:                         351
Notes for Book Club:                         353

PHANTOM
REALITY
1
LAURA C.
REDEN

I always wanted a scar. Nothing revolting. Just a gash. A sexy one that said I was dangerous . . . or that I could be. Like, you didn't know what you were getting into when you met me. I'd be mysterious, and often, I'd be known as "that girl." But as the tires lifted off the highway and the sky fell sideways through the windshield of my car, all I could think was, *Not like this. Not now.*

# CHAPTER 1

The loons let out their long, mournful wails across Baylor Lake, serenading us with their haunting symphony. The water was deep with deceit, and the summer air was warm and thick with secrets that kicked up like the dust when the light breeze blew. The dusk-lit sky illuminated the water's glassy surface, but there was no way of telling what lay below.

But all I could see now was the silhouette of Noah and the wide grin on his face that screamed of freedom and the beginning of our independence. It was too dim to see his blue eyes or the sandy golden hues of his hair. Too dark to see the fine lines around his eyes that I knew were there with that smile he wore. The one that had brought butterflies to my stomach for the past two years. And it was far too dark to see my dead grandmother standing by the water's edge.

"No way!" Asher exclaimed, admiring the view from the back porch. He stretched across the railing, taking in the lake's serenity. Yeah, he was excited. We all were.

"We get to stay here all summer?" Kimber asked in disbelief, as she wrapped her hand around the crook of Asher's elbow.

"This place is amazing, Kins! Why haven't we been here before?" Noah poked me in the side playfully, and I smirked, biting the inside of my cheek as I basked in his attention. The cabin had been left to my great uncle Tanner when his parents passed. My family had visited every summer since. But this summer was different. The twelve of us were here for two months, celebrating our high school graduation. Some of us were here to say goodbye before moving away for college, others were here for the memories, and I had my suspicions that at least one of us was here to hook up. *Levi.* But it was probably more than just him. We were a rowdy bunch, and we were young and full of promise.

That wasn't why I was here, though, and that's not why I'd invited the group to come with me. While it's true I'd wished for Noah's heart while blowing out my eighteenth birthday candles, I was here to celebrate my independence. I'd been planning the trip with Lainey our entire senior year, and nothing was going to change that. *Nothing.*

It was the first time we'd be away from our parents for an extended length of time. This summer, we hung in the balance between needing to be looked after by our parents and being fully capable adults, living on our own. Come fall, most of us would set off to realize our full potential. But this summer? This summer, we had each other. We would be a safety net for each other if one of us fell. We would look out for one another. We would be our own family of misfits.

"I'm going in!" Mason yelled. He ripped his T-shirt off and threw it to the floor. Scarlett May threw her hands up in the air and hollered before taking off her top. Her bra was a sweet baby blue, full of intricate eyelet lace. Emma's eyes grew large as she watched Scarlett May strip down to a matching lace thong. It sent the boys into a frenzy of adrenaline and testosterone, and before I knew it, they were all taking their clothes off. I felt it too. The heat flushed my cheeks and rolled down to my belly, making me want to do something crazy—something stupid.

Luggage was dropped and backpacks tossed. Shoes were kicked off and flew through the air, some rolling down the hill toward the lake. I was transfixed by the shadow of Noah's obliques, my eyes traveling further down. My breath quickened.

"Last one in's a rotten egg!" Asher yelled in a full run. Kimber threw her duffel bag to the ground, and I shrugged off my backpack onto the wooden planked deck and shimmied out of my jeans. Every single one of us stripped and ran down to the dock, even Emma in her plain cotton bralette. The grass was dry, and the pine needles were sharp beneath my feet. My heart raced with excitement as I ran side by side with my best friends to the old wooden dock to begin what promised to be the best summer of our lives.

I had the faintest memory of running past my gran. It wasn't that I saw her there in the flesh; it was more like I felt her presence. I knew she was watching. Always watching. She'd died of cancer just three days shy of my eighteenth birthday, and ever since, I'd been having dreams about her. Realistic dreams. Lasting dreams. The kind that stuck with you long after you woke. Her presence haunted me when nobody was there and my mind fell quiet. Losing her was harder than anything I'd ever gone through in my short life. But her presence thereafter, terrified me.

I loved my late gran—more than anything—but that didn't mean I wanted her looming over me. Watching me from the shadows. Her passing had been painful enough. So much so, I could barely acknowledge it. I'd rather forget. Push it away and never look at it again. But she wouldn't let that happen. And to my surprise, she'd apparently followed me to Baylor Lake. I didn't know why, but I knew it made me feel legitimately nuts.

There was a part of me that thought I could hide all

that crazy behind my friends. Bury it in my feelings for
Noah and forget all about the pain of losing somebody I'd
loved while I busied myself at the Water's Edge Concert,
the Fourth of July Baylor Parade, and Summerfield State
Fair. It was going to be the best summer yet, and I was sure
by the end of it, I'd no longer be haunted by dreams of my
late gran. And I'd no longer feel the hollow ache in my
heart when I was reminded of her. I'd leave this lake house
a woman, no longer a girl afraid of the things she couldn't
see. I was ready to put the childish fears to bed.

It was no surprise that Mason Fry was the first one in
the water. He flipped off the dock and landed with a heavy
splash. We were all a little crazy here, but Mason was
known for it. In a world of impulsivity, Mason was the one
you could count on to do something outrageous. Seconds
later, Asher dove in. His body was like that of a Greek god,
and his goddess was Kimber, who stood at the edge of the
dock with her arms wrapped around her tiny waist.

"Come on!" Asher yelled, slapping the water. Kimber
plugged her nose and took the leap with much trepidation
and a small squeal. Ethan Patrick pushed Emma in, and I
laughed at her as I leaped onto Noah's back, wrapping my
legs around his tight core. He grabbed the backs of my
knees and took off running down the dock. I held my
breath as he launched into the air, and for just a moment, it
was like I was flying.

I had my whole life ahead of me . . . and my legs

wrapped around Noah's waist. Something in me felt different. Like I was on the brink of a new life. And I had the power to make of it whatever I wanted. Whatever I longed for. Change was just around the corner, and it was mine for the taking.

I tightened my grip across his chest as we plunged into the lake. The water was chilly and invigorating. Just what we needed after a long idle plane ride. I let go of Noah's sleek body and dared to open my eyes underwater. My eyes stung as I searched for him, but the water was far too dark to see anything. I kicked to the surface and filled my lungs. As I did, Trinity dove in next to us, and I turned just in time to see Lainey jump in. Her dog, Gunner, was barking at the end of the dock, pacing back and forth. It didn't take long before he dove in after her, and his brown head popped out of the water as he swam to her side.

Lainey was my best friend. She was cautious and timid, and she suffered from anxiety. I had always thought it was a trait passed down from her mother. Her mom had barely let her come to the lake house. We'd begged and begged for the better part of our senior year, and bringing the dog was one of her conditions, among many others. Call every night, don't stay out late, don't take drinks from strangers, don't walk alone. The list went on and on. The dog was her comfort, though, and we'd all agreed he would be our group's mascot. Everyone cheered when Gunner leaped into the water.

Noah grabbed my waist, and while his hands fumbled around on my bare skin, I splashed water in his face, an oversized goofy smile on my face. I reached out for him, but Trinity got to him first. She dunked his head under the water, stealing the bits of attention that kept me fed. But I was hungry for more, and she was getting on my nerves. I swam away so I wouldn't have to see him flirting with her. It was easier to deal with when I closed my eyes to it.

Trinity was bold, but more than that, she was malicious. She didn't really want Noah. I knew that. She only wanted me to know that she could have him if she wanted. I couldn't stand it, always being trumped by her, but she was a part of our group, and whether I liked it or not, I was the one who'd invited her. I hadn't been able to stand the thought of being socially uncomfortable all senior year as we planned a trip for the group but excluded her. So, against my better judgment, I'd invited everybody. And I can't say I was surprised when she continued her hunt for Noah. Just because it was my cabin we were staying at didn't mean she'd back off from my crush. And if anything, she had more to prove now.

"The water is so refreshing!" Lainey said, swimming up to me.

"Isn't it?" I asked, reaching for Gunner as he swam laps around us. He was a strong swimmer, and after a long day on the plane, this was exactly what he needed before a good night's sleep. The dog required lots of exercise, and if he didn't get it, he'd tear up the yard, digging holes by the dozen; I'd seen him do it. "Swim boy, swim!" I called out, laughing at the way his head bobbed.

I glanced at Noah as he wrestled with Trinity in the water. I tried not to imagine all the things I couldn't see below the water's surface. Like an iceberg, I knew only a fraction was visible.

It was everything I wanted in that moment—to switch places with Trinity. Whatever power I thought I had over Noah paled in comparison to hers. I dipped under the water, letting the air leave my lungs slowly in little air bubbles as I sank into a pocket of warm water. It was peaceful there—the voices muted and the buoyancy suspending my arms. I wanted to stay there forever, but I needed to breathe. I kicked, bringing myself back up to the surface. And when I opened my eyes, I saw a dark figure standing on the dock. The dusk sky had nearly given way to nightfall, and I couldn't tell who had gotten out of the water. But when Noah left Trinity for me, none of it mattered anymore.

"Kins! You've got to save me!" he called out, his long strides propelling himself toward me.

"Oh yeah? Or what?" I teased, backpedaling. *Come and get me.*

"Or what? Or what!? You just wait right there because I'm gonna get you!" he said, picking up speed. He swam past Asher and Kimber, who were locked in an embrace, and I licked my lips in anticipation.

"Give it your best shot," I said. I weaved my hands back and forth, treading the cool water and slightly pushing away from the group. I wanted to get Noah alone. The smile on my face faded when I peeked above Noah's head and saw the figure still watching, waiting. An unsettled feeling spawned in my stomach. But when Noah reached me and grabbed my hand, I screamed with delight, splashed him in the face, and turned away from him, swimming deeper into the lake where perhaps a kiss could be stolen.

"You're going to get it now!" He swam after me. I didn't know what *it* was, but I wanted it. I wanted it really bad. Though I still intended to make him to work for it. I kicked hard, swimming as fast as I could. But Noah Hampton was a swim captain—and football player—and he closed the distance between us with a few powerful strokes. I felt him grab my foot, and I screamed out, slowing intentionally to get caught. *Catch me.*

I ached for him to grab more than just my toes, but when he grasped my thigh, the thrill I felt was short-lived. The lust turned to panic in a matter of seconds. I was pulled under the water violently with such force, I barely had time to grab a breath of air. It didn't feel like the hands of a lover or the touch leading to a first kiss. I didn't know what had a hold of my thigh, but I knew it was too strong and too fast to be human. I opened my eyes to see the surface disappear in a flurry of white bubbles.

My heart pounded against my chest as I tried to free my leg from the jaws of . . . Hand! It was a *hand*! Somebody's hand had a death grip around my leg. I clawed and scraped at flesh as I thrashed around in the water, fighting with every ounce of my strength. For a moment, I thought I was gaining momentum, and when my hand broke the surface, I splashed wildly. But there was nothing within my reach to take hold of. Nobody there to help me. No safety net.

My lips breached the surface, and I let out a guttural scream for help before I was pulled back under the water. I took one tiny gulp of air with me. It wasn't enough. The pressure built as I plunged into the depths of the dark lake. I gave it everything I had, but when the pockets of warm water surrounded me, I knew it was too late. I was too deep. And too weak.

A calmness came over me as the fight fled from my veins, and I gave in to the threat. A butterfly caught in a web, the fangs sinking in, spreading the venom and slowly paralyzing it. *So, this is it? This is how I die?* I had no other choice, ensnared deep within the malevolent grip. I watched my life pass before me as I searched the water for answers. And when all I saw was blackness, I closed my eyes in preparation for sleep. There were no answers for me to claim that night, only fear.

Sparks of light flashed behind my eyelids—brainwaves firing off their last sparks. Images flashed of a red door, crows by the hundreds, and a tall stone tower. A large circle dazzled me with lights and drew me in. A Ferris wheel rotated in my mind's eye. It was so welcoming, and I was thankful that, as death was upon me, I could conjure one last beautiful sight. Something to take the focus off my last fleeting moments. And for the first time, I was comforted that my gran's ghost was nearby to take me home.

I watched the Ferris wheel sparkle with magic in the summer air until I abruptly felt the release of my pinched thigh. It hardly registered at first. I remained paralyzed as I began floating toward the surface. The pocket of warm water moved down my body as I rose, free of my attacker. I didn't wake until a breath of air filled my lungs, and then a crash of adrenaline coursed through my veins. I screamed instinctively, hammering the water as I spun around looking for help. But there was no one there.

Disoriented, I looked out into the open water and back again to find the dock. But the dock was nowhere to be seen. The lake was quiet, the water still. The loons sang their haunting calls, cutting through the blanket of darkness. I was alone.

Where was I? Where did everybody go? How had I gotten into the middle of the lake? And how was I going to get back? I feared the depths of the water. Was that thing still down there? Would it grab me again? I had no idea how much I was bleeding into the water, and I feared the scent would attract the predator again, and it would come to finish me off. I began to swim, only to stop after a few strokes. Which direction? I couldn't see anything. Even the blackened night sky was barely discernible from the lake's surface.

My heartbeat echoed in my ears, and the sensory deprivation threatened to swallow me whole. I didn't know right from left and could barely tell up from down had I not felt the water.

"Are you okay?" A guy's voice called out from the void and echoed all around me.

"H-Hello?" I called back in a breathy tone, spinning around in search of help.

"Hello there. Are you okay?" The voice rang out again.

"No! No! I need help! Please!" I said in a voice that didn't belong to me but to a young girl not yet ready to be on her own. A girl who was still afraid of the dark.

"I'm right here. Give me your hand." The water lapped against the canoe that appeared beside me, seemingly out of nowhere. I reached my hand out and took hold of safety. Warm, dry hands plucked me from the lake of nightmares, and I spilled across the bottom of the canoe, panting. My body was too heavy to move, and I moaned in relief and tried my hardest not to cry.

"Are you all right?" the guy asked.

I opened my eyes to find his face looming over me. I blinked several times, trying to grasp what had just happened. It was dark as a moonless midnight, and I'd just had a near-death experience, but there was something in this guy's barely visible face that brought me comfort in my time of need. I let my eyes wander across the shadows of his face as I tried to swallow the rising lump in my throat. I didn't want him to see me cry.

His outline was etched in the deepest shade of coal, his jaw sharp and dimples piercing. His face was unshaven, and his stubble glimmered in the starlight. I couldn't tell the color of his hair or the shade of his eyes, but I knew they were kind, and I could tell he was worried. I said nothing—only blinked over and over again, trying to regain my composure.

"Hello?" His voice soothed my trembling bones.

His words were fleeting. I looked past him. When had the stars come out? I was certain that we'd just arrived at the cabin and it was still dusk. How much time had I been under the water? How had I survived? The stars twinkled in a hypnotizing manner, and I watched them as my breath slowed and my heart returned to a normal rhythm.

"Hello?" he asked again, his worry growing.

"Ya-yeah. Yes," I stammered, drawing my attention back to the guy in front of me.

His dimples disappeared. "What the hell are you doing

all the way out here? We must be miles from the nearest shore."

I raised myself on my elbows. "I . . . I don't know. I don't know how I got out here." And the second the words left my lips, I regretted them. I sounded like a lunatic. And judging by this guy's body language, that was precisely how he perceived me. "I, um, I live at Rock Creek Cove, if you could take me there?" I pointed behind me with a shaky, wet finger.

The guy frowned and pointed behind his shoulder in the opposite direction. I arched my back and craned my neck, looking in every direction. There was no way for me to tell where we were, and I had no idea how he knew. He then spun the canoe in the opposite direction and began paddling. "You really don't know how you got out here?" he asked, his voice a little softer.

"I'm sorry. I—"

"Don't be sorry. I just want to make sure you're okay. Did you hit your head?" he asked.

I reached my hand into my hair and rubbed my scalp. There were no lumps and, as far as I could tell, no evidence of an injury. My head did hurt, though, now that he mentioned it. "What did you say your name was?" I asked, sitting up and trying to get a look at my thigh.

"I didn't. It's Walker. And you are?" he asked, paddling the canoe effortlessly.

"I'm Kinsley Wilde. It's nice to meet you, Walker," I said, extending my hand.

He held the paddle in one hand and reached for my hand with the other. "Walker St. James. And it's nice to save you. Here, take this. You're shaking like a leaf." He shrugged out of his flannel, and my eyes trailed his silhouette.

"Thank you," I said, taking the shirt and pulling it on. His warm beachy scent lingered on the flannel. It reminded me of the summer I had spent by the sea with my family learning to surf. My stomach clenched, and I shivered, pulling it tightly across my chest.

Slowly, I ran my hand down the length of my thigh, feeling for damage. The flesh ripped to the bone . . . the exposed muscle numbed by my fear. But my skin was smooth. Not even an indentation where I had been pierced. And the wetness trickling down my calf that I had been sure was blood, was no more than water.

The lake was still and quiet except for the rhythmic sound of the paddle as it propelled us through the water. It was late, and the two of us were in the middle of nowhere, but I still felt oddly safe in his presence. Being alone with a stranger paled in comparison to the thing in the water's depths that had nearly taken my life. Or maybe it was his cologne that took me back to better times. Times when the worst thing imaginable was failing to stand up on the surfboard by the end of the day. Or my favorite flavor of

Icee selling out . . . again. Either way, the lump in my throat had dissipated and my heartbeat finally slowed to normal.

"Wow, what a beautiful night," I said, surprising myself. As the canoe glided through the water, I crashed from the height of terror to a low and tranquil state. A pendulum swinging from one extreme to the next. Baylor Lake was a beautiful spot for stargazing, but tonight was extraordinary. And it was calling to me. I couldn't remember it ever being so remarkable. The Milky Way was tinged pink and teal, and the stars twinkled like golden embers. I lowered my gaze to find Walker smiling at me.

"It's quite something," he said, looking up into the sky. He didn't say much, and neither did I. We spent the rest of the trip stealing glances at each other and admiring the Milky Way. Rock Creek Cove came out of nowhere, and Walker eased the canoe alongside the dock. He dropped the paddle and tied a small rope to the dock cleat. He offered his hand as I climbed out of the boat. His touch was so warm and strong that I wasn't ready to leave it.

"Thank you for the lift," I said, fiddling with the cuff of his flannel. That wasn't all I wanted to say, but it was all that came out.

"Anytime," he replied, climbing out after me. We stood eye to eye as my words failed me. I didn't know how to thank this guy for saving my life. And a part of me didn't want to say goodbye at all. So I said nothing. I gave him an awkward half-wave, turned on my heels, and started for the cabin. I walked down the dock barefoot, my bra and thong still wet and my long brown hair dripping down the back of his flannel. But my lack of words and indecency were the least of my worries. There was something evil in that water, and I feared it was only the beginning.

# CHAPTER 2

Every light in the house was on, and I could hear the music from the water's edge. They were all there. Safe and warm. Partying. Why had nobody been in the cove searching for me? Where was the ambulance? Where were the police? My friends? Had my absence gone unnoticed by everybody? Even Noah? Who had been swimming after me? Or Lainey and Emma, my best friends? Nobody was out searching? I stared at the cabin—my cabin—as an outsider looking in, and my stomach sank. Something was terribly wrong.

As I stepped off the dock, I looked back toward Walker. He'd been standing there, waiting to make sure I got home safely. He'd been the only person who cared about my safety, and he was a complete stranger. Did he think it was sad that nobody was out looking for me? Did he pity me? I looked away, embarrassed, as I rubbed the nape of my neck and hobbled up the grassy hill to the cabin. The pine needles poked at my bare feet. As I came closer to the cabin, I could hear the boys arguing over something stupid and meaningless. It only hurt me more. My life was a minuscule dot on their radar.

"Good afternoon, dear! It's so good to see you," my neighbor called from his back yard, startling me. Mr. Vandal stood at the edge of his property holding a shovel. He didn't seem to notice that anything was wrong. That I was in my bra and underwear. Wet. My face probably as pale as a ghost and drawn down with sheer sadness. But how could he? It was too dark for him to see that I'd been through the wringer or that I'd been dropped off at the dock by a stranger. He couldn't have known that I was one of twelve, and I was all alone because nobody cared about me. That I was shut out of my own cabin as my best friends celebrated the beginning of summer without me. It was only the beginning, but still, I found his chipper temperament peculiar. And it was far from afternoon; it was sometime late in the night. Perhaps even early morning. I didn't know.

"Hello Mr. Vandal, how are you?" I asked with a sigh.

"Are you here with the whole family?" he called out.

"No, actually I'm here with a group of friends for the summer." I nodded toward the cabin, hitching my thumb over my shoulder at the bright lights and bass pumping through the cabin walls. I smiled apologetically.

"All right then," he said. Mr. Vandal wrestled with his shovel before disappearing into his house.

"All right then," I whispered under my breath. The Vandals had always been a little weird, but that had been odd, even by their standards. I frowned, examining their house briefly before turning back to mine. Why was he gardening at this hour?

The bugs swarmed around the light bulb on the back porch, and I stood there with my hand on the door's cold knob for a moment, feeling overwhelmed and alone. I looked back toward the dock one last time, but if Walker was still there, I never would have known it. I squinted into the night but couldn't see past the glow of the porch light and the buzzing bugs. I wondered if I'd ever see him again.

When I entered the cabin, Levi and Mason were arguing about who could chug a beer faster. Asher and Kimber were making out on the sofa, and Noah and Kai were playing pool. Nobody had seen me come in, and nobody seemed to care that I'd been gone. Life had resumed in my absence, and even though I was back now, I might as well have still been missing. I closed the back door softly as I searched the kitchen and game room for Emma and Lainey. Surely they would be upset that I had been gone. The music blared and my head pounded. I reached up to my temple, squinting against the brightness. Maybe I *had* hit my head.

"Okay, go!" Scarlett May yelled, as she held her phone

and the timer ran. Her hair was dried and waved. Her makeup was freshly applied. She'd had time for makeup? A chill crept over my skin, leaving goosebumps in its wake. They were all dressed for a night out. A night to be remembered. And I felt ill thinking of Scarlett May applying her lipstick as I sank to the bottom of the lake on my last breath.

Levi and Mason threw their heads back and chugged their beers. Suds dribbled down Mason's chin and onto his shirt. They were clothed, and I was standing in nothing but my wet underwear and a stranger's soaked flannel. I pulled it tight, not realizing I'd taken it with me but thankful that I had. It was like a bad dream. The kind where you're in public and look down to realize you're naked. Exposed. Different. I was different. Too different. I wanted to run away. And not just from the insecurity that clung to me like the wet hair did to the sides of my cheeks, but I wanted to run from the feeling that I wasn't worthy of being noticed in my absence. I could have died out there. I nearly had. And this is what it would have looked like afterward. A party.

"Wow, watch it!" Ethan said as he bumped into me, holding his beer high in the sky so it wouldn't spill a single drop. Because that would be devastating. His eyes trailed down the opening of Walker's flannel to my wet belly and his cheeks flushed. The strong stench of tequila permeated the air and trailed after him in his wake. I grabbed hold of the kitchen countertop behind me as he staggered away. The flannel parted, exposing me further, and I quickly covered back up.

"Done!" Mason declared. I whipped my head around to see him throw his can to the floor. My floor. The one I helped my mom clean every summer. She'd be so mad if she only knew.

"No, dude! I finished first!" Levi shoved Mason's chest, and Mason shoved him back. I sidestepped out of their way, afraid to get knocked over. But even more afraid to be noticed. Because even though I'd started out as a strong pillar of this group when we'd arrived, something had changed. The Earth had spun on its axis and I found myself an outsider.

"Nooo! Mason won by a nanosecond. Like, just a nanosecond. But, hey! Hey! Hey, now. It's my turn! I race the winner! Loser fetches the beer," Scarlett May said, her words slurring together.

"No—" Levi started.

"Just go! And hold the timer—" she said, thrusting her phone into his chest.

I took a step toward the game room where Noah had been playing pool, but Trinity came out of nowhere. She slid her hands up his back and rubbed his shoulders. It stopped me in my tracks. He smiled back at her, and she took his pool cue in her hands. I was unable to look away as I watched him wrap his arms around her waist. She leaned over the pool table, and her body pressed against his, not a breath of air between them. My hair dripped lake water on the kitchen floor as I watched my long-time crush flirt with another girl. It was hard enough to watch him do it when I was around, but even more difficult to know he'd done it in my absence. Especially at a time when my life was threatened. Lainey was standing near Kai, but her eyes were glued to Ethan. Tears pricked the corners of my eyes as I bolted for the stairs. Not even Lainey cared.

I took the stairs two at a time. I passed Emma, whose hair was curled and makeup done, and I couldn't bear to stop and talk with her. I ran right past her.

"Where are you going?" she called out. "Hey! Kinsley! Did you go for another swim?" But I kept going, and I didn't stop until I reached the confines of the master bedroom. I slammed the door behind me and locked it.

I shut my eyes tightly, but the tears escaped and spilled over my cheeks. I lowered my forehead to the door, my lip curling as I sucked in uneven pockets of air. I almost died. I almost died! I thought I had! My knees buckled underneath me, and I fell to the floor, hunched over and drowning in my feelings of inadequacy. I almost died . . .

What would have happened if that thing hadn't let me go? If I'd succumbed to the darkness in the way I thought I had? If there were no more days of summer? No more life left to live? How long would it have taken my friends to notice I was missing? And how was it that the only person who cared at all was an utter and complete stranger? Was this what it all came down to? Was I worth so little that my thrashing arms, my hysteric screams for help, my drowning before their very eyes, went completely unnoticed by all eleven of them? Eleven chances to be looked after, cared for, and loved . . . all failed. The dog. Not even him, with his natural senses, had noticed me. The air left my lungs and my chest froze. I needed air but couldn't breathe. I didn't deserve to.

Long after I knew my face had turned purple, air finally rushed into my lungs, and I let out a long, somber wail. I knew I wasn't as popular as Kimber or Trinity. I didn't rule the school with my beauty. I didn't have Kimber's modelesque figure or Trinity's sex appeal. I wasn't as loud and gregarious as Scarlett May Marks, who was everyone's party favorite. I wasn't as smart as Emma or as kind as Lainey. I was plain. Maybe even a little forgettable, sure. But never would I have imagined that I was so . . . so . . . so *insignificant*, that I could just disappear —vanish—without ever being noticed.

I cried for a long time. I cried so hard, I thought I might die all over again. But it wasn't that easy. Nothing was. I soaked the borrowed flannel sleeves in my tears as the party raged on without me. *So, this is adulthood*, I thought. It wasn't quite the celebration of independence I'd had in mind. Never had I wanted to be this alone. I picked my limp body off the floor and started the shower. I let the hot water wash over my skin as my eyes remained unfocused on the white tiles and beige grout. The steam rose, and I slowly tilted my head back under the waterspout.

In a flash, behind my closed eyelids, I saw the bubbles escape my mouth and the water's surface disappear. I felt the tug on my leg, and I jerked and gasped for air. I reached out and pressed the palms of my hands against the cool, wet tile, and I breathed through my rising anxiety before it closed my throat. Would I ever be able to close my eyes in the shower again? I worried about closing my eyes in bed later that night. I knew I'd never be the same. What nightmares would I see?

After combing my fingers through my hair, I realized I'd left my suitcase in the kitchen and my backpack on the deck. I couldn't put myself through the pain of seeing everybody downstairs again. I looked through my mom's dresser until I found some of her pajamas. They still smelled of her, and it brought me some comfort to be wrapped in something of hers. I wasn't one to get homesick, but after the night I'd had, I wanted nothing more than for her to hold me. I was an adult now but wished this wasn't the case. The lump in my throat grew as I longed to be back in my twin-sized bed down the hall from Mom and Dad.

I lay in bed, afraid to call. I didn't want my parents to hear the fear in my voice, but I couldn't imagine going to bed without saying goodnight. I'd told them I would call when we got to the cabin. That was before the lake had swallowed me whole. I picked up the telephone, an old-school rotary dial phone my mom loved too much to get rid of. I used to play with it as a child. What once had been cream was now yellowed by time. As my finger circled the dial on the last digit, I hesitated. I was a terrible liar.

The phone rang only once before my dad picked up. "Hello?"

"Hi, Dad."

"Honey! You made it!" He was chipper, and I could almost hear the smile lines around his eyes through the phone.

I smiled, and the sting of tears threatened again. "Yeah! We did." My voice weakened, and I tightened my grip around the receiver. *Be strong.*

"Clara? Kinsley is on the phone!" Dad called out, his voice seeming so far away.

"Oh, oh, I want to talk to her!" my mom said.

"Okay, okay. Hold on. Kins? Your mother wants to talk to you. Just a sec."

"Kinsley? Is that you?"

"Hi, Mom. It's me." My voice was so meek, and I willed myself to be stronger.

"Is everything okay?" she asked immediately. *Shit . . .*

I paused for a second too long. "I—I . . ." It was the fatal flaw. Honesty. She knew me too well. I loved her too much. Lying had never been my strong suit.

"Oh no. What's the matter?" Mom's tone filled with worry, but I didn't want her to panic. I was old enough to deal with this on my own. I couldn't go running back to my mom. I was eighteen now and out of high school.

All the emotions from before my shower came swelling back. I bit my lip, attempting to feel the pinch above all else. "Nothing!" I said, but my pitch was too high. She sighed heavily into the receiver. I knew if I didn't make this about something else—something small— she would worry all night and possibly all summer. "It's just that . . ."

"Yes? I'm listening . . ."

"It's just that I don't think Noah likes me as much as I like him," I said. It wasn't a lie, unfortunately, but it wasn't the whole truth.

"Oh, honey." *She bought it.*

"What? What's the matter?" my dad asked.

"It's just boy problems," she whispered back. I could hear a door click shut, and I imagined she was taking the phone into the bedroom for more privacy. Just boy problems . . . I wished. "Well, dear, you just got there. Maybe it's too early to tell?"

"I think Trinity likes him. And it looks like he's interested in her, too. It's fine. It's fine. I just wish I didn't have to spend my summer vacation watching the two of them flirt in front of me," I said, dispelling the image of Noah swimming after me. His hand wrapped around my foot. I pulled a throw pillow into my lap and played with the tassels.

"Well, if he can't see how special you are, then he's not worth your time," Mom said. I rolled my eyes.

"You have to say that," I replied.

"What? No, I don't!"

"Yes, you do! All moms say that!" And it was true. They did.

"And what do you have to compare to?"

I smiled. "All the other moms I've had," I joked.

"So, what's first on the agenda? Are you guys going to the Water's Edge Concert?" she asked, changing the subject.

"Yeah, I think we'll go."

"Do you know who's playing this year?"

"Um, no. It's some band I've never heard of. But Scarlett May said that she's heard of them before and they're good."

"Oh, good!"

"Yeah. And I think I'll just unpack, get some grocery shopping in, and stuff like that," I said.

"Okay. Well, you've got a full-time job ahead of you keeping all those boys fed. I foresee a lot of pizza in your future," she said to lighten the mood, and it worked.

"Yeah. Probably." I looked down at the pillow tassel and the line fell quiet. "I love you, Mom," I said, my heart hitching like it might be the last time I ever told her.

"I love you, too, Kins."

"I know you do. Tell Dad I love him, too." I bit my lip. *Be strong.*

"Okay, honey. I will. Have a good night. Get some rest."

"I will. Oh! And Mr. Vandal said hi . . . sort of."

My mom laughed, and I chuckled. "I'm sure he did," she said.

"Goodnight," I said, happy that I heard her voice.

"Goodnight dear."

I listened to the click of the line being severed before I hung up the telephone, and then I chucked the throw pillow to the floor. I looked around the empty room, wishing that I had the company of someone. Anyone. I listened to the party rage on without me and sighed heavily. I just wanted to go to sleep. I wanted to forget today had ever happened. I reached over to the bedside lamp and pulled the string. The room went dark, and I lay my head down on the pillow. I was ready to be done with the day but not yet ready for tomorrow to come.

I didn't know how to face my friends. *Friends?* Were they still my friends? I tried to convince myself that there was a perfectly good explanation for it all and that I would find out come morning. I told myself that if I could only fall asleep, the nightmare I'd experienced in the lake would be nothing but a dream. But no matter what I told myself or how much of it I believed, I was still afraid to close my eyes.

I knew the second I dropped my lids I would fall victim to the cold depths of Baylor Lake. I'd re-live the torture of the attack all over again. I couldn't do it. I wouldn't. I forced my eyes to stay open. I forced my mind to be anywhere except for that lake. But my mind couldn't process the negative, and the more I tried not to think of it, the more I failed. Instead, I tried to detect what the voices were saying through the walls. The baritone of the boys' debates, the high-pitched hollers from . . . Scarlett May. It had to be Scarlett May. She was the only one obnoxious enough to literally scream for attention.

Eventually, my eyes closed, and I was so tired from the accident and so exhausted from the crying that I didn't even notice when I fell asleep. There was no terrifying lake or nefarious creature of the deep. No near-death drowning or house of fake friends. But there was my sweet gran . . . because not even the dreamwork of the night would keep her at bay.

GRAN STOOD WITH ME UNDER THE OVERPASS. WE held hands, her skin thin and cold, while a car flew through the air, spinning before our very eyes. And in slow motion, we watched it turn over, again and again. The blue four-door sedan with tinted windows spun like a ballerina twirling on stage, while shards of glass scintillated alongside it. The front bumper hit the road first. The front end smashed like an accordion, and the car momentarily stood perpendicular on the road before teetering over. It landed flat on its roof. The top of the car compressed under the force of the impact. The windows burst as the frame bent. The fog lights flickered into the distance, lighting up the condensation that hung like heavy weights in the night sky. Light-yellow fabric pressed against what was left of the driver's side window.

Gran turned to me slowly. Her droopy eyes showed no emotion. Her cheeks hung like those of a marionette, and though she'd once had the most stunning green eyes, they were no more than a silver fog of cataracts. "We should go," she said, leading me under the bridge. We walked away from the accident, and I never looked back. We walked until the road disappeared and there was no sky above and no ground below.

We walked until a rocking chair appeared near a roaring wood burning fire. Somehow, it did nothing to heat the frigid air. I shivered, rubbing my arms while looking around. There was no sky, no ceiling—nothing but a gray void beyond the cozy reading nook that sat before us. A stack of half a dozen books sat on top of a side table. Gran let go of my hand and took a seat. There was only room for one. She cracked the spine of a children's book and began to read. And though I saw her mouth moving rhythmically, I couldn't hear her words.

I had an odd feeling as I stood there watching her read. She looked different. Not better and not worse—just different. I couldn't tell what it was. Her hair was still stark white and brittle due to her age and the cancer. Her body was frail and bony. She rocked slowly back and forth as she read, and she didn't seem to notice when I began to slip away.

I woke with a jerk and a gasp for air, my hands full of bedsheets and my eyes wide with fear. It had happened again. The visit from my gran. I was positive that I'd have nightmares of the lake, but it was she who'd prevailed. I didn't know if I should thank her or look for a deeper meaning. Was it an omen of bad things to come? It was probably just repressed feelings. Something I should have said to her before she passed but didn't. She'd probably hang around until I was ready to say goodbye. But I wasn't ready, and I doubted I ever would be. But the more I thought about it, the more I wondered if she had been hanging around to take me home. But I'd survived the near-drowning in the lake, so why was she still here?

I'd been waking to dreams of her for nearly a week. And there was nothing like it. Nothing like seeing someone in a dream, only to wake and remember that they were gone. Really gone. That your reality is one they no longer live in. It's worse than any nightmare there ever was, because at the end of the dream . . . it's real, and your nightmare begins as your day does.

Gran and I had a special relationship. She had been close to my mom, but since I was the first grandchild, I'd had the privilege of spending lots of time with her. Undivided time. She loved to read me stories. All kinds of stories. But for the longest time, she had only read fairy tales. The classics. She'd read them so many times when I was young that she could nearly recite them from memory. Sometimes she did.

It was three days before my birthday when she'd passed. I'd never known anybody who'd passed before. I guess I was lucky. But it didn't feel like luck. Here one moment, gone the next. I didn't understand . . . and I still didn't. And I think that was the reason I was seeing her in my dreams, and sensing her when I was sure nobody was there. I think I simply wasn't ready to let go. And since I hid away the sorrow when I was awake, it haunted me while I slept.

CHAPTER 3

I woke to a headache that refused to let me rest. The music was still playing through the walls, though I was positive nobody was awake. I didn't know what to expect when I went downstairs, but I imagined they would be riddled with hangovers, regret, and, if I were lucky, a spotty memory. I myself wasn't so lucky. I remembered everything. Enough to make me not want to be here. Enough to consider catching the first flight out of Baylor. But I hadn't run. Not yet.

Barefoot, I padded down the stairs, and when I reached the stereo in the game room, I carefully leaned over Noah, where he lay sleeping on a plush velvet cream chair, and turned the music off. His shaggy, dirty-blond hair was swept over his eyes. I wanted to reach down and brush his locks out of his face, even though his behavior had hurt me deeply. How could he have been swimming after me and just lost interest so quickly? By the time I'd resurfaced, he'd moved on. They all had. I straightened my back, looking around the room. I was only mildly relieved that Trinity wasn't wrapped up in Noah's arms, but that still didn't erase the memory I had of them the night before. I passed by a red bra strewn across the pool table and cringed, thinking of what had happened the night I'd been forgotten by all.

Ethan twitched on the sofa, and I tiptoed away, careful not to wake him. I wasn't ready to face any of my friends. And if they slept all day, I'd have some time to collect myself away from their disloyal, watchful eyes.

The kitchen was a wreck, even worse than I'd imagined it would be. Empty cans were everywhere, pretzels smashed on the tile floor, and a shot of amber liquid had been spilled across the countertop. Somebody's swim trunks sat in a pool of water where the carpet met the tile, and wet towels were draped over every surface of the kitchen. I sighed when my eyes fell upon a vase I'd made my freshman year of high school in ceramics class, broken into several pieces on the floor. Nobody had even bothered to pick it up. I'd loved that vase. I closed my eyes. Had this trip been a mistake? Had these people never been my real friends? The sour feeling of regret settled in my stomach, and I felt like there wasn't enough oxygen in the air. I needed to get away.

I opened the door to the back porch, hungry for a

breath of fresh air. Everyone's belongings had been taken inside last night except mine. I found my shoes and backpack lying across the wooden planks. I picked them up and slung the bag over my shoulder. The heaviness weighed me down as I took my belongings upstairs, closing my eyes to the mess as I passed. I got dressed for a hike. I needed to get out into the open air to clear my head. Sort the facts from the painful feelings. What I knew to be true may very well have been a lie. I did that sometimes. I'd get so caught up in my own insecurities that I'd fail to see what was actually true. Maybe there was a good explanation for all of it. I just needed time to think.

When I snuck outside, ready for my hike, I was surprised to find Lainey awake, clipping a leash onto Gunner's collar on the back porch.

"Kinsley! You're up early!" she said, startled.

"I was thinking the same about you," I said in a weak voice. *She doesn't care . . .*

"Ugh, yeah. Crazy night, huh? I bet they'll sleep all day."

"Yeah . . . it was," I replied. I watched her intently as she pulled her medium-length brown hair into a low ponytail. There was no indication that she knew about my accident last night. Not a single hint of concern anywhere to be found. No time-lapse, no empathy behind her eyes, not so much as a furrowed brow. Lainey was her natural happy-go-lucky self. She may have been a little tired from staying up late the night before, but she harbored no guilt about leaving me to die alone in the dark, malignant waters.

"Are you going out for a run? Because I was going to take Gunner on a walk, but I don't know the trails around here. And we'd just run with you, but honestly, I don't think my body will allow me any type of cardio right now. It's a struggle just to take Gunner out. And I wouldn't have gotten up at all, except he wouldn't stop pushing his wet nose against my cheek this morning. And the last thing I want is for him to pee inside the cabin." Lainey rolled her eyes, exhausted by the responsibility of her dog not twenty-four hours into the trip. I could see this was going to have to be a team effort. Which was okay—we all loved him. Gunner's eyes squinted and he looked like he was smiling.

"I was just going to walk," I said, exhausted myself.

"Can we join you?" she asked, although it was really more of a statement. She had no reason to believe I wouldn't want her to join me. And the entire conversation made me question if last night had been real at all.

"Okay. I guess you can fill me in on what happened last night," I said, stepping off the back porch. The morning was warm already, and I could tell it was going to be a particularly hot day. I might have even thought it to be beautiful, if my life hadn't been turned upside down. I took the ponytail holder off my wrist and tied my long, dark, chestnut locks into a messy bun on top of my head.

"Well, you know. I mean, you were there," Lainey said, tight-lipped. "Oh, you mean because you went to bed early? You didn't miss anything. It really just went downhill after the pool tournament." I looked at my best friend's face. The freckles dusting her cheeks gave her an air of innocence, and I could tell that she wasn't being malicious—not in the least. She didn't have a mean bone in her body. So it must have been me. I was the one who was faltering.

"What pool tournament?" I asked, looking for clues.

"The pool tournament. You don't remember?" she asked, trying to read my face. "Oh, man! You don't remember? And I thought I drank too much!" Lainey laughed, shaking her head.

I frowned down at the path, which was wide enough here for us to walk side by side. All of the paths weren't this wide, though. Many of them had offshoots that wound tightly through the forest. Had I been drugged? I hated that my immediate thought turned to Trinity. But she was the only one who had a motive. I shook my head, dispelling the thought that one of my friends could actually drug me. It wasn't like that.

I'd lost a good amount of time last night between dusk and nightfall. Perhaps I had hit my head, and that was the reason I couldn't remember. I felt . . . off. My stomach was a little queasy now that I thought about it. And I knew that concussions could make you feel like that for days after.

Weeks even. Maybe Lainey was right and I'd been there all along. I reached up to the back of my head, checking for bumps and lumps—anything that would prove the theory—but found nothing.

"Honestly, I don't remember anything after we dove into the lake. I mean, there was this one bit when Mason won a beer-drinking contest . . . And Trinity hitting on Noah." I shrugged, shaking the thought from my memory. Out of all the things that could have happened last night, it was Trinity that I remembered. The way she'd slipped her hands around Noah's shoulders. The way he'd smiled at her over his shoulder.

"Oh yeah! I think Levi and Mason had a chug fest. And then at some point, Ethan joined." Lainey nodded and her cheeks turned the soft pink of embarrassment. "Don't get me started on Trinity! She only wants Noah because she knows you like him! She gets a rise out of seeing you fume. I think she's jealous of you because this is your cabin and she feels inferior being on your trip. Sometimes I even see her flirt with Asher just to get Kimber all riled up. And it works, you know. Kimber gets weird and stops eating for like a week. I don't know why Trinity gets such a high out of it. Why did you even invite her?" Lainey looked at me with one brow raised.

"I had to! I couldn't invite the entire group and conspicuously not invite her. Especially since we've been talking about it for nearly a year now. She would have found out and ended up coming anyway. Then she would have made my life a living hell!" I said in a low, weary tone. I couldn't imagine if she'd actually had a real reason to hate me. She was conniving enough as it was.

"Isn't that what she's doing now? Making your life a living hell? God, Kins, sometimes I think you're your own worst enemy," Lainey said, her head tilted in sympathy. I sighed, knowing that I had nobody to blame but myself.

"I guess so," I said. No matter what I did, though, if I was up against Trinity, I'd lose. Lainey and I exchanged a look of mutual defeat. She understood where I was coming from because she, too, had been the victim of Trinity Myers once before. Back in the day, when Trinity was the new girl at school, she'd quickly climbed the social ranks by spreading rumors. She'd told everyone that she was in a commercial for kids' swimsuits. But the lies didn't stop there. After she became popular, she started rumors about other girls, Lainey being one of them. I'd never believed that Lainey Summers had a crush on old Wigg, the overweight fifth-grade PE teacher rumored to wear a toupee, but many did, and it had stuck with her for some time.

"Hey, is it okay if I let Gunner off the leash?" she asked, looking around. I stretched my eyes as far as they could see. Not a soul in sight. We were approaching what I called the wall. The cabin sat in a clearing in the cove, surrounded by a wall of trees. A thick forest with winding pathways, blackberry bushes, and a rumored graveyard. I'd never seen it.

"Yeah, I think that's fine. Will he come back?" I asked, looking forward to the shade the trees would cast over us.

"Yes, he's a good boy! Isn't that right? He's such a good boy!" Lainey scratched Gunner's head as she unhooked the leash. He took off, sprinting down the path, hunting for birds, squirrels, and anything else that moved. His brown head and white speckled body disappeared in no time, but Lainey didn't seem worried, so neither was I.

"So, did I miss anything? From last night I mean?" I asked in all honesty, the feeling of deceit leaving my system. Bewilderment was the only thing I felt now, and it was stronger than ever.

"You really don't remember anything?" asked Lainey, studying me.

"Really." I looked down at my shoes kicking up dust on the trail and I winced at the pain I'd felt behind the locked door of the master bedroom. "Actually, can I tell you something?"

"Of course." Lainey wound the untethered leash around her hand.

"I have this one memory . . ." I didn't want to say it aloud. But I always told Lainey everything, and I feared what it would do to me if I kept it inside.

"Oh, yeah?" she asked.

"I have a memory of . . . drowning. I drowned last night

in the lake." I refused to look at her. Clearly, I hadn't drowned. I was right here, at her side.

Lainey took a moment. "Are you serious?"

"I didn't die, though," I muttered.

"Well, obviously!" she laughed. But I wasn't laughing. I felt ashamed. Like something bad had happened, and I didn't want anybody to know about it. They hadn't known.

"I mean, I was about to. But this guy . . . he saved me."

"A guy?" she asked, surprised. This wasn't a story she'd heard before. I looked at Lainey and she was both intrigued and concerned for my well-being. I was concerned too.

"Don't look at me like that! It was real! I swear it was," I said, doubting myself. Heat crept into my cheeks. Not from embarrassment, but from anger. I knew it was true, but somebody had been playing a trick on me.

Lainey sucked in a deep breath, and we both whipped our heads to the left as Gunner came bounding out of the bushes. He flew past us, breaking the tension, and she burst into laughter. I cracked a small smile, but it didn't reach my eyes. "Okay, Kins. So tell me about this mystery guy." She wiggled her brows and nudged my side.

"I don't know. He was just a guy. He came out of nowhere in a canoe—"

"A man in a canoe? That's hot—"

"It wasn't like that. He gave me a ride back to the dock. We didn't say much. But I felt like he was kind . . . and caring." I looked at Lainey. Her eyebrows were raised expectantly. I knew she wanted more, and a part of me did too. "I don't know. The whole thing was weird," I said, shrugging. I glanced down at my thigh, but there wasn't so much as a scrape from being pulled into the canoe, let alone bone-deep claw marks. I'd definitely hit my head last night. There was no other way around it.

"Well, it sounds like Noah better watch his back, because a local Baylor boy is ready to take his spot!" Lainey said, picking up the pace in her excitement.

"Stop that! It's not like that. I don't even know the guy! And he was . . . older."

"Like how much older?"

"I don't know. It was dark. But maybe, like, a few years. Five years?" It was hard to tell his age, but he was no boy. He wasn't like the other high schoolers I'd known and dated. It wasn't something that I could see in his face, but more of a feeling. He was an old soul. Responsible . . . like he had the weight of the world on his shoulders, and plucking a damsel in distress from the midnight lake was all in a day's work. He'd made me feel protected in a way that no other guy ever had. I only assumed it came from a few extra years of independence. The very thing I had expected to gain this summer but had already regressed from.

Lainey bumped my shoulder and made a low

humming sound. "Stop!" I shoved Lainey lightly. She stumbled just off the trail into a clump of bushes.

"Do you see that?" Lainey pointed to the purple flowering bush beneath her feet.

"What? The flowers?" I asked, taking a step closer.

"Yes. That little purple flower is called rampion bellflower, also known as rapunzel. It's one of my favorites, but I don't see it too often. I love that it grows rampant out here." I looked at the bushes covering the forest floor, and most of them had the little purple flowers she spoke of. I hadn't noticed them before, but now that I looked, they were beautiful in their own right.

We hiked to the water's edge and let Gunner cool off in the lake for a few minutes before turning around. Lainey pointed out several species of plants and trees, telling me which berries were edible and which to avoid. We spotted a few birds along the way, of which my favorite was the downy woodpecker. She described how the males have a beautiful stripe of red across the back of their heads. It kept me looking high into the trees as we walked back to the cabin. And I felt lighter with my face up to the sun, the filtered light gleaming into my eyes. There was nothing a good friend couldn't help by just being close by. The morning air had warmed significantly by the time we returned. And from the smell of bacon that permeated the air, I knew the rest of our friends had finally woken up. At least I was less afraid to greet them. But by all means, it was only a *little* less.

My stomach clenched as I followed Lainey in through the back door, Gunner by our sides. He collapsed immediately upon entry into the living room. Scarlett May stood in the kitchen, whisking eggs and wearing sky-high pajama shorts. Her hair, blonde and blunt, was still wavy from the night before. She glanced over at us as we came in, but it was clear that I was the only one who remembered the neglect. I wrapped my arms around my waist, trying to support myself. Her strength only made me feel small and weak. Forgotten. I scanned the room for Noah, but he was nowhere to be found.

"Thanks for making coffee," I said, pulling a mug out of the cabinet. It was another one of my ceramic creations. Not good enough to keep at home, but good enough not to throw away. I liked how the thumb imprint was fitted for my hand specifically. I also liked how nobody had broken it. Yet. I filled my cup with coffee and creamer and then drew in a long, medicinal sip.

"I hope you don't mind, but I had to make eggs and bacon. It's a tradition for my family every time we come to Baylor Lake. Us kids are woken up by the smell of a bacon-and-egg breakfast. And when I saw that nobody else was going to do it this morning, I figured, if you want something done right, you've got to do it yourself," Scarlett May said.

"Oh, no, I don't mind. I actually appreciate the

cooking. So make yourself at home. Now . . . if I could just get someone to help clean up, because this place is a mess," I said, looking around the kitchen.

"I didn't realize you've been to Baylor Lake before," Lainey said, as she placed a bowl of water on the kitchen floor for Gunner.

"I have an aunt who lives in Baylor. My family usually visits here once a year. Normally, we go in the winter, so I'm not familiar with this heat. But I know the town pretty well," Scarlett May said.

"Oh, nice," Lainey said.

"Oh yeah! I grew up on the Baylor Lake ghost stories. They were the only ones my dad ever told us. We used to go to the farmers' market on the weekends if it wasn't rained out. And we know all the locals. I have a really good friend who lives here, and he throws the best lakeside parties. You'll love him. I actually have plans to go visit my aunt later today, but it looks like she'll have to pick me up because I don't see a car in your driveway." Scarlett May looked at me inquisitively.

"Right. We don't keep a car here. We usually only come for the summer, and most often we stay at the cabin. There *is* a golf cart, but that won't take you into town," I said.

"Wait, did you say Baylor Lake ghost stories?" Emma asked, stretching. Her shirt was oversized and her hair a mess. Kimber stumbled into the kitchen after her. She looked like she hadn't slept a wink; her eyes were puffy and red. She opened the refrigerator door and pulled out a bottle of water. I glanced at Kimber briefly, looking for clues that she remembered last night's events, but she paid me no attention. Typical. I looked at Emma, but she was enthralled with the idea of hearing a morning ghost story. She loved her stories. Emma was the only person I knew who could read for eight hours straight.

"Everybody's heard the Baylor Lake ghost stories. Right, Kinsley?" Scarlett May looked to me briefly before flipping the bacon with tongs.

"I don't think I've ever heard them," I said, scratching my head, my fingers still searching for hidden battle wounds.

"Are you sure this is even your cabin? Everybody knows about the Baylor Butcher." Scarlett May had a way of making you feel small with her sharp, lashing tongue. My cheeks flushed, and I gave a small shrug.

"What's the story?" Kimber asked, her voice groggy. Asher came to her side, taking the water out of her hands and guzzling the rest of the bottle.

"Yeah, tell us." Emma pulled up a seat like an eager child ready for story time.

"Long, long ago—I can't believe you guys haven't heard this—there was this man who was a serial killer. He used to go on dates with women all the time because he was ruggedly handsome, and on the third date or so, he would kill them, chop them up into tiny pieces, and spread their bodies into the lake at night." Scarlett May spun around with a butcher knife in her hand for theatrics. I flinched, my nervous system still reeling from the night before.

"Eww!" cried Lainey, scowling.

"Gross." Kimber clutched her stomach and looked like she might be sick.

I felt a bit nauseous myself, remembering the feeling of my nails clawing at the hand under the water. Did that hand have a body? A breath? A soul? Or was the hand no more than a haunted dismemberment of a Baylor Butcher victim seeking vengeance? Or, perhaps I had heard the ghost stories before and forgotten them. And last night was no more than a reflection—a distant memory. Maybe it was a dream? Or, more likely, a nightmare.

I looked down at my fingernails and imagined that they'd been packed with scrapings of something dank and dingy. Fleshy bits of evidence of my frantic attempts to free myself. I spun to the sink, washing my nails vigorously. *It was just a dream. Just a dream.*

Asher stole a handful of bacon from Scarlett May's platter, and she slapped his hand with the back of the spatula. "One day," Scarlett May scowled at Asher as she continued.

"Bacon!" Mason yelled, reaching for a handful.

"Wait until I'm done," Scarlett May snapped and swatted the spatula about. "One day, when the Baylor

Butcher had come to his third date with a beautiful girl who had made him yearn for more time, he stalled. He chose not to kill her. Instead, he finished his date, a canoe ride across the lake during sunset. He thought that maybe she'd be the one to stop him in his tracks. To turn his life around. He'd gotten away with murder, and he'd never kill again. But when he tried to set up a fourth date, the woman had escaped, never to be found again."

I dried my hands, running the dishtowel under my nails. I hadn't heard this story before.

"What happened next?" Emma asked.

Ethan waltzed into the kitchen and went straight for the coffeepot. "Seriously, guys?" He held up the empty pot. I smiled at him apologetically. I had always liked Ethan. Not romantically, but in the sense that I could tell he was good to his core. Still, he hadn't noticed when I'd gone missing either. My smile faded.

"I'll make more," I said curtly, taking the empty pot from Ethan's hand.

"So, the butcher haunted the lake and the woods every night from dusk till dawn, searching for the one who got away," Scarlett May said, finally placing a platter of eggs and bacon on the kitchen island. In a blink of an eye, the food was gone. Everyone awake, except for Kimber and I, inhaled it.

"I guess I'm done swimming in that lake!" Kimber said.

"At least after dusk," Lainey replied.

"What? Are you afraid of a little ghost story? Afraid that the lake turns into poison and the woods into a web of nightmares as soon as the sun goes down?" Scarlett May laughed at the absurdity of it all.

But my stomach knotted, because that's exactly what I was afraid of. A web of nightmares.

# CHAPTER 4

It had been a lazy morning. With the exception of myself, everyone else had been hungover. Most of them slept until while I busied myself cleaning up after their mass destruction from the night before. And although everyone was tired and lacked the energy to contribute to the cabin, they were all raring to go again come nightfall.

It was an endless loop of celebrating our freedom. After all, we deserved it. Eighteen years of being under somebody's thumb at all times. No more parents, teachers, or coaches. We'd made it, and now nobody could tell us what to do. We would go to college because it was our choice. But when it came to cleaning up after ourselves . . . well, needless to say, it wasn't happening. Nobody would help. At first, the idea of a constant party and lack of responsibility and structure exhausted me, but somewhere along the way, I desired it. I grew sick of looking at my friends as an outsider. I didn't want to be the only one who cared anymore. I needed to let go. Just one night. No responsibility, worry, or skepticism. I didn't want to think of it. I wanted to turn my mind off and act on pure instinct, chasing the joy and adrenaline wherever it might be found.

It was somewhere between my first and third drink that I stopped seeing the messes made, the spills on the carpet, and the wasteful byproduct of half-eaten bags of chips and near-full soda cans abandoned. I stopped fretting over the ceramic pieces I'd made and how I could never replace them if they were broken. I turned off the nagging voice in my head by drowning it, and I narrowed my focus to Noah Hampton. It was more fun this way. He was messing with the stereo, trying to find the perfect song. I'd convinced myself that nobody had abandoned me the first night at the cabin. That it was all in my head. And every time I saw Walker's flannel, I'd just look away. It was the only way I could heal. The only way I could move on. And I needed that.

I quickly glanced around the room. Trinity was out front with Kimber and Scarlett May, so I had some uninterrupted time with Noah.

"Are you looking for a particular song?" I asked, peeking over his shoulder.

Noah smirked at me, his dark-blue denim eyes peering

out from beneath his shaggy, sandy hair. "I might be," he said, inviting me in. A low hum escaped my chest.

I felt my cheeks heat as laugh lines appeared around his eyes. His face was so close to mine. My gaze trailed from his eyes to the crevices around his mouth and then to his lips. I wanted to kiss him, but it was that exact thought that made me lose my confidence. I faltered for just a second, and I looked down to the floor, shattering the moment. Disappointment washed over me. I always did that.

"I might be able to help," I suggested.

"Oh yeah? Here. Find me the perfect song." Noah handed me his phone. My fingers grazed his as I took the cell phone. Noah and I had flirted before—on many occasions—but that didn't mean it wasn't like the first time every time. I smiled, the butterflies fluttering up and down in my stomach, looking for a way out. It was hard to pry my eyes off him, but I did so in search of the perfect song. One that would describe everything I felt inside, not only in that moment, but for him in general. I had known Noah since I was a kid, but it had only been in the last two years that my feelings for him had grown into something more. I was pretty sure he felt the same way. I scrolled through many songs, but none of them were perfect. It was a tall order. I felt his gaze on me as I scrolled through the songs, my thumb hovering over each and every one that confessed feelings of love or lust. But as I recited the words in my head, I decided against them all. Nervously, I peeked up at him.

Noah placed his hand against the wall, his body stretching out around me. I leaned into him, scrolling through songs as he lowered his head close to mine. This song was too angry, this one too mushy, this one was too old. I bit the inside of my cheek and craned my neck, looking up at him. It wasn't the perfect moment for our first kiss, but it could do. I was positive that any first kiss with Noah would be romantic, regardless of timing. Our eyes would be closed either way. He looked down at me, smiling, and leaned in just a hint, right when Mason and Asher stumbled into the room. Our connection was severed by the commotion.

"Are you going to put some music on? Or are you just going to stand there?" Asher complained, his stance wide, his presence imposing. Asher was the quarterback of the football team and arguably the most popular guy at our school. He and Kimber had been prom king and queen, and the rest of us were living in their shadow.

"I am! I'm working on it. It's a hard decision, you know?" I said. Noah pulled away, his warmth leaving my side. I frowned, returning Noah's cell phone, and he took it with little thought. Our hands didn't graze each other this time. The moment was squashed, thanks to Asher's demand. *Music now, peasants!*

"Just pick something!" Asher yelled as he grew impatient.

"There!" Noah called back, selecting a random song. One that in no way, shape, or form was a confession of love. Asher took a seat on the couch, and Noah followed. I paused for a moment, surveying the room, before sitting to Noah's right.

"This guy says he's eaten glass before. Can you believe that?" Asher asked as he gripped Mason's shoulders. Lainey came into the room, picking up the TV remote.

"You've eaten glass?" Lainey said, flipping through the channels. Her thumb hovered briefly over the channel button as a reporter spoke at the scene of a car accident. Our hometown of Clover scrolled in bold letters on a bright red banner across the screen. My attention piqued just as she flipped the channel, landing on a documentary about large cats. I peeled my eyes away from the screen as she turned the volume down and split her attention between the cheetahs and Mason's speculative diet of glass. I frowned.

"I've got a stomach of steel. I can eat anything you put in front of me. I'm a machine!" Mason howled and beat his chest. I chuckled, and Lainey leaned into me, giggling. Mason Fry was a true rebel. His hair hung to his shoulders and was a mess. He always looked like he'd just woken up —or perhaps had an early morning surf session. He was dangerously daring and brave. More fun than anybody I'd ever known. And at his core, I believed he was a pretty great guy. Had he not been so obnoxious, I might have gone for him. But his need for attention was insatiable, and it often had the rest of us rolling our eyes.

"It's true. I've seen him do it before," Noah said as he leaned back, extending his arm around the back of the sofa, encapsulating my shoulders. I pretended not to notice but slouched a little deeper into the plush sofa and his side.

"You've seen him eat glass before?" I asked.

"Oh yeah! He used to do it all the time freshman year. It was our favorite trick. Somewhere along the line, I thought maybe he'd grow up, but no such luck. He really does have an iron stomach, though."

"What did you say?" Mason asked Noah.

Noah leaned into me and whispered in my ear, "We can't egg him on, or we'll have no light bulbs left, and we might have to spend the night in the ER!"

I raised my eyebrows and chuckled. I had no intention of watching Mason eat glass, and I wanted to keep what lighting fixtures we had intact. So when Lainey changed the subject, I was glad.

"Did you know the cheetah can run sixty miles per hour?" she asked, eyes trained on the TV.

"I can run sixty miles per hour!" Mason argued. I threw my head back on Noah's arm and moaned. Noah and Lainey laughed, and Asher just stared at Mason, seeming to consider if it was possible.

"No, you can't!" said Asher flatly.

"I can run sixty miles per hour. I can do it right now. And I'll do it naked!" he said. The entire room erupted in laughter. It wouldn't be the first time I'd seen Mason naked. He was a fan of streaking and often gathered huge followings. One time, he'd led a pack of sixteen naked sophomores across the football field at halftime.

"Want to make a bet?" Asher asked, knowing very well that Mason would strip and run, but not at sixty miles per hour.

"No! Don't egg him on!" I said, leaning over Noah's lap and swatting at Asher.

"I'll take that bet! I want to see this!" Noah said. Lainey laughed and shrugged as if she didn't care one way or another, but I knew she wanted to see it too. I slapped my forehead. Who were these people?

"See what?" Kimber asked as she, Scarlett May, and Trinity walked in from outside. The moment Trinity walked in, Noah's arm pulled back to his lap and he leaned forward, casting me into his shadow. My side turned cold, and my heart sank with disappointment. Had it been a coincidence? I didn't know, but it crushed me all the same.

"Mason is going to run sixty miles per hour with his pecker out," Asher said, laughing.

"Wow, okay. We're doing this?" Kimber asked, looking around the room.

"Sixty bucks. Sixty miles per hour. My body is just the

cherry on top for all you ladies." Mason seductively traced his hand down his torso to his groin.

"Eww!" I groaned.

"I've got twenty on this," Asher said.

"Same," Noah replied.

"I'll throw in twenty," Lainey said, with a coy smile and a shrug.

"Lainey!" I shoved her shoulder, and she laughed out loud. I questioned her motive. If she liked Mason, I might have understood. But I happened to know that Lainey Summers liked nobody like she liked Ethan. She'd never *admitted* that she liked Ethan, but a best friend knows. She couldn't hide the blush under her freckled cheeks every time she said his name.

"What? He can't run sixty miles per hour, you guys. Honestly? You're letting him do this?" Kimber asked.

"True story. He can't do it," I said and shrugged. Noah stood up and walked to neutral ground. My eyes flicked to Trinity's and hers to mine. I tried to hide my disappointment. Mason took off his shirt and beat his chest like a gorilla one more time. All the girls in the room laughed, and the boys shoved each other around, getting excited. This was the stupidest thing I had ever seen, and I had seen some ridiculous stuff before. I stood up and looked for Emma, because this wasn't something she would want to miss.

"Emma! Mason is going to attempt to run sixty miles

per hour, and he's going to do it naked! You have to come see this!" I yelled.

"Mason is going streaking? Again?" Levi asked.

"Yes!"

"I'll go streaking!" Levi jumped at the chance to take his clothes off. Emma and I laughed and followed Levi to the front of the cabin. Mason was unbuckling his belt when we came out to the driveway. His shoes were kicked off and socks already cast aside. Levi wasted no time joining in. He took his baseball cap off and placed it on Emma's head, then started unbuttoning his shirt. Emma turned toward me with a small squeal.

"What are you doing, man?" Mason asked Levi.

"We're going streaking!" he said.

"I'm getting paid sixty bucks. I'm not sharing that with you."

"I'll do it for free. I can't make these ladies watch your ass run down the street when they can have the pleasure of watching mine. That's just cruel," Levi said.

Levi kicked off his shoes and hopped as he peeled the socks off his feet. He threw his dirty socks at Scarlett May's face, and she screamed, batting them down to the ground. We all laughed at her. I hadn't laughed this hard in a long time. Who knew all I needed was a naked nighttime race to feel so alive? My summer was officially back on track. Mason and Levi stood side by side, naked, on the road that stretched before the cabin. The air had cooled from the hot day, but not as much as the boys claimed as they cupped themselves in their hands. The gravel was sharp, but I doubted they would feel the pain under the rush of adrenaline.

"All right, are you guys ready?" Scarlett May asked, holding her arm high in the air.

"Wait!" Asher said, ripping his shirt off and tossing it to Kimber.

"What are you doing? Babe?" she asked in a whiny tone.

"What? I can't watch a race without entering, I've got to compete. It's in my blood," he replied. I grabbed Emma's arm and squeezed just above her elbow. Her eyes grew to saucers as Asher pulled his clothes off. He had a nice strong build that made us giggle like schoolgirls.

"You sure you don't want to get in on this Noah?" I called out, hoping. Praying. But he shook his head like it was a terrible idea.

"I can't believe this!" Lainey said, the whites of her eyes bright in the night.

"On your mark. Get set. Go!" Scarlett May yelled.

Levi, Mason, and Asher took off, running full speed down the street. Their arms outstretched, pushing and pulling each other as they ran. I laughed so hard I folded in two, fearing I'd pee my pants right there in the street. But it wasn't until Emma grabbed my shoulder and pointed to my neighbor, Mrs. Vandal, as she walked out to the end of her driveway to take out the trash that I stopped breathing altogether and then really lost it. Tears squeezed from my eyes as I staggered, nearly falling to the ground. Emma wasn't as strong. She *did* fall, taking Lainey down with her. I nearly tripped over the two of them, laughing even harder. Harder than I had in my entire life. I missed the race, I laughed so hard.

I heard the boys yelling a laundry list of profanity as their voices became smaller the more distant they became. It could have been my imagination, but I thought I heard Mrs. Vandal mutter in disbelief, and when I did, my knees became so weak they buckled. Emma tried to help herself up, but she only pulled me down with her. The three of us sprawled in the street, the boys' voices echoing in the cove.

"Look at them! And they thought they could run sixty miles per hour! They couldn't even get to the end of the street," Lainey said in hysterics.

"Quick! Grab their clothes!" Trinity hissed. Trinity Myers was usually the reason for the sour taste in my mouth or the cold chip on my shoulder, but at that moment, she was my hero.

"Yes! Oh my god, yes!" I bounded to my feet, stumbling and scooped up various boxers, T-shirts, socks, and pants. Emma held Levi's hat on top of her head and took off running to the cabin. Trinity and I bumped into one another, hands full of stolen clothes, and I all but forgot that she was the closest thing I had to an enemy.

It was for this very reason that Trinity was so popular; she was mean . . . in the most entertaining of ways. It was always at somebody's expense. But tonight, when I wasn't the target of her entertainment, I easily hopped on board. I became her partner because the fun was too great to pass up, and the boys—they'd done it to themselves, really.

All of us except Kimber ran into the house and locked the doors behind us. Kai took it upon himself to close the windows and lock them too. And Scarlett May took out her cell phone, ready to document the three naked cheetahs by way of video and, regrettably, social media.

It wasn't long before Mason and Levi came pounding on the door. Asher and Kimber were attempting to sneak into the garage, but Kai had locked that too. When I thought I couldn't laugh anymore, I did. Levi stood in front of the window, hiding his bits behind his hands while Scarlett May snapped picture after picture. The others filled the house with hooting and hollering while running to check the locks at every entry. Mason ran wild throughout the yard, doing cartwheels on the grass and making us all laugh even harder. He ate it up. We all did. They endured a rough ten minutes in the "cold" before Trinity had a new idea. The perfect sequel to her first.

"Let's throw their clothes in the lake! That way, they have to jump in to get them!" she said.

"That one's on you!" Kai said, holding up his hands.

He didn't want to be responsible for taking it a step further, but I did.

I helped Trinity scoop up the clothes. We peered out the windows, making sure we wouldn't be caught. And when the coast was clear, we unlocked the door. Slowly and quietly, we stepped off the porch. My heart was pounding in my chest. Once we made our way to the grassy knoll, we took off running in a sprint for the dock, laughing the whole way. Ethan tripped and went down, somersaulting several times before coming to a full stop. The rest of us, on our feet, continued running down the dock. Once we reached the end, Trinity threw handfuls of clothing into the lake. But I stood, frozen. The black water did its mesmerizing dance. Hypnotizing me. Reminding me. Drawing me in.

"What are you doing? Throw them in!" Trinity yelled. I stood motionless, feeling the phantom hand reach up my thigh and yank me under the water. My gaze fell unfocused. I went somewhere else—a world I didn't want to know existed.

"Give me that!" Trinity grabbed the boxers and jeans out of my hands, snapping me back to the present, and threw them into the water just as Levi yelled.

"Hey!" he yelled. "Hey, over here! They have our clothes!" I watched the water ripple out from the clothing until the heavier jeans had been swallowed whole. I was paralyzed. I felt like somebody was watching me. But from where? For how long? I scoured the shore, looking for eyes in the dark.

"No!" Asher came out of nowhere, running down the dock. Kimber stood in the grass, hiding behind her muffled laughter.

"Look at those cheeks!" She giggled. Mason was nowhere to be found.

We hung around long enough to see the two of them jump in after their clothes, and a part of me knew they would never surface again. In that moment, I felt the sobering effects of fear. This wasn't fun any longer. Something was wrong. Something was terribly wrong. I watched for what felt like minutes strung out in slow motion until their heads breached the water. Relief washed over me, making me dizzy.

I reached down to help Levi out of the water, and Noah came up behind me, grabbing my waist and startling me. I nearly leapt into the water in shock. I screamed louder than I would have liked, and an image of a cold, gray, dismembered hand reaching out of the black water flashed through my head. I felt the blood drain from my face. I turned around and slapped Noah on the shoulder, and he laughed. I still felt the eyes on me.

"Where's my money? Pay up," Asher said to Noah. We all laughed at Asher's ridiculous request. Nobody had agreed to pay him—only Mason, and Mason was still running naked in the woods.

"Do you think he really believes he ran sixty miles per hour?" Lainey asked, leaning into me.

I looked at her and smiled. "Actually . . . probably," I said, and we both laughed. The group walked slowly up the hill and back to the cabin, recalling elements of the race. Emma told everyone how the next-door neighbor had seen it all too. The group laughed hysterically as Asher tied Kimber's tiny sweater around his waist. Levi wrung out his clothes.

It was in these memorable times that I always felt like somebody was watching me. I tried to brush it off, but it picked away at me until striking a nerve. An owl called out, and I gave in and peeked back over my shoulder. Just one look to tell myself I was crazy. One look to confirm that nobody was there. But somebody *was* there. A dark figure stood at the edge of the dock. We had just been down there moments ago, and nobody had been around. I stopped and squinted into the night, stretching my sight as far as it would take me. I saw a large shadow cast on the water. A canoe? Was that Walker?

I stood frozen, split between emotions. On one end, I was excited to see him again. I'd been curious about him. And I'd felt safe by his side. A part of me wanted to explore that under more normal circumstances. And I'd be lying if I completely ignored how handsome he was. But there was another part of me—an even larger part, perhaps —that worried about his presence looming down by the dock. If he was there now, then I really had been in the middle of the lake on our first night, and it wasn't something I could sweep under the rug as a false memory or twisted dream. If I really had almost drowned, then I had never hit my head. And all the friends who had left me in that lake to drown weren't really my friends at all.

I looked back to Noah, Emma, and Ethan, who trailed behind the group, and it was clear that nobody would miss me if I slipped away. It had already happened. A pattern being painted before my very eyes. And for the first time in a long time, I was pleased by that. I wanted to see Walker again—to thank him for saving my life. But also to give him back his flannel. But I didn't grab his flannel when I headed out to the dock. I only grabbed Gunner's leash and told Lainey that I was taking him to go to the bathroom. She hardly blinked an eye, happy for the help.

I gripped the leash tightly in my hand as I made my way down the hill. There was a heat in my cheeks that told me I was flushed. Hopefully it would be hidden in the dark of the night. Was he waiting there for me? Had he come here to check up on me? What was I going to say to him? And the one question in my head I wouldn't allow myself to ask: why hadn't I brought his flannel?

CHAPTER 5

The red leash was wrapped around my hand so tightly it nearly cut off the circulation to my fingers. I squeezed it tighter still. I wanted to see Walker again. Only I hadn't imagined it would be this soon . . . or ever at all. I hoped I would have more time to think of something clever to say, to gather my wits. But I had nothing. I had no idea how to thank him. And at this point, I didn't know if he had really saved my life, or if I had made up the whole thing. But the fact that he was there at the edge of the dock and his flannel had been lying across the foot of my bed for days could only mean one thing. Whatever had happened to me the first night we got to Baylor, it was real.

I reached the dock, my shoes padding over the wood planks and Gunner prancing happily at my side. Walker stood with his hands balled deep in his pockets, his stance wide. He'd come here looking for me. And it was more than any of my friends had done. A smile crept up my cheeks, and I lowered my head so my hair spilled over my face.

"I didn't expect to see you here so soon," I said, closing the distance between us.

"I came to check on you. It looks like you're doing just fine," Walker said, motioning to the raging party going on inside the cabin on top of the hill. Rock Creek Cove consisted of the Vandal's cabin and ours within a large clearing. The party was hard to miss. I looked back, a bit embarrassed at my friends' antics. There was no courage left from the drinks I'd had before the races started. The flashes of nightmare had sobered me up and dried me out.

"Oh, yeah . . . *that*. I have a group of friends staying the summer with me. They can get a little . . . rowdy," I said, shrugging. I studied his face. His dimples were deep, his face scruffy, and his eyes . . . I still couldn't discern what color they were. It was dark tonight, but not as ominous as the night we'd met. I could see a little more of his face in the shadows, and every bit was a welcome surprise. He was handsome, even more so than I remembered.

Walker sat down on the dock with a small groan, hanging his legs over the edge. Gunner came over to investigate, and Walker reached out to pet him before leaning back on the palms of his hands and looking up at me with his dark, mysterious eyes. I looked nervously back at the cabin. The lights were on, and the music was loud, even in the distance. I bent down and unhooked Gunner's leash, letting him run off to relieve himself and give us some privacy. Lainey said that he would come back, and I assumed this was true even when she wasn't around. I watched him race off and then loosened the leash around my hand. I took a seat next to Walker, but I didn't dare hang my legs over the edge.

"Is that your dog?" he asked. His warm, beachy scent brought up images of a sunny day. A frisbee. A dog galloping into the surf.

"Oh, no. That's my friend Lainey's dog. His name is Gunner. He's a really sweet dog. He just needs a lot of exercise. He'll come back," I said. We watched the dog disappear into the night, and I questioned my better judgment in letting him go. But it didn't last long, because right then, a pair of boxers surfaced in the lake before us.

"Oh . . ." I gasped.

"Do you see that?" Walker asked, his brows furrowed. It wasn't how I'd expected the conversation to go. I wanted to minimize our immaturity, not highlight it.

"So, there's this thing called The Naked Cheetah Races," I began.

"Really?" he asked, amused. I felt myself shrink just a little.

"It's where you race naked down the street as fast as you can. It's not really popular yet, but I think it will catch on." My eyes were trained on the boxers until they drifted underneath the dock and out of sight.

"Does that underwear belong to one of contestants?" he asked.

"Well, yes. We just figured that, after the naked races had finished, we would throw all the contestants' clothes in the lake, so they would have to jump in the lake . . . naked." It sounded so much more malicious out loud than it did in my head.

"And this is a tradition?" he asked.

"It might be the first annual race. Only time will tell."

He chuckled, and a relieved smile spread across my lips.

"Hey, I never got a chance to say thank you," I said. Walker looked at me, and in that moment, I knew that everything I had experienced that night was no lie. No charade. And no devious dream. I had thought maybe I was crazy, that I had made the whole thing up, or had an injury, but the look on Walker's face said it all. This was very real. Which made it very dangerous. I owed him everything.

"I don't know how to thank you for saving my life, but I do know that if you hadn't been there in the middle of the lake, I may never have gotten back alive. And I can't imagine what that would have done to my family. I just can't thank you enough. Honestly." My eyes watered, and I wiped a tear away before it had a chance to spill over my cheek.

Walker nodded, looking down at his feet dangling over the dock's edge. He gave me a moment of silence, and I tried to clear my throat of emotion. "I'm just grateful I was there, too," he said. A wash of relief came over me because, even though I knew from looking into his eyes that the night had been real, I hadn't known if we were on the same page until he'd said it out loud. And it felt good to finally be in sync with someone. Anyone.

"So, you're here for the summer with a group of friends?" he asked, looking back at me.

"Yeah. Eleven of my friends, one dog, and me. We've been planning it all senior year."

"High school?" Walker raised his eyebrows. I'd assumed he was older than I was, but not by much. Clearly, he was taken aback.

"We just finished high school. We flew here right after high school graduation. It's our summer of freedom. How . . . How old are you?" I asked and immediately regretted it. *So rude.*

"Twenty-four."

I looked at Walker. It wasn't too much of a difference. I smiled, trying to read his face, but I detected some sadness there. He looked out over the lake, and I watched his pensive gaze deepen. Was he upset that I was only eighteen? That was stupid. It's not like we were dating. I shook my head, dispelling yet another thought.

"After this summer, I'll be going away to college. For many of us, this is our last true break. Then come the bills, the rent, the jobs," I said.

"What are you going to college for?"

"Art history." I shrugged. Art history was never something I was passionate about, but it would have to do. I liked art enough. It just wasn't my first choice. "I just left an internship at a small art gallery in town. It was okay. The husband and wife that owned it were a little peculiar though." A frown spread across my face as I remembered all the times I had walked in on something that seemed fishy. I'm not sure if they were cooking the books or laundering drug money through art sales, but I knew something didn't add up. I'd been thankful my internship was only a matter of months. And I learned quite a few things, regardless.

"You don't sound too excited."

I twisted the leash in my hand and scanned the grounds for Gunner.

"I don't know. I like art enough, but if I was being honest with myself, I would have chosen something else. I think I'm really good at art. Not like painting or sculpting, not even drawing, but I'm good at selling it. I'm good at looking at the brushstrokes and knowing what technique was used, or even what era the art had come from. I really excelled at it in school. At first, it was just an easy grade, but then I thought, maybe it was an easy living, too. It's an odd talent, and I figured I should just run with it."

"Well, if you have a talent, I think it's great you're furthering your abilities. But why do you say you like it . . . *enough?*"

"I just like other aspects of art better, but I'm not good at them. I can't make a living off them. And I figured it would be smart to choose the option I thought would be most lucrative," I said.

"So you choose art?" he laughed.

I shook my head with a sheepish smile. He was right. I'd probably make a better living being a waitress, and I wouldn't have to go to college for it. Sometimes I thought I had it all figured out, and other times I knew I was a mess.

"Where does your *passion* lie?" he asked, his smile not yet fading.

"Um, nooo . . ." I said, tucking my hair behind my ears. But he just waited expectantly. The silence ate at me, and I finally caved.

"It's kind of embarrassing, but I really love movies. I can play movies in my head, anywhere, anytime. I fall asleep at night playing movies in my head. Daydream all day. I can imagine the best of times, and I can imagine the most tragic of them. I know where the music should start and how it should build. It's like a symphony, and I want to create that more than anything. So when you ask where my passion lies, if I were being honest, I'd have to say screenwriting." I ran my free hand through my hair nervously and didn't dare look at him. I didn't want him to ask the million-dollar question. Because the embarrassing part wasn't *what* I was passionate about but more the fact that I could never do it justice. Being dyslexic was like a hand that always held me down, held me back, and I knew not to go up against it. For I would lose, every time.

"What do you do?" I asked, not giving him any time to ruminate over my dream.

"Well, you talk about what's lucrative, and for me right now, it's bartending. You wouldn't believe the amount of money I make bartending. But it's taxing. Most nights, I go home feeling lonely—so lonely. It's really hard when you're in a room full of people and it only makes you feel more alone." He sighed, long and heavy. "But when everybody is drinking, and everyone is on a date or with friends, and you're the only person there who is sober, responsible, and alone, it can be mentally and emotionally taxing."

Walker looked into my eyes for a long moment, and I could almost feel his pain. I didn't know a thing about him other than that he was lonely, and it was enough to break my heart. He had saved my life. The least I could do was be a friend to him.

"So, if bartending is lucrative for you—if it pays your bills—then what is it that *you're* passionate about but can't squeeze a penny out of?" I asked.

"Most nights, I work air traffic control at the airport. I love it. And it actually does pay the bills. But I'm still learning, and I have a little way to go before I climb the ranks. And so, I bartend on the weekends."

"Do you mean you tell the planes where to go?" I asked.

"Yes. I watch the skies. I talk to everybody in the air and tell them when the coast is clear. I'm like a traffic light for the sky." He looked up at the stars, and I followed his gaze. I imagined planes flying through the sky and stopping at his command. Stoplights made from twinkling stars.

"Why do you bartend if you're making money doing what you love?" It made little sense to me.

"Like I said before, nights can be lonely. And since I spend nights doing air traffic control, I'm awake while the rest of the world is asleep. It only made sense for me to get another job during the nighttime hours. At first, I imagined being around a lively group of people would cure the emptiness, but what I didn't realize until months into the job was that it only made it worse."

Walker steepled his fingers under his chin, and I imagined what his stubble would feel like on the palm of my hand if I caressed his face. I took a deep breath, prying my eyes from his jawline. *Emptiness. So sad.* "I get that," I said, looking back at the cabin.

"You do?" he asked.

I inhaled, looking away from him, out over the water.

When somebody saves your life, all other boundaries seem to prove nebulous. No topic was off limits.

"I do. I'm in this cabin with eleven of my closest friends, and I've never felt as alone as I did that night. The night of the . . . the night we met."

"The other night? You felt alone?" he asked.

"I don't think anybody even noticed I was gone," I said, my voice choking up a bit. I bowed my chin to my chest and fiddled with the leash in my hands, turning it over again and again.

"That's impossible," he said.

I smiled because that's exactly what I had thought. I shrugged, trying not to cry. Looking away, I caught a glimpse of something in the distance. At first, I thought it was Gunner running through the woods, but then I realized it was much taller. As if the dog had stood upright and run on his back two legs. I arched my back, craning my neck to get a better look.

Walker followed my gaze, looking into the woods himself. "What in the . . ." he mumbled.

The blur came at lightning speed, and when it breached the wall of pines into the clearing, it was clear that it was no dog. Mason was running full speed, buck naked. A wash of disbelief poured over me, and I burst into laughter. I covered my mouth with both hands, suppressing what I could. Walker started to laugh too, and we sat on the dock watching a naked guy running through the clearing at top speed. Sixty miles per hour? No, but pretty darn close. He kept looking behind him as if something was chasing him. As if he were running for his life. Not far behind him was Gunner.

"Ahhh!" Mason yelled as Gunner closed in on him. I looked at Walker, tears filling my eyes once more. This was far more embarrassing than the underwear floating in the water or my top-secret dream to be a screenwriter.

"That must be a contestant?" Walker asked.

"Clearly, he came in last!" I said.

Mason slammed the door behind him as he rushed into the cabin, locking Gunner outside. I watched the dog sniff around the grassy knoll after his prey had fled, and I was happy that he'd returned home. The hazing going on inside the cabin was audible from the dock, and it made me smile. I could only imagine what they were saying to Mason, but I was positive that Scarlett May had videotaped it all, and I could watch it later.

"So, the races are every Friday night. Sign-ups are inside . . ." I said as our laughter died down. I peeked at Walker when the air between us fell silent, and he had a small smile on his face as he stared out over the water. It was a far better look than the pensive, lonely gaze he'd been wearing when we'd first sat down.

"So, do you live around here?" I asked.

Walker shook his head. "No. I'm just here visiting, like

you." My eyes locked onto his canoe, tied to the end of the dock.

"Where are you staying?" I asked.

"I'm staying at the Williams' cabin. It's across the lake. They rent it out as often as they can. I stay there sometimes when work becomes too much and I need a break from all of it." Walker's voice was ragged now.

"You mean, when you need a break from being lonely, you come to the lake to get away from everyone?" I teased. Apparently, it was something we both did. Walker smiled at me, and I felt the warmth creep into my cheeks once more. He caught me staring at his lips, and I looked away, thankful he couldn't see my swarthy hue betray me.

"Now you're getting it," he said with a full smile. He wore it well, but something told me he didn't wear it often.

"Actually, I do," I said.

The cabin door opened and slammed closed, stealing my attention. Out came Lainey and Kimber, arms interlocked. They leaned against each other, swerving from side to side. I knew my time with Walker was coming to an end, and I'd have to say goodbye.

"I still have your flannel!" I blurted out in an attempt to make further plans with him.

"Oh, you can keep it," he said, swiping a hand through the air.

I'd like that very much, but I still needed a reason to

see him again. It's not like I was old enough to keep him company at the bar where he worked.

"No, I'll get it back to you." I insisted. "Will I see you again?" I asked. Hopeful.

"Yeah, of course. I'll be here for a while."

Lainey and Kimber barely made it to the dock without tumbling to the ground. Squeals and screams were heard as they slipped on the wet grass—and once again when Gunner pushed up beside them. I watched as they swerved dangerously close to the dock's edge. I stood up anxiously, the leash wrapped around my hand. Walker stood too, and I gave him an awkward shrug of apology. I knew he was lonely, and I could have sat there all night talking to him if he'd let me. If we weren't interrupted. But there were naked men running from ferocious beasts in the woods and inebriated girls in stitches stumbling down the dock. An entire night to connect might be in our future, but it wasn't tonight.

"Okay, so I'll see you again then?" I asked worriedly.

"You sure will," he said, stuffing his hands into his pockets. I started toward my friends, saving them from walking the plank that they'd inevitably tumble over. And even though the water was shallow, I knew it was the home of something nefarious.

"Where'd Gunner go?" Lainey asked, slurring her words. I searched the hilltop. Gunner was digging a hole just beyond the cabin. I sighed. It was my fault.

"He's right over there. He didn't go far."

"What are you doing out here?" Kimber asked, eyes searching. I looked behind me. Walker stood, assessing the situation. I smiled, turning back to Kimber and Lainey.

"Nothing!" I reached out to grab Kimber's arm as she stumbled over her own two feet. "Easy there. Or you're going to fall into the lake," I said.

"I'll be careful. I can do it. Watch this. Watch." Kimber closed her eyes and tilted her head back, trying to touch each pointer finger to her nose. She failed miserably, stuffing her right finger into her eye and her left into her cheek. I cringed inside.

"Oh yeah, I can see that," I said.

"Gunner! Gunner? Come'er boy!" Lainey yelled. Gunner came running down the hill, abandoning his hole. When he reached us, I clipped the leash onto his collar, thankful he'd come back. We reached the end of the dock, and Lainey wrapped her arm in mine, her weight making me stagger too.

"But seriously, who were you talking to?" she asked.

I turned back, looking at Walker. Like a gentleman, he was still there, waiting to make sure I got back into the cabin safely. I smiled, butterflies fluttering in my stomach, and said, "Nobody!" in a coy tone, denying myself the truth.

## CHAPTER 6

The room was dark and empty. Not a thing could be seen except for Gran's chair lit by a blazing fire, though I felt no heat. Goosebumps prickled the nape of my neck, and a shiver spilled down my spine, quaking deep in my bones. I'd been to this place before; that much I was sure of. I felt a sense of familiarity as I looked around me. Gran's chair was empty, and a book lay open with a bookmark nestled between the pages. I looked into the void, as far as my eyes could stretch, but there was nothing there . . . there never was.

I'd been here before, but I couldn't remember when, or why. A dream? Was I dreaming? I looked down at my hands, opening and closing them. They moved in slow motion. I turned them over, examining them closely. Something was off, but I couldn't pinpoint what. It was like I had been peeking behind the curtain during a magic show.

I pressed my fingers against my palm, slowly and steadily, until something odd happened. My fingertips disappeared as they sank into my flesh. I couldn't feel it. I couldn't feel anything but cold. I watched as they poked out the backside of my hand.

I did it again in disbelief—this time faster . . . harder. My fingers drove through the meaty part of my palm and jutted out the other side. A small sound escaped my throat as I pulled my hands apart and whipped my head around, looking again to see if anything was out there in the void. But I was alone. Just me and the thudding of my heart like a caged animal driven mad.

Hypnotized, I grabbed at my arm fast and fierce, but it was different. I was able to hold my arm with a firm grip. What was happening? *Am I here? Am I not here?* I concentrated on doing it again. I tried to prove to myself that I saw it. My head hurt as my hand glitched through my arm. I was no more than a figment of my own imagination. A ghost. I wasn't supposed to be here. I swallowed the lump of anxiety building in my throat. I was in some state of subconsciousness. A higher level of awareness. But why? How?

With a creak of the rocking chair, I whipped my head up. Gran was there, as if she had been sitting there the whole time. She looked at me and smiled, though I felt no peace in her pleasure. No love in her eyes.

"This is a dream," I heard myself say.

Gran slowly turned the page, as if my presence meant nothing to her, and continued to read. "This isn't real," I said, repeating myself.

"This is as real as you make it, my dear," she said, eyes still transfixed on the page.

"No, this is just a dream. Only a dream." I looked back at my hands and realized why they looked so weird. There weren't any wrinkles where my knuckles should have been. It was smooth skin, like it had been manipulated by a computer-generated image. I ran my hand over my face, feeling my features. My lips, the bridge of my nose, my icy breath.

"Oh dear, you have so much to learn. And so little time," she said.

"What do you mean, Gran? Is there something you need to tell me? Is that why you're here?" I asked. I didn't think she was supposed to be here. I *knew* that *I* wasn't.

Gran slowly closed the book and placed it on the table before her. "In fact, I have something to tell you. You see, there are answers to the questions you seek. There are answers out there, waiting for you to find them. If only you would find them, dear," she said, in a dark, mysterious tone. It wasn't the voice I'd grown up listening to.

"What do you mean, answers?" I asked.

"Dear, there is a girl out there who needs your help. A girl who's lost and lonely. Even more lost than you are now. And there's no way out." She motioned to the black void. "You're the only one who can find her and bring her home safely. You need to find her."

"A girl?" I didn't care about a girl. I only wanted to know where I was. And why I was so cold.

"A girl. You must find her," she insisted.

"Well, how? How do I do that?"

"Find her!" Gran bellowed. I didn't hear her voice with my ears; instead, I felt it throughout my body, shaking my bones and echoing into the distant emptiness of the void. The fire faded out, the orange flames shrinking down to glowing red coals before disappearing in a trail of smoke. As impossible as it would seem, the place grew colder. The chills raked through me until I was frozen. I turned to stone, unable to move an inch except for my eyes. My skin was tight and dry, and I felt as if I might crack in half and shatter against the floor. Gran grew dim as the shadows spread across her face, and she began to disappear. I knew my time was closing in.

"Gran? Where do I find her?" I asked without ever moving my lips. The thought echoed far away and went unanswered. The room had turned dark as coal and Gran was no longer there. Nothing was. No chair. No fireplace. No books.

"Gran! Gran! What does she look like? How will I

know?" I yelled into the darkness. My voice called out for miles but reached no one.

I used all my strength to break out of the stone—to escape the fixation that encapsulated me. I jolted awake, covered in a blanket of sweat and gasping for air. I gripped the sheets in my hands, panting, and looked around, taking in my surroundings. I was in the cabin, the master bedroom. And though it was the middle of the night, it wasn't as dark as the void, nor as cold. My head pounded, and I brought my hands up to my forehead, squinting. It wasn't a fight I could manage alone. I threw the blanket off me and swung my knees over the edge of the bed, my toes touching down on the soft plush carpet. I slipped on some shorts and tiptoed downstairs in search of pain medicine.

I didn't know if my headache was from the few drinks I'd had the night before or the recurring dreams of my gran that tormented me, but I knew I would no longer be able to sleep with the throbbing between my ears. The stairs creaked as I made my way to the kitchen. The air hit the sweat on my shirt, leaving me chilled. A green sleeping bag was sprawled on the living room floor, a body stuffed inside. I figured it was Mason, who had been known for his unconventional sleeping habits.

There were only three bedrooms in the cabin—all of them upstairs. Asher and Kimber were sharing a room, since they were the only couple in the group. Emma and Lainey shared the third bedroom because they were my closest friends. And I, of course, had the master. Everyone else slept wherever. On various sofas, recliners, and sometimes, I'd come to learn, the back porch.

"What the hell?" A small moan came from a sleeping bag when I turned the kitchen lights on. I quickly turned them off again, trying not to disturb the sleeper. I fumbled around, thankful it was my cabin and I knew where the first aid kit was kept. By the light of the refrigerator, I managed to take out a couple of pain killers and pour myself a glass of water.

Before I had finished my water, Noah surprised me in the kitchen, wearing only a pair of boxer shorts. His sandy hair was a mess, and his face pink from sleep. "Hey," I whispered, my shirt wet and clinging to my chest.

"Hey," he replied. His eyes traveled down and back up lazily.

"What are you doing up?" I asked.

"I've got this headache that won't quit. Do you have ibuprofen?" he asked.

"Yeah, I just took some, too. I've got a raging headache also. Right here," I said, rubbing the top of my forehead.

"Mine's in the back," he said, rubbing the back of his head.

As Noah and I stood in the kitchen, both rubbing our heads, I flashed back to a memory of when we were young. "Do you remember that one time, when we were at your house and our moms were hosting a book club meeting?" I asked with a coy smile.

"I remember her book clubs, but which time?"

"The time we hit our heads together on your trampoline, and we were too embarrassed to go inside and interrupt the meeting," I said, still rubbing my head.

"Oh, that time. How could I forget? I thought I was going to die!" Noah whispered, cracking a smile. I stifled my laughter as I tried not to wake up whoever was wrapped in the sleeping bag in the living room.

"I thought we were dying too. It hurt so bad."

Noah and I had grown up together. Our moms were friends and often hosted random parties together—book club once a month and the occasional Tupperware party or Bunco night. Basically, any reason to get together and uncork the wine. Often, I would go with my mom, and Noah and I would play in the yard while our moms got toasted.

We grew up as good friends, but somewhere along the way, when puberty had struck and our feelings began to develop for the opposite sex, things between us grew awkward. Many years passed where we wouldn't speak to one another, and I no longer went to his house for our mothers' meetings. Eventually, in high school, we started talking again. We picked up right where we'd left off and became fast friends again. Our groups combined—his the athletic, popular group and my threesome of Lainey,

Emma, and me. It wasn't until the last couple of years that I had developed feelings for him. I believed those feelings were mutual, but I couldn't be sure. I knew staying at my cabin all summer would either flush out our feelings or chase them away.

"Hey, do you still get those nightmares? The ones about your shed?" I asked.

"No, not often. But every once in a while, one will resurface." Noah seemed embarrassed, but I wasn't judging him, just trying to connect. He'd had a rough time with nightmares when he was a kid. Something about the shed in his back yard always seemed to scare him. I was never sure where the fear stemmed from. And every now and then, I would think about it and try to figure out what the missing piece of the puzzle was. But as far as I could tell, it was just his mother's potting shed and nothing more.

"That's good," I said, finishing my water. The room fell quiet, but neither Noah nor I made a move to leave the kitchen. Neither one of us wanted the conversation to end. And presumably, neither one of us could sleep with our headaches. I kept the conversation going with the only thing I knew about nightmares. Mine.

"I've been having nightmares myself," I confessed, as I recalled the one that had woken me up. I tugged at the hem of my shirt, and it peeled away from my chest.

"You've been having nightmares? What about?" he asked, no longer embarrassed about his own.

"I don't know. They're kind of weird. It's always this empty dark place. My gran is there, and it's as if she never died. Like she thinks she is still alive. Only I know better. I know she shouldn't be there with me, and a part of me wonders if she's trying to get a message through. But that's stupid."

"That's not stupid. That's awesome," he said. I looked up from the countertop into his denim-blue eyes. They were compassionate, and I knew he only wanted the best for me.

"You think so?" I asked, wrinkling my nose.

"Yeah. I've heard enough stories like that to believe that maybe there's some truth in them. What does she say?" he asked with honest curiosity.

"Well, the one I just woke up from . . . she was there in this room of . . . of . . . nothingness. She told me I needed to find a girl," I said, thinking about it for the first time since waking up.

"A girl?"

"Yeah, a girl. But that's pretty much it. She didn't say where I would find her, or what she would look like. She only said that I needed to find her. Bring her home."

"That's all? Do you have any idea what it means?"

"No, but she said that the girl needed my help." I shook my head, dispelling the stupid idea that my grandmother was talking to me from beyond the grave. A large part of me didn't believe it myself, but there was a small part that wouldn't let it go—an itty-bitty part that believed that maybe she was alive somewhere. That I was special enough for her to cross worlds beyond ours, just to talk to me. Maybe she had gone through all of this effort to reach through the veil of the living to get some special message to me. I didn't know who this girl was, and I didn't intend to go find her. But the riddle would keep me up at night. That much, I was sure of.

"How are you doing with your grandma and all? I meant to reach out earlier, but honestly, I didn't know what to say. I know you two were close," he said, biting his lip the way he did when he was nervous.

I could feel the warmth of emotion heating my skin. Gran and I had been close. I missed her deeply, but I knew my mom missed her more, and for that reason, I felt invalidated in my hardship. I brushed it off like I was stronger than I was. "I'm doing all right," I lied.

"You know you can talk to me, right? We've been friends forever," he said. *Friends? But was that all?* I looked at him but saw nothing behind his eyes—other than a well of sympathy for my pain. It could have been the love you had for someone because they grew up with you, like family, or it could have been more.

"I know I can talk to you. It's just hard. It's hard to think that somebody so significant in your life can be there one minute and gone the next. If I'm being honest with you, it's turned my universe upside down. All the things I thought were important before just aren't anymore. And I don't know if it's some sort of depression from her passing or a simple change of perspective. But everything I see and everything I think . . . it's different now." I looked down at my fingers interlocking with one another as I fidgeted. A part of me focused on the resistance of my fingers against my hand, and I remembered what it had been like in my dream when I was fluid.

"I get that. Do you feel like these new perspectives on life are better than before?" he asked.

"Better?" I thought back to all the times I'd questioned the loyalty of my friendships or the motives behind their actions. I thought about all the times I'd sat on the edge of my bed alone, wondering what the point was. If I should even bother with college if it couldn't buy me happiness. "Not better. Just different," I lied again, as a movement caught the corner of my eye.

Mason staggered into the kitchen, his sleeping bag still around his lower half as he clutched it tight around his waist. Both Noah and I stared at him curiously. Was he sleepwalking? Was he still drunk? He slid his feet along the kitchen floor as he moseyed toward the refrigerator. He didn't notice either of us as he opened the door and pulled out a cold beer. He cracked it open with one hand and guzzled back what I could only assume to be half the can, if not more. He was about to close the fridge when he saw something else and opened it back up. It felt like Noah and I were watching a National Geographic documentary.

Mason reached into the refrigerator with his other hand, and his sleeping bag dropped to the floor, exposing his bare butt. I sucked in a quick gasp, and Mason spun around to see Noah and me standing behind him with large, watchful eyes.

"Oh shit! Oh . . . It's just you guys," he said, somewhat disappointed. My eyes dropped below his waistline, and Mason turned back to the fridge and pulled out a slice of pizza. He set everything down on the kitchen counter before pulling up his sleeping bag once again. I forced my gaze away, but my eyes were still wide with surprise.

"You sleep naked, man?" Noah asked.

"My clothes are wet, douche bag."

Noah and I snickered. He had more clothes in a bag somewhere. He totally slept naked.

"Because somebody threw them in the lake. Whose bright idea was that anyway?" Mason asked through a mouthful of cold pizza.

"Don't look at me!" I said, holding up my hands.

"I don't know, but it was brilliant," Noah said.

"Brilliant? I should throw your clothes in the lake and see how you feel, asshole," Mason said, taking another bite. My eyes dropped from Mason's face down to his leftover pizza, and my stomach growled.

"Is there any more?" I asked.

"Yeah, there's a bunch in there." Mason turned to open the refrigerator and dropped his sleeping bag once again, only this time he bent over, giving us a view of his undercarriage.

"Eww, stop that!" I hissed. Mason tossed a Ziploc bag full of pizza onto the kitchen counter.

"There's the pizza, but I already gave you what you *really* wanted," he said with a hip thrust.

"You wish," Noah said.

The three of us stood in the kitchen chatting quietly while we ate our midnight snack and Noah and I waited for the ibuprofen to kick in. When my pain was no more than a memory, I told the boys I was going to try to get some sleep. I swiped my hand across Noah's back as I passed to say good night. My fingers kept contact as long as they could. Noah gave me a look that said he'd much prefer my company over Mason's, and I smiled before turning away.

I tiptoed up the stairs with a full belly and a smile on my face, hoping for a more restful night. But when I crawled into bed, all I could see was the framed photograph of my gran sitting on top of my parents' dresser. Ornate golden corners and a grainy old photo. She'd had the most beautiful eyes—green like emeralds— but as she'd aged, they'd turned cloudy and gray. She was like that in my dreams. And that's how I knew they were nightmares. Because she was still hindered by her cataracts and cancer.

I closed my eyes to sleep, but I couldn't think of anything other than the mystery girl. The most haunting thing that wracked my mind wasn't the girl, but the part where my gran had said there was no way out.

As I waited for sleep to take me, I imagined Noah in the kitchen. His sleep-mussed sandy hair and boxer shorts. But this time, a very different scenario. One where we didn't talk about my gran or nightmares. One where I had the courage to kiss him instead. One where the kiss was so passionate, it led to much, much more. But somewhere along the way, Noah turned into Walker. And I couldn't tell if that was the reason for the increased passion or not. I fell asleep before I could figure out what it all meant. And when the sun rose, all that really mattered was the fact that I rose with a smile.

CHAPTER 7

I sipped on my coffee as I pondered my dream from the night before. I wasn't planning on looking for a girl, but if I did . . . if I did, who would it be? A slow chill crawled down the nape of my neck, inching its way to my spine. There was something at the edge of my mind trying to get in. But I couldn't quite recall what it might be. I picked at it. Something Scarlett May had said. A story. It began to fester, and before I knew it, there was no more coffee left in my mug. I poured myself another and stared off into the distance. My eyes dry as I remembered the Baylor Butcher and the girl who had gotten away.

The girl had escaped her own death by just one date. She'd followed her instincts to safety. And had she seen him just one night later, she might not have been alive. She probably went into hiding. *Hiding.* A girl who was hiding needed to be found. Had the girl my gran spoke of been the same girl that had escaped the Baylor Butcher? No. I was stretching.

But *if* the girl I was supposed to find had been the girl from the stories, then how was I to help? I had nothing in common with a stranger who had dated a monster long, long ago. At least, nothing that I knew of. It was then that curiosity lit inside me. A small flame at first, but it was being fed, and growing brighter and hotter. I needed to find out who this girl was to see if we had a connection. I hesitated to ask Scarlett May any more questions for fear of her sharp tongue, but she was the obvious place to start.

I looked around the living room at the slow-moving zombies before me. Several people were awake, but none of them alert. Many of them were like me, a mug in their hand and a distant gaze on their face. It was time I started taking matters into my *own* hands. I had a mission. A mission that wasn't driven by my late gran, but one that had been ignited by my own curiosity. Who was she?

"Hey, Emma? I'm going to run to the grocery store in a little bit. Is there anything in particular that you want me to pick up for you?" Emma rubbed the sleep from her eyes while she thought about it.

"Some yogurt would be good. I like to eat that for breakfast," she said.

"Yogurt. No problem," I said, writing it down.

"Do you want me to go with you?"

"I don't think that'll be necessary," I said, looking away.

I had much more than grocery shopping to do. I wanted to talk to some of the locals about the Baylor ghost stories, and I couldn't exactly do that if I had a friend tagging along. Not without follow-up questions, that is.

I took my notes and went to find Lainey, who was a vegetarian and surely had a long list of specialty items for me to gather at the grocery store. I found her upstairs brushing her hair in the bathroom.

"Good morning," I said, leaning against the doorjamb.

"Morning."

"I'm going to the grocery store. What kinds of things should I pick up for you?" I asked, tapping the pen on the pad.

"Oh, I can just go with you," she said, fumbling around in her bag for toothpaste and a toothbrush.

"No, that's all right. Why don't you stay here and enjoy the lake? It's going to be a nice day," I said.

"I don't mind at all. Plus, I have a lot of weird things to pick up that you're probably unfamiliar with." Lainey shoved her toothbrush into her mouth and looked at me sideways.

"You like those vegetarian sausage patties, right?" I asked, jotting it down.

"Yeah, but it has to be the brand with the green box. They have another one that comes in a blue box and they are gross. But seriously, I'll just go with you!" Suds ran down her chin, and she leaned over the sink.

"Actually, I was just going to run some errands and then hit the grocery store on the way back home. I'll probably be gone most of the day," I said.

"Okay, why don't I write it down for you then," Lainey said. I waited patiently for her to finish brushing her teeth and write out her list.

Lainey had been an animal lover from the time she was a young child. She'd stopped eating meat after watching a documentary about how farm-raised fish made it to the market. A long time ago, I'd asked her if she missed it, and she'd said that she didn't.

"Thank you. I'll just call if I have any questions," I said.

"Yeah, and if you change your mind, I'm happy to go with." Lainey turned back to the mirror for one last look.

I ventured downstairs in search of Scarlett May. I found her on the back porch talking on the phone. The way she spoke made me think she was talking to a crush. There was a smirk on her face, her cheek lifted, and a sparkle brightened her eyes. She was dressed to impress in studded jean shorts and red cowgirl boots. Everyone else in the house was still in pajamas, with the exception of Mason, who I assumed was still naked in his sleeping bag. Scarlett May hung up the phone and looked at me with raised brows but didn't say anything.

"Are you going somewhere?" I asked, checking her out.

"I'm meeting my friend Sampson today." Jack

Sampson was a family friend of hers. Whenever she came to visit the lake, she and Sampson would get into all sorts of mischief. She'd been planning for the group to meet up with him and his friends for a bonfire. I wondered if they were more than just friends by the way she was dressed and the light in her eyes when she spoke to him.

"I'm running to the grocery store. Is there anything that you need?" I asked.

"Yeah, get eggs and bacon. Probably coffee too." Scarlett May stuffed her cell phone into the back pocket of her shorts and started to head for the door.

"Oh, I just had a question real quick. You know how you were telling us about the Baylor ghost stories? I was wondering if you had any more details on the girl who got away? Like a name, or perhaps—"

"You're not serious, are you?" she interrupted.

"What do you mean?" I felt the shrinking of my presence, like a reprimanded dog shaking before its owner. She cocked her head to the side, looking at me as if I were stupid. Was I? Stupid?

"You don't really think she has a name, do you? For me to have a name would mean that the ghost stories were real. And ghost stories aren't real. They're no more than fables meant to scare the living daylights out of young children. And last time I checked, you're not a young child." Scarlett May stared at me with her head still cocked. "Well, are you?" she asked.

"What? Am I what?"

"A child?"

"No, I—"

"That's what I thought. So don't get spooked by the kiddie story." She spun on her heels and then peered over her shoulder and whispered, "It's not real . . ." Then she left me on the back patio, stewing in my humiliation. The door slammed shut, making me jump.

It was going to be a beautiful day. The sky was clear, and the green grass was glistening with morning dew. The lake itself was like glass, with not a soul in sight. Nobody except Mrs. Vandal. She watched me as she watered her rose bushes. I gave her a curt wave, and she looked away, ignoring me. Yup, it was going to be a beautiful day in Baylor, but that wouldn't clear the gloom I felt building inside me.

I found Ethan with Asher in the game room. They were using the pool table as a dining table, their breakfast plates on top of the green felt; my dad would be furious. "Do you guys want anything from the grocery store?" Ethan Patrick was Asher's biggest fan. I think he liked him even more than Kimber did. Both of them had dark hair, but only Ethan's was sun-kissed, shining red under the sun's rays. Ethan styled his hair much like Asher did, and he even dressed like him. I sometimes thought of Ethan as Asher's shadow, and I wasn't the only one.

"You're running to the grocery store?" Ethan asked.

"Why don't I come along and give you a hand? That's a lot of people to shop for," he said, blushing. I'd known Ethan had a crush on me since second grade, the same way I'd known when somebody had been watching me, even if there was nobody there. Typically, he took failure well, but there was something about this trip that was different. I imagined he had goals of his own to achieve this summer. His last chance to make a move. It's how I felt about Noah.

"I appreciate it, but I'm going alone. I have a bunch of errands to do in town, and grocery shopping is only my last stop. But I'm happy to pick up whatever you need." I tapped the pen on the pad that was nearly full of special requests. Lainey didn't talk much about Ethan, probably because she felt he liked me too. But I knew she had feelings for him, which made it difficult for me. I usually tried to minimize my time with Ethan so she would feel more comfortable.

"Just make sure you get lots of meat. I think I went through the sandwich meat in one sitting yesterday," Asher said.

"Lots of real meat, and lots of fake meat. Got it," I said.

I called a cab to get into town. It was too far away for the golf cart to handle. Most of the visitors around the lake needed temporary transportation, so cabs were crawling around all the local attractions. With the list stuffed in my back pocket, I had the cab drop me off on the main street, just before the grocery store. There was only one store in

Baylor, and it was slim pickings. The floors were scuffed and in desperate need of renovation. The shelves were stocked, but mostly with off-brand products. I wasn't sure if I would be able to find anything that Lainey wanted. Especially the green-boxed sausages.

I grabbed a cart and strolled through the aisles, slowly looking for not only the items on my list but locals who looked like they'd heard a story or two before. The air was frigid, and the wheel on my grocery cart squeaked every time it rotated. I didn't know which was worse, the squeak or the elevator music that piped through the speakers. If I had chosen the grocery store to start my research on the Baylor ghost stories, then I had chosen the wrong place. There wasn't a soul in sight.

By the third aisle, I passed a mother with a young child. Young enough to have nightmares about the questions I had planned to ask. I smiled at them politely as I passed by.

I came upon a store clerk. A young man—probably in his twenties—with a face full of acne. He was stocking shelves and pretended not to notice me. "Excuse me? Do you know where the lunchmeat is?" I asked. Even though I had already walked past it three times, looking for people to start my investigation.

"Aisle twelve," he said, eyes fixed on the cans of corn before him. I tightened my grip on the shopping cart, but I didn't move.

"I have a really weird question that maybe you can help me with? I'm in town for the summer, and I've recently heard of an old tale about a butcher. Something about a man who haunts Baylor Lake. Have you ever heard of something like that before?" I asked.

"I'm sorry ma'am, I don't know of any ghost stories." The store clerk stood up and abandoned his cans. I watched his tall thin figure walk away. I scratched my head, looking up and down the empty aisle.

I had just about finished my shopping when I found a large man, both tall and wide, taking a bag of trash out back. I seized the opportunity. "Excuse me! Excuse me!" I yelled as I pushed my cart, squeaky wheel and all, as fast as I could. When I approached the store clerk, he was much more intimidating up close than from afar. He was an older gentleman and quite rough around the edges. And there was a smell. Putrid in its own right.

"You talkin' to me?" he asked, with a furrowed brow.

"I was curious if you had a moment? I'm doing a little research on some town gossip, and I was wondering if you've heard any Baylor ghost stories before?" I asked, my heart beating a little faster than normal.

"Which Baylor ghost story? There are several. Which one you wanna know about?"

"You've heard them!" I was so excited that I finally had someone to ask my questions that when he walked out the back of the grocery store, I didn't hesitate to follow him. I left my cart inside and stepped into the back alley. It was an unsightly place, filled with dumpsters and a few parked cars. Trash lined the curb, and the cars looked like they'd been there for months. Spider webs stretched from the tires to the street. Slightly uneasy, I looked at the man's nametag. Jim.

"My friend recently told me of a story about a man who used to, um, kill his dates. She said that one lady got away, and since then, he's haunted the lake. But that's all that she told me, and I was curious enough about it to start doing some research," I said hopefully.

"Why are you so curious?" he asked, throwing the trash bag into the dumpster.

"Oh, I don't know. I was just intrigued by the history of it all. Is it real?" Jim walked straight toward me, and I feared he wouldn't stop. He was uncomfortably close, and I had to take several steps back.

"It's real, all right. The man. The ghost. The one who got away," he said, stepping forward. I stepped backward.

His blue button-down shirt gaped between buttons, exposing the skin beneath his navel. He reeked of something sour. And I imagined it was the smell of not bathing for days on end. The sense that I had done something foolish washed over me. My eyes flicked to the door and back.

"Do you know any of their names?" I asked, my voice quivering as I took another step back.

"I don't know their names, but I know how he did it. He got the women to go on dates. And then he loaded them into a boat. He went out to the middle of the lake where nobody could hear their screams." He began to whisper. "Then, he took a saw, and he—"

"I was only looking for names," I said, "but thank you." With that, I turned to the door, quickly grabbing the handle. It was locked. I tried the handle again, pulling it down with force, only it didn't budge. I heard the jingle of keys behind me.

"Piece by piece, he threw their bodies into the lake. Using their flesh as fish chum. A hand here. A head there. They say he was a fisherman. Best damn one around. Fish love human blood," he said in a deep, breathy tone, spit gathering at the corners of his lips.

"Oh, thanks for your time. But I have to get going now." A tremble began inside me and worked its way out.

"Do you know what happens when little girls go looking for the one who got away?" he asked, dangling the keys to the locked door. I spun around, my heart starting to hammer in my chest.

"No," I said in a whimper.

"They become fish chum. And there's a tournament coming up, don't you know?"

"I'm sorry I took up so much of your time. I really have to be going now," I jiggled the door handle, but it wouldn't budge.

"The butcher haunts the lake until he finds her. If he gets her, he comes back to life with renewed power. Is that what you want?" he spat.

"No! No, I don't want that! I'm sorry," I pled.

"Then don't go poking your nose where it don't belong!" His belly pressed up against me and I was suffocated by his odor. I feared it would be the last thing I remembered. He pushed me against the door, grabbing my shoulders, his fingers squeezing into my bones as I screamed. The door pushed open and I was shoved forward, grabbing a hold of Jim to steady myself.

Just then, the acne-riddled store clerk appeared out of nowhere and barked at Jim in an authoritative tone I hadn't imagined he had in him.

"Jimmy! Get back to work! You're not allowed to talk to the customers! Do you want to be suspended again?"

Jim released me and spat on the floor before ridding me of his death stare. I gasped, throwing my hand across my chest. I could feel my heartbeat steady under my hand.

"Ma'am, are you okay? Jimmy's a little crazy. He's not supposed to talk to people. That's why he's on trash duty. We try to keep him in the back. I don't even know how you got out here." The clerk was upset. With Jimmy *and* with me.

"I'm okay! I'm okay."

"Shit!" hissed the clerk under his breath as I gathered myself. The store clerk unlocked the door, and we both went back inside. He strode away, leaving me alone. I looked frantically for Jim, but he was nowhere in sight.

I gathered my abandoned cart and hurried to the front of the store. The squeak of my loose wheel was sharp in my ears and even more unnerving than before. The elevator music was hauntingly calm.

A woman began checking me out, scanning multiple packs of lunchmeat. She looked nice enough, possibly like she might have grown up in Baylor. I was sure that she was the one I should have asked about the stories from the very beginning. But I was far too frightened to ask her about the fables now. I paid with a shaky hand and continued to look over my shoulder as I left the store, wishing I'd let Ethan come with me.

As I waited for my cab, there were two things I was sure of. First, the Baylor Butcher was real. Dangerous even. And there was a story there to be unearthed. Second, I had no business uncovering it. I was an out-of-towner and didn't belong to this world. I never wanted to see Jim or smell the stench of his unwashed folds again. And if he said not to look for the girl who got away, I wasn't about to.

CHAPTER 8

than met me at the front door and helped carry the grocery bags inside. We set them on the countertops, and Emma and Lainey dug through the loot. It was like Christmas morning in June.

"You'll never believe what happened to me!" I said, placing the yogurt in the refrigerator.

"What happened? Ethan asked.

"So, I randomly asked this guy who worked at the grocery store if he knew anything about the Baylor Butch—"

"What? Why would you do that?" Lainey asked.

"I . . . I . . . I overheard him talking about it, and I was curious. Anyway, that's not the point. The point is, I followed him outside into the back alley—"

"You did what?" Ethan asked, head cocked to the side.

"It was an accident. I didn't mean to. It just sort of happened that way," I said.

"Okay. So, what happened next?" Emma asked.

"Once we were out there all alone, the door locked behind us, and I was trapped with this big scary guy!" I said, holding my hands high above my head to show that he'd been roughly the size of a yeti.

"I knew I should have gone with you!" said Ethan. Lainey's eyes flicked from me to Ethan and back again.

"No, it all turned out fine. But he ended up grabbing me and shaking me violently."

"What? He touched you?" Ethan hissed.

"Yeah. He grabbed my shoulders and shook me! He towered over me, and he smelled so bad. And we were all alone! I don't know what would've happened if the other store clerk—who turned out to be the manager—hadn't come out and saved me," I said, taking out several loaves of bread for sandwiches and piling them in the bread box.

"Geez, Kinsley, you shouldn't be following creepy guys into back alleys. Didn't your mom ever teach you that?" Emma asked.

I sighed, knowing it had been a stupid idea. But the truth was, I hadn't been thinking much at the time. I'd become so consumed with the idea of finding this mystery girl that I'd lost my senses. It wouldn't happen again.

Kimber came into the kitchen and took several snacks out of the bags and began reading the labels.

"It was stupid all right. I'm just glad I made it out of there," I said, shaking my head in disbelief.

"Next time, Kinsley, I'm going with you," Ethan said. I smiled at him and nodded. I was careful not to lead him on, but I really wished I'd had somebody by my side when I was out there today, even if that meant making Lainey jealous.

We had just finished putting the groceries away when Scarlett May came in and told us about the plans she'd secured for the night. Sampson was going to have a bonfire at his place across the lake, and he'd invited everyone. Maybe a night out was exactly what I needed. I put away the part of me that was still wanting to find the missing girl —the compulsion I felt to uncover a name, at the least. A simple name. It couldn't be *that* hard to find.

It was well after dinner when everybody was getting ready to go to Sampson's house. Several of us girls packed into the bathroom, fighting for real estate in the mirror. Scarlett May had changed her blouse but stayed in the short-shorts and cowgirl boots. Kimber tied her hair up in a top bun. Maybe it was her hair, or maybe it was her impossibly thin, lanky build, but I would've bet money that she could leap into the air with the elegance of a professional ballerina.

"Sampson is so cool. You're going to love him. He's a mechanic and can fix anything. Maybe we should give him Kinsley's golf cart to fix," Scarlett May suggested.

"What's wrong with my golf cart?" I asked, swiping a smoky shade of eyeshadow across my lids.

"Nothing . . . if you have nowhere to be. It's just a little slow. He can put a turbo engine in there, and we can zip around the lake in half the time," she said.

Trinity tied a braid in her long, dark, ominous hair. Her light hazel eyes popped like those of a rattlesnake—alluring, but poisonous. It was no wonder she was so popular. She was drop-dead gorgeous . . . when her mouth was closed. I did what I could with my makeup. I had to try and keep up with all of my beautiful friends. But no amount of makeup would make my brown eyes shine. There was a small fleck of green at the bottom of the left one—a memento from my gran—but my eyes were still a muddy brown, and no amount of eyeliner would change that. My mom used to say they were full of wonder, but I always thought it was her motherly way of saying they were round and slightly oversized. At some point in my life, I'd looked in the mirror and recognized that I was plain. I'd never be as pretty as Trinity, and I'd accepted that long ago.

I left the girls in the bathroom to change my top one

last time. I wore a white blouse that I'd loved fifteen minutes ago, but after seeing Kimber in her white tank, I knew I needed to change. I stood in my closet flipping through the few shirts I'd brought when I heard something behind me. I looked to my left, where I thought I heard a whisper tickle my ear. There was nothing there. Not so much as an open window. Slowly, I turned back to my closet and yanked a black T-shirt off the hanger. It was more casual than I wanted, but it would have to do.

As I slipped the T-shirt over my head, my eyes were covered for a split second, and I heard the whisper again. I pulled the shirt down, and I spun around, whipping my head from side to side. A small light shone on the bedside table. The windows remained closed. An old antique wooden table sat in the bedroom's corner, the paint on its legs chipped. There was nobody there. My heart thumped in my chest as I felt eyes spying on me. My instincts told me to leave. To *run*. And that's what I intended to do. I grabbed the door handle, eager to join the girls in the bathroom across the hall. But when the whisper touched my ear again, I heard it, and I heard it clear as day. *Find the girl.*

I couldn't tell if it was my gran from the breathy voice. It was only a whisper. But I gathered it was her from the demand she had given me the night before as she sat in her rocking chair. It was the first time that I'd heard her voice— as quiet as it had been—outside of my dreams. I'd sensed that she was watching me before, but I had never heard her speak. With my hand glued to the doorknob, I stood frozen—not in fear, but bewilderment. A knock came from the other side.

"Kinsley? Are you in there? We're getting ready to leave," Lainey said.

"One second," I said, gathering myself.

I was caught between the fear that big Jim had instilled in me in that dingy back alley and the not-so-subtle urgency that my gran had pushed down on me. To find the girl or not. It might be a dangerous road to travel, but my loyalty lay with my grandmother. I'd do just about anything to make her proud, and if she wanted me to uncover something hidden—something lost—then I'd do it. Or I'd at least try. Even if it scared me a little. At that moment, I decided to stay behind.

I desperately needed another night to take my mind off all the craziness swirling inside my head, but if my gran had come back from the dead to tell me this one thing, could I really ignore it? I opened the door and joined the girls down the hall. "I think I'm going to stay back tonight. I'm just not feeling that well," I lied.

"What!? You have to come," Lainey said. Her face was a mixture of disappointment and confusion.

"Suit yourself," Trinity said.

"Sorry. I just got this headache out of nowhere. I think I'm going to just lie in bed and maybe read a book." I rubbed the side of my head for dramatic effect, squinting my eyes as if the pain were too much to bear. I followed the group of girls downstairs to see them out.

"Damn, I'm going to miss you. I'll text you updates," Emma said.

"I've never seen you read a book . . ." Lainey called me out. My eyes widened.

"It's her loss," Scarlett May said, her boots clacking on the kitchen floor. I forced a smile. It *was* my loss. I knew that. I didn't want to be home alone researching an old ghost story. I didn't want visits from my dead grandmother. I wanted to go to the bonfire, to see all the guys, and to whisper in my friends' ears. I wanted to have a drink, let loose, and be present. It was a loss.

Noah came into the kitchen, his shaggy hair styled, and his denim-blue eyes trained on me. "What's this I hear about you not going to the bonfire?" he asked.

"I have a headache," I lied, rubbing my head again.

"Why don't you take some pain medicine and come along? I'm sure it will fade soon."

"Maybe. I think I'm just going to stay here. I've got a book to keep me company. I'll go next time," I said, regretting my choice already. Lainey shot me a glare that I chose to ignore. Noah's eyes looked sad, like he'd miss me at the party. I already missed him as it was. I wanted to continue our conversation from the night before—the conversation we'd been sharing before Mason had joined us in his birthday suit.

"Well . . ." Noah looked around the room, his hands stuffed into his jacket pockets. "I could stay here with you?" he asked. And it was more than a question. It was an invitation to spend one-on-one time with him. A vision flashed through my head of me lying in bed with his head across my lap. The cabin quiet and still and my hand in his hair. I shook my head, dispelling the thought.

"Oh, you don't have to do that." I felt my cheeks flush. It was then that Trinity took notice. Like a dog catching sight of a rodent scampering by.

"Do what?" she asked, looking between Noah and me.

"Are you sure? I don't mind," Noah said. A part of me wanted to agree, just so that Trinity couldn't have him.

"Do what?" she asked again.

I looked at her nervously and then back at Noah and nodded my head. I wanted him to stay more than anything, but Gran's whisper echoed through my head. A haunting reminder I had work to do.

"Nothing. Kinsley just isn't feeling well, so I said I could stay back with her," Noah said to Trinity. Her face hardened, and her jaw flexed.

"You're not going to miss the bonfire to sit in this musty old cabin all night, right?" she asked, a deep crevice forming between her eyebrows. Noah looked at me once more, just to make sure.

"No, I guess not," he said. Something in his voice told me he was disappointed. Perhaps, as much as I was.

"Great! Then you can be my date!" Trinity slipped her arm in his and pulled him away. He stole a look at me one last time before the door closed on his way out. And when the cabin fell quiet, I groaned with regret. If I ever lost my chance with Noah, it was because of this moment. This choice. And that damn ghost story.

I listened to cab doors slam closed and the tires turn over on the asphalt as I stood, unsure of what to do with myself. I gathered up a pen and paper and fired up my laptop. But before I could focus, my stomach growled. I remembered there was some pasta in the refrigerator that Kai had made for lunch but hadn't finished. I knew he wouldn't mind if I finished it. Kai was a gentle soul. Gifted athletically. Book smart too. He would always come up with inventions late at night. Some unrealistic, some quite good. I had no doubt that he would change the world, one small gadget at a time.

I ate the pasta cold, too lazy to heat it in the microwave. Gunner came to my side, asking for scraps, and I fed him a noodle here and there. He wagged his tail, excited for more, and I was grateful that I wasn't completely alone. I was still a little rattled by what had happened at the grocery store.

When the pasta was gone, and Gunner wouldn't leave my side, I opened the back door to let him outside. I sat down with my laptop and opened a browser. I started with "The Baylor Butcher," but only local butcheries populated the search. I tried searching "local ghost stories of Baylor Lake," but local tourist spots like bed-and-breakfasts, the Crumpet Café, and the Summerfield State Fair were all I got. I spent a good hour exhausting the search engine, to no avail. I sighed, thinking that my sacrifice to stay home had been pointless.

Gunner scratched at the back door, startling me. But as I turned to let him in, I heard a noise upstairs. It sounded as if something had been knocked over, falling on the carpet with a thud. I swung the door open, eager to let Gunner inside. He came in, nose in the air. Had he smelled an intruder? I watched him carefully. He looked as if he were hunting something unfamiliar. He froze mid-step, one paw in the air, and my body went rigid. I scanned the kitchen for anything I could use as a weapon. I drew a thick, sharp meat cleaver from a wooden block and gripped it tightly in my hand. Gunner slowly put his paw down and stalked toward the stairs. I followed in his wake.

Another thud came from upstairs . . . but this time it was louder. There was something up there all right. My every instinct told me to run straight out the front door. But I didn't listen. Not because I didn't want to, but because the fear kept me rooted in place. My legs were heavy and the floor was like molasses. Gunner growled, and I raised my cleaver high in the air.

I looked up the staircase, and it seemed to stretch for miles. My cell phone buzzed in my back pocket, and I screamed aloud, dropping the cleaver and leaping backward. The knife stuck to the floor and stood on end. I knew if it had landed on my foot, it would have meant a severed toe. The thud of the knife striking the floor sent Gunner barking ferociously—something I had never seen him do before. I took my phone out of my pocket, and as luck would have it, it was Lainey on the other end.

"Hello?" I answered, breathy.

"Hello? Kinsley, hello?" Lainey said on the other end. I could barely hear her through the commotion.

"Lainey! Your dog is going nuts! He won't stop barking at something upstairs! I think somebody is up there!" I hurried to get it out.

"H—hello? H—home . . ." The phone broke up, and I could only make out pieces of what Lainey was saying.

"Lainey? Can you hear me?" I said frantically. A door slammed shut upstairs, unleashing Gunner from his pointing stance. He bounded up the stairs at full force, skipping several stairs at a time. A growl ripped through his chest. My breath stalled. I dropped the phone and it clattered to the floor. I yanked the cleaver out of the floor, and I stumbled backward until the front door pressed against my back.

I heard Gunner rip into something. *Somebody*. A body

fell to the floor. I could hear the wrestling through the floorboards as the cabin creaked and moaned.

Thoughts raced through my head. Was I being robbed? Was the butcher here to get me? Chop me into pieces? Use me as fish chum? How had they gotten in? How long had they been there? I felt the whisper in my ear, and I had the frightening thought that they'd been up there when I was changing. When the cabin was full and I'd felt safe.

I imagined Jim, the store clerk, hiding in a closet upstairs, and it was enough to send me running. I turned to bolt out the front door, but I heard something just then that broke through the deafening adrenaline.

"Kinsley? Where are you going?" somebody asked.

I whipped my head around to find Ethan standing at the bottom of the stairs, calm and collected. I gasped and ran into his arms.

"Wow! Are you okay?" he asked, almost seductively in my ear. I gasped for air. I looked up the stairs and realized everything had fallen quiet. Gunner was no longer barking, and the wrestling had stopped.

"There's somebody here!" I hissed, my eyes snapping from Ethan's face to the upstairs landing.

Ethan turned slowly to follow my gaze. "Somebody's here?" he asked, brow furrowed.

"Yes! Gunner ran up there and attacked them!" I said. Ethan drew in a long, deep breath, studying my face.

Slowly, his eyes left mine and landed on the cleaver gripped in my hands.

Embarrassment ripped through me. It was so quiet. Like there had been no threat. And Ethan was looking at me like he wasn't sure if I'd imagined the whole thing.

"Is he up there now?"

"Yes!"

"Stay behind me," he said, taking my hand in his and treading quietly.

My hand, slick with sweat, gripped his as I followed him step by step. Everything in my body screamed not to go upstairs. Why were we going upstairs? I was afraid of what we might find. Was Gunner okay? Was that intruder still there? I didn't think there was a safe way to jump out the second-story window. I looked down the hall, afraid of what I might see. It scared me to find nothing.

Ethan looked back at me and I pointed to the master bedroom, breathing laboriously. He nodded before continuing. "I, I think it was in there," I stammered, our backs pressed against the wall.

My heart was thumping in my chest like a rabbit caught in a snare. I pulled my sweaty hand from his and reached for my cell phone. I patted my back pockets, then remembered that I'd dropped it. Ethan took the cleaver from my sweat-slick hand. He had a better chance of defending us with the kitchen knife than I did. He wiped his palms on his pants before raising the cleaver above his head. I placed my hand on his back and cowered behind him. We slowly turned the corner into the master bedroom.

Expecting to find a massacre, broken lamps, and bloodshed, I was taken aback by the stillness of the dark room. I flipped the lights on, and there was no sign of a struggle. I looked around the room. My abandoned white blouse lay on the floor just before the closet. Everything else was perfectly in its place. Ethan turned to me questioningly.

"Maybe it was in Asher and Kimber's room?" I whispered, pointing across the hall. Ethan shrugged, and we turned to check out the other rooms. I hid in his shadow as we trekked down the hall. Every single bedroom was clear. Ethan began to relax, but I became more and more unnerved.

As we went downstairs, a chill ripped down my spine when we found Gunner sleeping on his dog bed. I wasn't the only one who'd noticed him. Ethan looked back at me, pointing to the dog fast asleep.

"I swear, he fought off the intruder. I heard the whole thing!" I said as Ethan returned the cleaver to the butcher block. Fear shifted to anger. "What are you even doing here?" I snapped. It was a mixture of terror and embarrassment; it wasn't something I was proud of.

"When I heard that you had stayed back because you weren't feeling well, I thought about the trouble you got into at the grocery store and how I wished I'd gone with you. I took a cab back from the party so I could check on you. And clearly, my instincts were right. You shouldn't be alone," he said sternly.

I hated everything about that. I hated that Lainey liked Ethan and that I needed him. I hated that I felt like I was leading him on or that I owed him for saving me. And I hated he was the one who had come back and not Noah. His words echoed in my head. I shouldn't be left alone. I was eighteen years old—an adult. But if I couldn't go to the grocery store alone, or even be in a cabin alone, then I was still only a child. A helpless child afraid of her own shadow. One with a wild imagination that would get her into trouble.

# CHAPTER 9

I looked around the room restlessly. I couldn't stay here. Not because it was only Ethan and me—and he was looking for something more than I could give him—but because something inside had stirred, telling me I wasn't safe. I looked at Ethan, wondering when he had arrived and if he'd ever left for the party in the first place.

"I want to go to the party. Only, I'm not sure how to get there. Could you take me? You can drive the golf cart." I looked toward Ethan, anxiously awaiting his response. I knew it wasn't what he wanted. He wanted to stay in the cabin, alone with me. He wanted to bond. And he wanted me to look at him as my knight in shining armor. But how far would he take it? Had he staged the whole thing so that I'd go running into his arms? *Impossible.*

I could never look at Ethan like he wanted me to. Not because of Lainey, but because of Noah. Because I only had eyes for the boy I had grown up with. The boy who'd been my friend long before I developed feelings for him. My heart resided with Noah Hampton.

"Are you sure you feel good enough to go to the party? I thought you had a headache? And you look pretty upset. We could just stay here and watch a movie or something?" Ethan suggested. I swallowed down the lump in my throat and shook my head. It's what he'd wanted the whole time. For me to be scared and seek his comfort. I couldn't stay in this cabin one more second. I grabbed my phone from the floor where I had dropped it in the heat of the attack and stuffed it in my back pocket.

"Well, I'm going to go, and you can either come or not. But I don't want to stay here." Before I could get out the door, Ethan was on my heels.

"No, I'll come. Plus, you don't know how to get there. And I've always wanted to drive a golf cart." He was standing closer than I was comfortable with, but I was thankful that I didn't need to drive through the woods at night alone. I was too rattled as it was. We fired up the golf cart, and Ethan's face lit up. He came to life behind the wheel like a young boy excited to play with a new toy. I taught him what little he needed to know in a few quick seconds, and before I knew it, we were pulling out of the driveway. At first, the ride was a little touch and go, but he quickly got the hang of it.

I pointed to a trail that ran parallel to the main road

around the lake. It weaved in and around the massive pine trees through the dark forest. I gripped the handle above my head. The night was cool and the wind on my face refreshing. I closed my eyes, breathing in deeply and exhaling the fear that had coiled inside the pit of my stomach. The panic from the break-in paled in comparison to the worry and horror I felt wondering if my mind might be slipping from me. I was too young and too healthy to have a mind that was deteriorating into a false reality. But something was off. Something didn't add up. And I was the only common denominator.

My eyes flew open as the golf cart launched over a large rock and my seat lifted off the bench. Ethan laughed, a little embarrassed about the rough ride. I gave him a small smile back. The trail was uneven and the ride bumpy; it was to be expected. But Ethan took my smile as something else entirely. He reached over and grabbed my hand. I quickly recoiled. His smile dropped, and even in the dark, I could see the shame spread across his features. I was mortified that I had made him feel that way. Guilt overcame me.

"Ethan . . ." I began.

"No, you don't have to do that," he started, too embarrassed to hear what was about to come next. His hands gripped the steering wheel tightly, and he refused to look at me.

"Ethan, I'm sorry—"

"You don't need to be sorry. I know. It's not you, it's me, blah blah blah. I've heard it all before."

I bit the inside of my cheek, rolling the flesh between my teeth. The golf cart launched over another molehill and I accidentally bit down, drawing blood. "Ah!" I called out, cupping my mouth. The taste of copper spread throughout my mouth and dressed my lips.

"Are you okay?" he asked, letting off the gas. I leaned over the edge of the golf cart and spat out a mouthful of blood.

"Ahh, I just bit my cheek." I spat once more. I looked at my hand, unsure of what to do with the crimson on my fingertips.

"Here," Ethan held out his sleeve.

"I can't use that! It will stain," I said.

"It's okay, it's black," he insisted. Thankfully, I found a small rag tucked inside a pocket near the center console and spared his sleeve.

"Ethan, I really like you. Just not the way I think you might want." I ran my tongue over the wound and found that it had begun to swell.

Ethan sighed, looking away and tightening his grip on the steering wheel.

"It's complicated. If things were different, if I didn't have feelings for somebody else . . ." I shrugged.

"It's Noah, isn't it?" I didn't have to say anything. He already knew. I nodded, and he did too.

"And Lainey?" he asked.

"You know?"

The sounds of the forest came alive as his disappointment silenced us both. "It's okay. I'm fine." Ethan started the ignition again and our bumpy ride continued. I reached out to his forearm and gave it a squeeze. A gesture he would have adored ten minutes prior. But now, I knew it pained him. I looked out at the passing trees as we drove the rest of the way in the dead of night, and the cool breeze washed away the awkward conversation. The harsh feelings wafted in a trail behind us for the forest to feed on.

I knew we had reached Sampson's cabin by the volume of the bass bouncing from one tree to the next. An orange halo glowed around the bonfire by the water's edge where a group huddled. Ethan handed me the keys to the golf cart and, without a word, disappeared into the crowd. I was the worst person alive to have hurt him. And after he'd saved me, no less. I knew I wouldn't be able to talk to anyone about it either, because Lainey would be crushed if she caught wind of it. Alone, I ventured into the cabin in search of my friends. A small group of girls hung around the kitchen island, pouring drinks and talking about guys.

"Did you see the one with the sandy hair? He's wearing that jacket with a red patch," one girl said, pointing to her shoulder where a patch would reside. Immediately, I knew she was talking about Noah. The red patch was our high school mascot. I knew the jacket well because I'd borrowed it one time and hadn't given it back for a week.

"Oh yeah! He's cute! But I think he has a girlfriend," the girl responded. I frowned, approaching the island. It wasn't true.

"Can I get one of those drinks?" I asked.

"Yeah, sure!"

"He has a girlfriend?"

"It's that really pretty girl with the long dark hair and light eyes. You couldn't have missed her," the girl said. *Trinity.* Something came over me.

"That's not his girlfriend!" I blurted out. The group of girls stopped and stared at me blankly. "Sorry! I just . . . I just overheard, I'm sorry." I stammered and felt the urge to flee without my drink.

"So he doesn't have a girlfriend then?" the inquisitive one asked. I'd shot myself in the foot. That's exactly what I did.

"Um, no, he doesn't," I said, taking my drink and excusing myself.

"You should totally go for him then." I heard on my way out the back door. I spotted Lainey and Emma, only they were talking with Ethan, and I wanted to get as far away from that situation as possible. I pressed on through the crowd until I found Noah. Trinity was wrapped around his arm. I took a step back, hiding behind a couple of guys in line for the keg, and I watched for a moment.

Trinity whispered something in his ear, and whatever it was, it stole his attention. His brows lifted, and I could tell that he was intrigued. I didn't have to know what the proposition was to know how it made me feel. My stomach dropped with jealousy. I could tell why the other girls had thought that Trinity was his girlfriend. If I hadn't known any better, I would've thought the same thing. It was then that she grabbed his hand, pulling him away from the crowd. He followed . . . hesitantly, but he followed nonetheless.

I watched him look around the crowd, searching for faces, presumably mine. And when he didn't see me, or whomever it was that he was looking for, he went with her. Trinity shrugged off her burgundy leather jacket and threw it over her shoulder. Her hips swayed from side to side in a way that reminded me of a leopard stalking its prey through tall blades of grass. I took several steps back, watching as long as I could. I followed them inside the house. I peeked around the corner from the kitchen down into a hallway and watched her lead him into a back bedroom. My heart broke, and a wave of nausea passed through me.

"Hey, do you know where that guy went?" It was the girl who had made me the drink.

I looked back toward the bedroom, and the door was

now closed. "No, I haven't seen him. Sorry." I said. I crossed my arms over my chest, tapping my fingers on my red plastic cup, fuming inside. My face was hot with betrayal, and I stared blindly off into the sea of people. I acknowledged the pain and deceit and then quickly tucked it away into a dark corner of my mind. It's what I did best. I only let it sting for a second, and then I drowned the discomfort with my drink. I got another on my way outside. And since I couldn't join my two best friends, and my crush had been stolen from me, I joined the group down by the bonfire.

I took the only open seat, a blue camping chair with cigarette burns in the arms. I ran my tongue across the sore in my cheek, using the sharp pain of the cut to cover the ache in my chest over Noah and Trinity. I wished I had never invited Trinity to the cabin. Before, I'd thought it was unavoidable, but knowing what I did now, I wished I had put my foot down. I wished I would have said straight to her face that she couldn't come. That she wasn't invited because she wasn't my friend.

I briefly wondered if I should stand up for myself now —barge into that room and declare that she get off him. But the truth was that Noah was just as guilty as Trinity was . . . though *guilty* wasn't really fair. He was in that room because that's where he wanted to be, and he didn't owe me anything. We weren't a couple. And I had never once told him how I felt about him. I was a coward, and this was what I got. I accepted in that moment that it was my fault and my fault alone for whatever happened. What was happening right now behind that locked door. Because it was I who allowed her to walk all over me. And it was I who wasn't brave enough to have told Noah to stay back at the cabin with me. It was my fault. And whether Noah liked me or not didn't really matter anymore, because it was clear that I wasn't the only one he had eyes for.

"Guys, this is Kinsley Wilde. She's the one who owns the cabin where we're staying. Kinsley, this is everyone. That's Sampson, Skid, Tina, Pat, and Lola," Scarlett May said. I looked around the bonfire and waved meekly. Everyone was warm enough. Tina sat on top of one guy's lap, who Scarlett May had called Skid. I presumed they were dating. But after seeing Trinity and Noah together, I couldn't be sure.

"This is the girl I was telling you guys got attacked by Big Jimmy today," Scarlett May continued.

"Oh gosh, yeah, that happened today," I said, nodding. I could feel the warmth spread across my cheeks. It wasn't from the heat of the fire.

"Big Jimmy is dangerous. You have to stay away from him! Everybody in Baylor knows that!" a guy with a backward hat said—Pat, I think.

"This one time, Big Jimmy slept in his car in the middle of the forest for a month straight. Nobody knew where he had gone, but they knew he was off his medication," Sampson shared. "The hounds found him, and he had to stay in the loony bin until he was right again."

*Makes sense*, I thought.

"He's legit crazy," said a girl—Tina, I think. "And if he goes off his medication, he gets mean. He's gone to jail for assaulting a woman before, and they just let him off because he has mental health issues or whatever. And I heard the grocery store can't fire him because his instability is a disability."

"Makes sense to me. He seemed pretty crazy in the alley. I'm pretty sure he hadn't showered in quite some time, and he was angry. He snapped for no reason," I said.

"How did you find yourself with him in the back alley, anyway?" Tina asked.

"It's kind of embarrassing, but I was asking him about the Baylor Butcher." I shrank a little at Scarlett May's glare. *You're not a child, are you?* I tried to ignore how her look made me feel small and insignificant. "I overheard him talking about it, and since Scarlett May had shared the story with us a little while ago, I was just curious. He started talking as he was taking the trash out back, and I just sort of followed him without thinking. The door closed, and we were trapped. *I* was trapped." The story was embellished, but only a little.

"The Baylor Butcher! I haven't heard that story in a long time!" Skid said with amusement.

"Skid?" I asked, pointing a finger. What kind of name was that?

"Adam Skid. It's my last name," he said.

"Oh, okay," I said and nodded. "Well, it was my first time hearing the story. So, I guess I'm a little late to the party."

"You've never heard it before? I love that story!" Tina said.

"What? You love it?" Scarlett May admonished.

"It's such a beautiful story," Tina said with a shy shrug. Her hoodie was covering most of her face, but I could tell that there was something more than a morbid sense of beauty in her mind's eye.

"I think we're thinking about different stories here. The one we're talking about is the one where the guy butchered all his dates and threw pieces of their bodies into the lake," Scarlett May clarified in a dry, cutting tone.

"What? No! That's not the Baylor Butcher ghost story!" Tina argued. My ears perked and my back straightened. Was there a different side to the story? Of course there was. There were two sides to every story.

"What—" I began.

"Yes, it is! That's the one I grew up with," Scarlett May argued.

"Is there a different version?" I asked Tina. The fire crackled when Sampson threw another log in the pit.

"Yeah, I can't believe you guys haven't heard this one before. It's a love story."

"Tell the story, babe," Skid said, patting her leg.

"You guys want to hear a love story?" she asked everyone.

"I do!" I said, almost too enthusiastically.

"Oh, here we go. Kinsley and her wild obsession with ghost stories," Scarlett May muttered loud enough for me to hear on the other side of the fire. I ignored her.

Tina sat up from her boyfriend's chest and leaned forward. "Long, long ago, there was a butcher. See? Same story. Only he didn't butcher people; he worked as an actual butcher. I swear things get so mixed up, the more mouths they get passed through. But I swear this is the true story."

"It's not, but continue," Scarlett May said, and Sampson laughed. My eyes were trained on Tina, waiting for more. I was vaguely aware that my interest in the story was helping to cover the gnawing ache that I was losing my chance with Noah.

"The butcher was so in love with this girl—more in love than anybody had ever been with another. Their love was known across many towns, traveling nearly statewide. They were a pretty big deal. One day, when the butcher was taking her out to propose, they got in a terrible accident. His car crashed alongside the lake and tumbled down into the water. He survived, but his girlfriend didn't. He was so distraught that, after a year of grief, he took his own life in hopes to be with her. But that didn't happen. It's said that he haunts the lake looking for her because he can't move on without her. But she's not here because she left to go to heaven. And he's trapped here because he damned himself by taking his own life. Now, he's in his own personal hell, here in Baylor. He looks for her every evening around the lake and in the forest. But he'll never find her, and he'll never move on," Tina said.

My heart sank. Hearing the story brought me deep sorrow. It was just an old story, but I felt the pain as if it were my own. I slipped my hand over my heart, rubbing the ache. "That's so sad," I said.

"It is! It's so sad, but it's so beautiful. He still looks for her every evening. And he'll keep looking for her for the rest of eternity because he loves her that much. Some people call him The Phantom of the Lake," said Tina, turning to Skid. "Would you look for me, for the rest of eternity, babe?" she asked.

"Yeah, I would!" Skid said, thrusting his pelvis into her. Tina slapped his shoulder, and Lola laughed. I smiled, wishing that I had had somebody to joke with. But Noah was—a flash of Trinity straddling him in bed crossed my mind—occupied . . .

"I heard they're buried next to each other in the Baylor Cemetery," Lola added.

"I know! It's so cute!" Tina said, leaning back against her boyfriend.

"I still think he was a murderer," Scarlett May said.

"Who hurt you?" Sampson said, laughing. We all joined him.

The conversation moved effortlessly away from the ghost story and fell upon my deaf ears. I watched the orange flames dance in the fire and listened to the crackling logs. If it had been a love story, then what was in the depths of the lake that had tried to take my soul?

If it had been a love story, then why had Big Jimmy become so violent over it? I pictured the lake in the evening when the fog bank would settle in and the loons would call out to one another. It had always been haunting, but in a soothing, eerie way. In a way that spread a sense of serenity throughout my body and mind but still managed to raise a few hairs on the nape of my neck. I imagined that the fog carried within it an epic love searching for its soulmate. And a small smile crept across my face.

I wanted more than anything to think that the Baylor ghost story was a hopeful one. That true love did exist. That there was one person out there meant to find another. And when they did, nothing could break their bond. Like souls that were fated to belong to one another. It made me hopeful that I'd find my soulmate one day. If I hadn't already.

But as I imagined the fog bank of low-hanging clouds, I

also imagined the dismembered hands reaching out of the water, grasping for one last chance at survival. It soured my stomach, giving me heartburn. I shook my head, in limbo between the darkest horror and the greatest love story. Only, I couldn't decipher which of them was right. The truth was on that nebulous line between fact and fiction. Reality and illusion.

# CHAPTER 10

The bulk of us came home that night, but it didn't escape me that Trinity hadn't returned. I was thankful she'd stayed back because I wasn't ready to look her in the face. Neither was I ready to look at Noah, but I wasn't as lucky on that front. Many times, I saw him stealing glances in my direction, and every time, it turned his cheeks a swarthy red of regret. I didn't know how far he had gone with Trinity, but the details didn't matter. He'd made his choice when he'd closed that door, and it hadn't been with me. I hated that I still had feelings for him, even though I knew he lacked the loyalty I so deserved. We were friends long before we grew feelings for each other, and I knew friends wouldn't treat each other the way he'd treated me tonight.

"Did Scarlett May come home?" Lainey asked.

"No, I think she's staying at Sampson's tonight," I said.

"She must be staying there with Trinity," she said, shrugging. At the sound of Trinity's name, my eyes met Noah's, and he all but fled the room. I sighed, throwing my head back. The tension in the room was suffocating.

"Who knows? She can stay there for the rest of the summer for all I care," I said to Lainey. She raised her brows and nodded. She understood that like no one else here. "I'm exhausted. I'm going to bed," I said.

"Yeah, me too."

As Lainey and I headed for the stairs, I overheard Mason's booming voice.

"Did you get with Trinity tonight?" he asked. And I knew instantly that he was talking to Noah. Lainey wrapped her arm around me as she watched the disappointment spread across my face. We hovered on the staircase, eavesdropping.

"No man," said Noah, his voice low and disgruntled.

"Yeah, you did!"

"No, seriously."

"You're such a liar, man."

I rolled my eyes and stomped up the stairs. Lainey followed. He was such a liar. I'd seen him go into the back bedroom and shut the door behind him. Even the girls at Sampson's cabin thought that he and Trinity had been together. It was clear for everyone to see.

"I'm sorry, Kins. That really sucks," Lainey said, hovering in the doorjamb.

"No, it's fine. I can't help who Noah likes, and it's my fault for inviting her. I knew she was like this, and I really just wish I hadn't let her come."

"That doesn't mean it's your fault," she argued.

"I guess it really wouldn't have changed anything. I just don't want to spend my summer watching them hook up. It's cruel and unusual punishment." I frowned. "Sometimes I think I do it to myself. Like I don't deserve happiness, so I invite people like Trinity to rain down on me. Or I let myself fall for someone who can't give me what I need." I rolled my tongue over the inside of my cheek, still swollen from me biting down on it in the golf cart.

"Don't say that. You had nothing to do with this. And you deserve all the happiness in the world. I really do think that Noah likes you. I mean, does Noah even know that you like him? Because on the one hand, he has Trinity, who is a sure thing. And on the other hand, he has you, and he probably doesn't even know you like him. You guys have been flirty for years, and nothing has ever come of it. He probably just assumes that's the nature of your relationship."

I took a moment to think about what she said. She was right. I'd never told Noah how I felt about him. How could I expect him to know it?

"You're right, Lainey. And that's just another reason it's my fault. I never told him."

"Well, it's never too late," she said with a hopeful smile.

"Oh yeah? Are you going to tell Ethan you like him?" I asked, hand on hip.

Lainey's cheeks turned red. "I don't like Ethan," she hissed. But both of us knew that wasn't true. And I was being an ass.

"Sorry, I'm just irritated. And I'm super tired. I think I need to go to bed."

"Well, try to get some sleep." Lainey headed for her room.

"Good night," I said before closing my door.

Once alone in the master bedroom, I took a deep cleansing breath; it was anything but refreshing. I inhaled the memory of Gunner fighting off the intruder on this very floor. In this very room. And for a brief moment, I saw it. I saw the man in black, a ski mask covering his face, and Gunner at his throat. I saw the broken lamp and the tipped-over nightstand. The commotion of them rolling around on the carpet and the snarling of the dog. I jumped back, my back hit the door behind me, and it all disappeared.

My heart pounded as I opened the door and ran out into the hall. I heard Noah and Mason talking in the stairwell, and everything seemed normal. It was only a daydream. A vision. Slowly, I crept back into the master bedroom, where I had seen the attack that never happened.

I checked the bathroom and closet multiple times before crawling into bed. And even then, I felt the room spinning with the presence of an intruder. I hesitated before turning out the light, my fingers on the pull string as I stared at the lamp; I was sure it had broken. I forced myself to be brave enough to close my eyes. And I prayed for sleep to overtake me.

When morning came and I realized I'd survived the night without the torment of a nightmare, I was only mildly relieved. I'd need much more than a single night without a nightmare to feel all right. Nothing was okay. Noah had chosen Trinity over me. He chose a girl who didn't even like him over a long-standing friendship that had blossomed into so much more. And that was just the tip of the iceberg.

I decided to throw myself into finding this girl—though I was sure it was nothing but a ghost story. Still, though, if my current reality had nightmares coming to life before my very eyes, then maybe there was more to finding this girl than anybody realized. Maybe there was a reason for it all, and like my gran had said, the girl needed me.

I'd overheard Lola speak of the cemetery last night, where supposedly the butcher and his girlfriend were buried next to one another. And the best part about cemeteries? Headstones. That was where I'd find the names. It was as good a place as any to start my research, and therein lay my mission. Find the cemetery . . . find the name.

I got dressed and headed downstairs, somewhat surprised that I had slept in. Kai and Ethan were making breakfast when I entered the kitchen, and Mason lay in his sleeping bag telling stories from the night before. Lainey and Emma were on the back porch drinking coffee, and it appeared that Trinity and Scarlett May hadn't come home last night.

"Good morning," I said to everyone. Kai greeted me, but Ethan shied away. Guilt sat like a heavy brick in the pit of my stomach. I walked past Mason, kicking him gently as any good friend would, and then went to the back porch.

"Morning," I said.

"Good morning. You slept in," Emma said.

"First time in a long time," I said. I looked out at the lake. The fog bank was clearing. I remembered the love story I'd heard the night before, and in that moment, it seemed so clear to me which side of the ghost story was the prevailing truth. In all the beauty that lay before us, there was no question that this ghost story was rooted in love.

"Hey, Lainey, can I take Gunner for a walk?" I asked.

"That would be great! Because I caught him digging a hole in your yard again." Lainey shook her head, annoyed.

"I'm going to have to pick up some grass seed before the summer is over," I said, and Lainey nodded.

"Don't worry, I'll make sure everything is taken care of; your mom will never know," she said.

I tucked my phone into my back pocket and set out on a hike with Gunner. He was just as eager as I was. He pulled against the leash, and I quickened my step to keep up. I didn't know where I was going, but I had heard a long time ago that the cemetery was hidden within the forest. I had a faint memory of passing it when I was a child. And there was only one hiking trail I didn't frequent.

As I entered the wall of trees, the shadows from the pines offered welcome shade, and I let Gunner off his leash. He took off, galloping down the path for a moment before bounding into the bushes. I let my eyes wander through the forest in search of clues. It was about a two-mile hike that I had planned, ending with a giant boulder that was a popular place for locals to jump into the lake. I was sure there was a small trail off the beaten path that led to the cemetery. I couldn't remember exactly where it had been, but I was confident that I would remember when we came across it.

"Gunner?" I called out, hoping to see his little brown head bobbing above the bushes. But I caught no sight of him hunting. Still, I figured I'd run into him before getting off the main trail. After some time walking alone in the forest, I finally felt at ease. I even spotted the downy woodpecker that Lainey had told me about the last time we'd walked. I craned my neck to watch as the bird pecked a hole into the tree. He had a distinctive red spot on the back of his head, but I couldn't remember if Lainey had told me that meant it was male or female. I enjoyed the view either way. The sound of his pecking echoed throughout the forest, bouncing from tree to tree.

When I came across an opening, a hint of a trail off the beaten path, I knew it was the one I had been looking for. The bushes had overgrown most of the trail, and it looked like nobody had hiked it in some time. I regretted wearing shorts, because I knew my legs would get cut up from the thorns in the bushes. But it wouldn't deter me. Nor would the fact that I couldn't find Gunner. I took one last look around, scanning the tops of all the bushes for a little brown head, and when he couldn't be found, I trudged on, taking the overgrown path. At first, the thorns were really irritating, scratching the flesh just enough to break the skin. But the farther I got, the more terrain I recognized, and the less I cared about my legs.

When I came upon the clearing where I recalled the cemetery had been located, it shocked me to see something else entirely. A large stone tower, nearly three stories high. It looked like it had come straight from a medieval fairy tale. The only things missing were the fire-breathing dragons and a spellbound princess. I knew I had never seen the tower before. But that was suspicious in itself, because the tower appeared to be so old. It looked like it had been built ages ago, and I was surprised that I had never heard stories about it when I was young. I looked around the grounds, but there wasn't a headstone in sight. Disoriented, I worried that I had gotten myself lost. I pulled out my phone, and as luck would have it, I had no service.

While I was here, lost in the middle of the forest, I might as well relieve my itching curiosity. I had to know what was inside. And this chance might never come along again. I walked up to it, placing my hands on the stones, and it surprised me that they felt warm to the touch.

"Hello? Is anybody there?" I called out. I don't know what I thought—maybe that somebody had inhabited it. But as I walked around the base of the tower, it was clear that there was no way in. The tower had been sealed up, stone by stone. But I couldn't imagine the point of a structure with no way in. Or no way out. I took several steps back, looking toward the top, and on one side of the tower was a window. I scratched my head, staring and waiting for a way inside to magically appear. But when it didn't come, I got the odd sense that I should be on my way. That I might not be safe all the way out here.

As soon as I made the decision to leave, I felt it. The same sense I'd had when my friends and I had run down the dock to jump into the lake. I felt the eyes watching me. I looked around, my breaths becoming more frequent and shallow. No movement but the subtle rise and fall of tree branches swaying in the breeze. I turned back the way I came, quickening my pace through the angry bushes. If I could only get to the main trail, I thought. Twigs snapped several feet behind me, as if there was something closing in on me. But when I looked back, dizzy and breathless, there was nothing. Nothing my eyes could see—nothing from this world. My legs were painted red by the time I got back to the main trail. It was there that I thought the chase would be over. But the feeling of something closing in on me only grew more keen.

I whipped my head from side to side, totally disoriented. My breath became jagged as I jogged down the trail. Slowed down by the frequent backward glances. Time I didn't have to spare. I quickened my step from a jog to a run the moment I heard the gravel stir behind me. When I looked, I thought I saw a subtle shift in the air. A density suspended over the main trail. But I couldn't be sure and wasn't about to stop to investigate. I felt it though. I felt the predator hunting me. I felt the adrenaline rush through my veins, and I knew I had been singled out as prey.

"Gunner! Gunner!" I yelled. The voice that escaped me wasn't my own but a husky cry for help.

I glimpsed something in motion close upon my flank. I couldn't tell what it was, but I knew it was after me. My run turned into a sprint. My legs thrust as fast as they could to save my life. My heart rate redlined. "Gunner!" I screamed.

Each time I looked behind me, I saw the thing closing in at an impossible speed. And each time, I found it within myself to run even faster than before. I let out a scream with a breath I couldn't hold onto. And then, out of nowhere, the trail ended, and a cabin appeared in a peaceful clearing.

"Help! Help!" I screamed, tripping over my own feet. The gravel gouged into my wrists and forearms as I sprawled onto my stomach. I rolled onto my back just as the figure leaped for me, snatching its prey. I shut my eyes and threw my arms over my face, cowering in anticipation.

"Help!" I screamed one last time.

Time stilled as I waited for claws to pull me apart, slash by deadly slash. Teeth to rip the limbs from my body. My life to end before it had begun. But the attack never came. Instead, a hand grabbed my shoulder, and I screamed, kicking out on instinct. My foot made contact with a very hard mass, and I heard a disgruntled groan. My eyes sprung open to see Asher grabbing his thigh. Mason stood there too, breathless and confused. I looked from the boys back to the woods. The trail was still, the air reminiscent of a light summer day.

I couldn't see the vile thing that had chased me, and from the looks of both Mason and Asher, they hadn't seen it either.

"What the hell, Kinsley?" Asher said.

"What—" I gasped breathlessly, looking all around me,

my hands on the warm sandy pathway. "What happened?" I asked.

"You're asking me? You screamed for help and then kicked the shit out of me!" Asher said.

"Did you see? The thing?" I gasped, dusting my hands. Kai and Noah had just reached us, and they, too, were breathless, their faces red from running out to the forest.

"Are you okay?" Noah asked.

The truth was, I didn't know. My legs were bloodied, but I was positive that was from walking through the overgrown bushes. My hands and forearms were shredded, but that was road rash. The real threat . . . That had been invisible. A figment of my imagination. So, I guess the answer was no; I wasn't all right. Far from it. My mind was the most dangerous predator in those woods. And I was out to get me.

"I . . . I . . . I don't know," I said, as he helped me to my feet. My body ached, and my lungs burned.

"What happened to your legs?" Mason asked.

"Why did you kick me?" Asher asked.

My eyes dropped to Asher's thigh, and there was a dusty footprint from my shoe painted on his shorts.

"I'm sorry I . . . I was being chased, I thought you were the . . . the thing," I said, looking between the guys.

"What was chasing you?" Asher and Kai looked into the woods, and I looked too, following their gaze. The woods were quiet, not so much as a breeze to lift a branch.

"I don't know. I couldn't see it. But it was big, and it was fast."

"How do you know it was big if you didn't see it?" Kai asked.

"She just got scared—that's all," Mason said, batting a hand through the air.

"Damn, Kinsley! You really scared us!" Asher said.

I dusted off my butt, and I began the walk of shame back to the cabin where the rest of my friends stood on pins and needles, watching and waiting to see if I was okay. On one hand, I was mortified that I had cried wolf. But given the choice to have them run to my side and be disappointed or to fight my demons alone and have nobody notice, I'd choose the former. Because nothing hurt more than being forgotten.

"What happened?" Lainey asked, as soon as we were in earshot. The girls stood on the back porch, faces etched with worry. I looked at the boys. What they had seen differed greatly from what I had experienced. Two sides of the same story.

"It was like a wolf or something," I said. I caught the alarming glare that passed between Asher and Kai, and I looked down at my feet before I could see the look on Noah's face.

"What *really* happened?" Lainey whispered, as I got closer and the guys dispersed. I ran a hand through my hair, picking out a single twig. I watched the guys go back to their mundane activities. "Are you okay?" Lainey looked down at my legs. It looked like I had been mauled by a raccoon that tried to climb me like a tree trunk.

"It was a wolf, I think. A wolf was chasing me. And I lost Gunner," I said, worried.

"You lost Gunner?" she asked, trying to hide her dismay. My mouth fell open, but no words came out. I'd lost much more than her dog in those woods. And I didn't know how to tell her the truth.

# CHAPTER 11

Late into the morning, when Scarlett May had returned home and Trinity had not, we began to worry. Scarlett May had had a life in Baylor long before we came up for the summer. She'd spent time here with her family and friends outside of our little world. But Trinity was different. She didn't know anybody in town, and she was part of our core team. It had been easy to think that maybe she'd stayed at Sampson's house because she was there with Scarlett May. But now that we knew she hadn't, the alarm went off. Something was wrong. And I hated the part of me that was glad it was her. The part of me that thought maybe she had gotten what she deserved.

"So, you're telling me that Trinity wasn't with you last night?" I asked Scarlett May.

"No, was she supposed to be?" she asked.

"Well, no, but we haven't seen her. We figured she was with you last night."

"She was with Noah last night," Mason said. My stomach clenched. Scarlett May's brow lifted.

"And you haven't seen her this morning?" I asked one more time.

"I haven't seen her since you guys left last night."

I looked to Kimber, who was pulling on her bottom lip, eyes unfocused in front of her as she tried to recall the night before. They weren't the best of friends, but Trinity was to Kimber what Ethan was to Asher. She was her shadow—and a mean one at that, but it didn't stop them from being friends. Kimber, Trinity, and Scarlett May had always ruled the school. Kimber was the most popular, but that was because she had some kindness in her. She was the total package, minus the mental instability, but most never saw that part. Scarlett May was the outgoing one . . . and the one I liked to think of as obnoxious. She often spat cruel comments where they didn't belong. And Trinity was the mean one disguised in dark beauty. Many of the boys liked her, but it was the girls who could see through her long locks, bright hazel eyes, and wicked smile. It was her actions that always spoke volumes about her integrity.

I felt bad for Kimber, but there was that deep part inside of me—that smoldering ember—that was glad it hadn't been Emma or Lainey who'd turned up missing.

Surely if it were one of them, something tragic would've happened. But Trinity? Trinity was most likely on some grand adventure. She'd probably found the band crew who were set to play at the Water's Edge Concert in a couple of weeks and had been partying all night long. She'd come home with some epic story to tell that would make everyone jealous. Especially Noah. I wasn't worried.

"Have you called her?" Asher asked from the kitchen. Kai ran his hands through his hair and walked outside. Levi nodded as if it were as easy as that.

"Yeah, have you called her phone?" Levi repeated, as if it had been his own idea.

I pointed my finger to my chest, surprised as I looked between the wandering eyes in the room. I certainly hadn't called her. What would I have to say to Trinity? Other than asking her if she'd slept with Noah with the intent to crush his heart or mine. But I wasn't about to do that. *Why not, though?* Maybe I *should* confront her.

"I've called her a dozen times. Sent two dozen texts. And somewhere along the way, her phone stopped ringing. It's unlike her. Normally, she'd answer. She'd call me back or text immediately," Kimber said. Her blue eyes glistened with worry as she wrapped her pale blonde hair around her finger, twisting until it was strung tight.

"This is stupid. I'm calling her right now," Scarlett May said, with the phone pressed to her ear. We watched and waited as her eyes drifted slowly to the floor and she slipped the phone into her back pocket. "It went straight to voicemail," she murmured.

"Well, I think I'm going to go back over to Sampson's house and see if anybody has heard anything. Many people are still there, just barely waking up. Does anybody want to go with me?" Scarlett May asked.

"Yeah, I'll go," Asher said.

"Me too," Levi said.

"I was just about to run into town and tape flyers up for Gunner. I'll keep my eyes open," Lainey said.

"I'm going with her, so call us if you need anything," Emma said.

Kimber looked at me with worried eyes, and I knew I needed to satisfy her in some way or another. "Kimber, do you want to go drive through the woods in the golf cart? I know of some trails back there that she could have gotten lost on."

Kimber nodded, and we gathered our things as everyone but Kai and Mason headed out. Ethan and Noah were down the street, and nobody bothered to fill them in on the hunt for Trinity. Which was ironic, because Noah was probably the last person to see her. We split up, making plans to check in with one another in an hour or so. I wasn't expecting to find Trinity out in the woods. I was really only taking the trip to keep Kimber busy.

My distaste for Trinity grew as I watched the group pull together as a team. Unity in their worry for one of the members. But where had the search team been when *I* was missing? When I'd nearly drowned in the middle of the lake. And here Trinity was, sucking up all the love. Even though she'd burned down most of the authentic relationships she'd ever had. I stewed inside. Why hadn't I tried to talk to her before? I'd always run from my truth, but for the first time, I felt the need to say it. When she stumbled back from her epic night with the band, she and I were going to have a little talk.

I started the golf cart, and we pulled out of the driveway. Kimber grabbed hold of the overhead handle and cursed me for taking sharp turns. Had she not already been on edge, she may have enjoyed the ride. We dipped into the forest, and a sense of foreboding crashed down upon me. I was out here alone, and I was being hunted. The air shifted as the shadows enveloped us. The temperature dropped as we left the sunny clearing. I couldn't think of that now, and I knew I'd be safe as long as Kimber was by my side. My eyes wandered deep into the shrubs, jumping from treetop to treetop and whipping back and forth down the trail. I punched the gas.

Kimber was so worried about Trinity that she hadn't even realized how paranoid I was. I tried to take my mind off it by asking her questions that would force her to open up. It was good for the both of us. "When was the last time you spoke with Trinity?" I asked.

"I think she found me last night after she . . ." the

words hung in the air between us, and the gentle breeze did little to lift them away. *After she slept with Noah?*

"I know she was with him last night. I saw them go into the back bedroom," I said, clearing the air of unspoken words.

"Yeah, okay, so you know. She came to talk to me after that, but it wasn't long, and she didn't say much. She staggered off to talk to Kai about something, and that was the last time I saw her."

Kimber gathered her hair and pulled it over one shoulder, trying to fight the few tresses that were blowing in the wind. We came upon a fork in the road where I could stay near the main road or travel deeper into the forest where I thought the cemetery had been. And even though I'd been hunted like an animal of prey the last time I was there, I still chose to venture into the depths of the shadows.

"She went to talk to Kai? He never said anything . . ." I said.

I parked the golf cart by the boulder that many of the locals used as a platform to jump into the lake. There was also a rope swing, but I thought that to be far more dangerous. There were a few teenagers perched on the rock who didn't look too happy to have the company. We looked around briefly, and when there was no sign of Trinity, I started the engine again just as a dog barked. I looked over my shoulder to find Gunner eating scraps from somebody's bagged lunch.

"Gunner!" His ears perked up, and he barked once more. "Come here, boy!" I yelled, slapping my leg. He came running and jumped into the golf cart, smothering Kimber. "Thank god I found him. Lainey is going to be so happy," I said, feeling a sense of relief wash over me. I'd think twice next time before letting him off the leash. I stepped on the gas, and we continued down the trail.

"I just feel terrible because I was fighting with Asher and I probably didn't give Trinity the attention she needed. What if this was my fault? What if she needed me and I wasn't there for her?" Kimber asked, her voice cracking as if she might cry. She pushed Gunner's face away, and I ended up with a face full of his dog breath.

I wanted to tell her that was stupid and that Trinity was probably just partying with a random group from Sampson's house, but the strain behind Kimber's eyes told me she was more than worried. I felt the compunction settle in my chest, for I had been far too guilty of not caring as much as I should.

"Don't do that to yourself, Kimber. Trinity is going to be just fine. Now, why don't you tell me about this fight that you and Asher had? What was it about?" I asked, taking a turn toward the mysterious tower that I had found earlier. Who knew? Maybe Trinity was there now.

"It was stupid, really. I don't even know how it

started. I wanted to go back to the cabin, but he wanted to stay. It was a simple disagreement, but it ended with him calling me names. Sometimes we have these fights, and I wonder why he's with me in the first place. I see the way he looks at other girls, and I look nothing like them. They all seem so perfect, you know?" she asked through a veil of insecurity. She had no idea how beautiful she was. And I bet that when she looked in the mirror, she was blind to it.

"Did you want to go back to the cabin because he was looking at other girls?"

"Well, yeah! Why would I want to stay when my boyfriend is being tempted by the lake locals?" she said defensively. "Where are we even going?" Kimber looked out into the forest and not a single soul was in sight. "I doubt that Trinity is out here," she said.

"You know? I came across something the other day, and I thought it was a cool hiding spot. It was this enormous stone tower. Maybe she's out there. I'm sure people party there all the time," I said, shrugging to hide my own self-interest. The guilt crept in again. What if Trinity really was in danger, and I was wasting precious minutes? But as we came upon the overgrown trail that led to my mysterious tower, fear pricked the nape of my neck and coiled in my stomach, and Kimber got a text from Scarlett May.

"They said to meet back at the cabin. They're heading

there now. Oh no. That doesn't sound good, does it?" she asked.

"I'm sure it's fine. Totally fine." I pulled away from the haunted trail and felt the eyes watching as we motored away.

When we got back to the cabin, it was clear that it was anything but fine. The boys paced back and forth with nervous energy, and Sampson had followed Scarlett May and the others back to the cabin. Gunner leapt out of the golf cart, greeting everybody one by one, but nobody seemed to notice. Before we reached the back deck, Asher approached us with news of a found cell phone.

"Is that hers?" I asked Kimber, but she didn't need to say anything. The tears in her eyes were enough for me to realize that maybe this was more serious than I'd originally thought. The wishes of ill-will I'd made upon her last night crept into my mind.

"Where did you find that?" Kimber asked, her voice strained. I looked between Asher and Scarlett May as unspoken worry passed between them. "What? Just tell me!" she said.

"We found it in the back bedroom. It was just lying on the floor," Sampson said.

"She'd never go anywhere without her phone. Something is definitely wrong," Scarlett May said, summing up what we were all thinking.

"We need to talk to Noah. He was the one with her in

that bedroom last night. Where is he?" Levi asked. Unwanted images of Noah and Trinity together floated through my mind. Noah's smile in response to Trinity's kisses. His hands, sliding down the small of her back and beneath her jeans. I suddenly realized everyone was looking at me. Everybody relied on me to know Noah's whereabouts. Was it really that obvious? It made the whole situation worse. As if I were nothing more than a doormat he stepped over. I wanted to tell them all to shove it—that I didn't know where he was . . . and why would I? But the truth was, I did know where he'd gone because my eyes were trained to follow him. And everybody in that room knew it.

"Noah and Ethan rented a boat earlier. I saw them out front with fishing poles while we were heading back," I said. As if on cue, I looked out the kitchen window and saw them tying the boat to the dock upon their return. I nodded in their direction, and Asher strode outside and down the hill. We all followed, and I was afraid of what I might see. Or more so, what I might hear.

"Hey, man, Trinity is still missing. What the hell happened between you two last night in that bedroom?" Asher demanded. I turned away briefly, but who was I fooling? I wanted to know as much as the rest of them. We all walked down the grassy knoll to the dock. This was a conversation that involved all of us.

"What are you talking about, man? We didn't do anything!" Noah said, his eyes flickered toward me.

"Then where is she? She never came home last night, and she left her phone in that room. What happened?"

"I'm telling you! Nothing happened! She was drunk, and she wanted to hook up, but I stopped her. That's it. That's all. Nothing more," Noah said. *Lies . . .*

Kimber turned away crying, and I stared at Noah in red-hot anger. He looked far too guilty for nothing to have happened. And I had known him a long time—long enough to know what his guilty conscience looked like. He was wearing it now. His darkening complexion. The crevices in his forehead. The sweat beading in his hairline.

"Why was her phone left in the bedroom?" Mason asked. All of our eyes flicked back to Noah for his response.

Only Ethan hadn't taken his eyes off me. He was probably wondering if we had a chance now that Noah had been with Trinity. But the fact that Noah had deceived me didn't make Ethan any more appealing.

"I don't know why her phone was left in the bedroom. She was really drunk, staggering all over the room. It probably fell out when she . . ." Noah said, before stopping. His eyes trained on me, and my mistrust was visible for all to see. "When she tried undressing," he said, in a softer voice, one filled with regret. I imagined he wouldn't have found himself in this situation had he known I had been at the party.

"I'm going to call the local hospital and see if she's there. Who knows? Maybe there was an accident we didn't hear about?" Emma said. She turned away, walking back toward the cabin.

The boys argued a bit longer about what specifically had happened in that bedroom, but I couldn't listen to it anymore. I turned away, and it was Ethan who ran after me. I couldn't deal with both my emotions and his. Not only was I hurt by Noah, but I felt terrible for wishing for Trinity's demise on the same night that she'd vanished. And worse, I hadn't cared come morning, when I knew that something could be wrong. I was a terrible person, and I had no room in my heart to let Ethan down softly for a second time.

"Hey, Kins, do you think Noah has something to do with Trinity going missing?" Ethan asked, checking behind him. I stopped halfway to the cabin and looked at Ethan and then down toward Noah and the group. A flash of Noah's smile turned violent and feral, but I stopped it there. That wasn't him, and I couldn't let it play out in my head.

"What do you mean? Like did he . . . harm her?" I asked, confused about where he was going with this.

"I don't know. I mean, you know him better than anyone. Right? You guys grew up together. Do you think he could have hurt her?" he asked, his hair shining red under the sunlight. I wasn't sure if it was Asher's conspiracy coming through his shadow or if Ethan had conjured up this theory to make Noah look even worse, but I was thoroughly disgusted.

"Noah would never hurt anybody! Is that what you guys think? Do you seriously think he hurt her?" I snapped. Ethan took a step back, absorbing my anger like a punch to the gut. He shrugged, seemingly unsure of how to respond. I trudged off without him.

The clocks raced forward as the tension grew. Emma said there was no record of her at any of the local hospitals. Kimber wanted to call the police and make a missing person's report, but most of the boys strongly disagreed— Kai in particular. They argued to give it one more day for fear of looking guilty themselves. I understood not wanting cops involved, but I believed it was time. Lainey had mentioned calling Trinity's mom first, to let her know what happened. She said it would be worse if she heard it from the cops, and I agreed with that, but nobody wanted to be the one to call her. I suggested it was Kimber or Scarlett May, as they were better friends, but neither one of them wanted to step up to the plate. As the owner of the cabin, the responsibility fell on me.

I got the phone number and stepped outside, away from the argument, to make the call. But when I did, I found I wasn't alone. Kai rested his forearms on the back porch railing as he looked out toward the vast black lake. All the light had drained from the sky, and had I not heard the water lapping against the shore below, I would've never believed there to be a lake beyond the porch.

"Are you okay, Kai?" I asked, joining him.

"I saw Trinity." His stare was pensive, and his pain, palpable.

"What do you mean? You saw her *when*?" I asked.

"I saw her last night. After . . . she was with Noah. I think I was the last one to see her," he said in a soft voice, as if even he didn't want to hear himself say it out loud.

"Kai, you have to tell me what happened. You have to tell everybody what happened. We need to find her, and if you're holding information back, that's not going to help anybody."

"But I'm not proud of myself, Kins. I'm really damn ashamed, to be honest. And I don't want to admit it."

I ran a hand through my hair, sighing. "You can tell me," I said, placing a hand on his forearm and giving him an encouraging squeeze.

"Trinity was drunk. She went to hook up with Noah, but he turned her down. I wasn't so strong. God . . ." Kai hung his head. It seemed as if all the guys had fallen for Trinity's wicked good looks at one time or another.

"So, you guys hooked up then?" I asked.

"No. Actually, we didn't. We were going to. We were about to, when she realized she'd left her phone in the bedroom. She pulled me far into the woods where nobody would see. She pushed me up against a tree, and even though I knew it was wrong and that she was using me to make Noah upset, I let her do it." Kai steepled his fingers beneath his chin, pausing for a moment.

"She unbuttoned my shirt and kissed my neck. But when she realized her phone was missing, she told me to stay put. She said she would be right back. She ran off through the woods, and she never returned. I waited out there like a fool. It must have been an hour. I looked for her on my way back, but I didn't see her. By the time I realized she'd stood me up, I was too embarrassed to say anything. I didn't want to see her then, and when a cab showed up to take Asher and Kimber back to the cabin, I jumped in with them."

I took in a deep, steadying breath and let my eyes wander through the darkness. I imagined Trinity running back for her phone and getting snatched in the middle of the forest. Presumably by the thing that had chased me. She must have been so scared. And if I hadn't been worried about Trinity before, I certainly was now. I looked down at the cell phone in my hands and knew it was time to call Trinity's mother . . . but how? How would I tell her mom that eleven of us had lost her daughter to the dark woods?

"I'm so sorry, Kinsley. I'm such an ass. It was unlike me, and I regret it so much. And now I'm afraid that the cops are going to think I did it," Kai said, his eyes misty.

"No, nobody is going to think you did anything. But we

have to tell the cops, and we have to tell everybody inside, too. Because if you hide this information, you're going to look far more suspicious when they find out. And they will."

We looked back into the house, which had fallen quiet, and my stomach sank when I saw two cops standing inside my living room. They were already there. The red and blue lights were flashing against the side of the house as Kai and I shared a look of dread for what was to come.

CHAPTER 12

After the cops left that night, every conversation devolved into an argument. Somewhere along the way, it had been flushed out that Mason already had a strike against him for battery, and he was afraid of what a missing girl tied to his file might look like for him in the future. Levi had unpaid parking tickets, and anytime a cop would come close, he'd break into a sweat. But one thing the group had agreed on unanimously was that nobody wanted to talk. Noah hadn't said a word to the cops about his time in the back bedroom, and Kai hadn't told them about his time with Trinity in the woods. In fact, he hadn't told anybody at all. I didn't know if the group could see it, but it was clear as day to me, when Kai's face was painted red and his lips pursed closed into a thin, straight line, that he was hiding something.

You never know how a group of people are going to

deal with a missing girl, but I never thought the group would fall apart. They turned inward as all their skeletons were flushed out. Secrets were billowing into the open air like a poisonous gas. Their knowledge of the event at hand was simply tucked away. Trinity missing was no more our fault than the weather shift, a summer storm blowing in from the east. Yet everybody had their own reasons for hiding, and it only made us, as a group, look more suspicious. I, myself, had motive. And that scared the hell out of me.

When morning came, I asked Lainey if she wanted to take Gunner on a walk. I told her I wanted to vent, and she didn't need any convincing after that. It was a lot for anybody to handle, and time alone to straighten our thoughts had become a necessity. But I didn't just want to talk about Trinity; I wanted to talk about what had happened to me in the woods. I wanted to take Lainey back to the tower, and I needed to understand how my mind was playing tricks on me. I had to face my fear to get past it.

We set out on the trail, and our conversation went from zero to sixty a few steps in. Lainey dove in deep the second we stepped off the back porch.

"I have something to confess, but you can't tell anybody," Lainey said, her eyes full of worry and her brows scrunched to match. Honestly, knowing that I wasn't the only one with secrets hidden inside felt like a blessing. It only made me feel like I was normal, and that was the best of feelings for me. I hadn't felt normal since my gran died, and I had never yearned for something so mediocre in my life.

"I won't tell anybody," I said.

Lainey reached down and let the dog off the leash. She took a deep breath as she watched him run into the woods. I looked behind us at the cabin, and nobody was outside to hear Lainey's deep, dark secret.

"I was the one who called the cops. I know everybody said not to. To give it time. But I just felt like I had to. I had to file a missing person's report. It was the right thing to do," she said, staring at me as if asking for forgiveness. It pained me to think that this had eaten at her all night long.

"Oh, Lainey, I honestly would have done the same thing if I was brave enough. I'm glad you called the cops. It was something that needed to be done." Voices could be heard in the distance, and they grew louder as we walked down the main path. An older couple was headed our way.

"Yeah, but everybody is so mad. Everyone is going to hate me when they find out," she said, hanging her head.

"No, they won't. And hey, nobody even needs to know. Maybe it was somebody at Sampson's house. They don't know."

"You think?" she asked hopefully.

"Of course! Do you know what I did?" I asked. "I called her mom last night."

"You did?"

We fell silent while the couple passed us, giving them a small curt wave hello.

"Yeah. I didn't know how to tell her mom that we lost her or, worse, that something terrible had happened. I was sweating bullets outside on the back porch while everybody was inside talking to the cops. The phone rang four miserable times before it went to voicemail. I've never been so conflicted in my life. On the one hand, I was relieved that I didn't have to speak to her. But on the other hand . . . I knew I would have to do it again. But this morning, when I told myself that I should call her, I couldn't bring myself to do it. I faltered, thinking that maybe the cops had done it, and it was no longer my job."

I stared down the trail before us, knowing that I should have made that call. I could do it now, right? But the cell service was spotty in the woods. Lainey didn't have much to say about that as we walked deeper into the forest, the dirt crunching under our shoes as our feet fell in step with one another.

"I have a secret to tell you. Promise not to say anything to anybody?" I asked, looking behind me. I knew the forest had eyes and ears, and I didn't want it hearing what I was about to say.

"Kins, of course. This is confidential, like always."

"You know how Trinity hooked up with Noah at the party?" I asked.

"Or, so we think. He says he didn't. You don't believe him?" she asked.

"No, do you?" I asked, taken aback. Our pace slowed.

"Well, why would he lie?"

It felt like a dig. Like I wasn't reason enough to lie. Like a potential relationship with me wasn't worth covering his tracks for.

"I don't know. Maybe because he wasn't proud of it?" I said, omitting the truth. Lainey shrugged, and I felt like I had made the whole thing up. Like Noah had never had feelings for me like I thought he had.

"Do you still like him?" she asked, her question hanging in the crisp morning air. It was a question I'd asked myself over and over since I saw him close that bedroom door. I knew I still had feelings for Noah, but I was ashamed of it now. Those feelings were tainted with the guilt of knowing that I deserved more and I wasn't giving it to myself.

"So, what's the secret?" Lainey asked, pointing to Gunner as he flushed out a covey of birds. I took a moment to watch them fly away, noting the low drum of their wings. I loved birds in flight, and I wished my insecurities could be taken away with them. When the birds disappeared into the treetops, my eyes fell back to the forest floor, and the hidden trail of thorns appeared.

"It's this way. The thorns are pretty bad, so just be careful where you step." We took the turn, and Lainey called Gunner back to make sure he followed us. I mused over the fact that he came running when she called because he did no such thing when I needed him.

"So, it turns out that Noah wasn't the only one spending special one-on-one time with Trinity that night." It spilled from my lips like a hot, sweet syrup, thick with gossip.

Lainey's pants snagged on a thorn, and she cursed as it ripped a small hole in her pant leg. "Nooo!" she gasped.

"Apparently, after Noah, she turned to Kai. And Kai took the bait. She led him deep into the woods where nobody would see, and then she left him there. She never came back."

We stepped over a fallen tree trunk, and Lainey turned to me. "She never came back?"

"No. He said that she headed into the woods because she left her phone back in the bedroom, and that was the last time he saw her." I looked up from the trail, trying to find the tall, arcane stone tower that I'd stumbled upon before, but there was nothing there.

"And he hasn't told anybody?" she asked.

"He . . ." I stopped and stared at the clearing. A multitude of trees freshly cut. A dozen stumps two feet tall, exposing their pale heartwood. I was sure that we were in the right spot. How could a tower the size of a lighthouse be there one day and gone the next? "He didn't want to tell anybody. I don't know why he mentioned it to me," I said, looking for the tower in every direction.

As we approached the clearing and my eyes traveled down to the ground where the base of the tower should've been, I was surprised to find the old, historical cemetery, hidden in plain sight.

Both large and small headstones sank into the overgrown forest floor. The stones were crooked, and many had crumbled as if they'd been here since the beginning of time. Letters had been etched into the rock as if one by one, each symbol drastic in variation. A small picket fence lined the cemetery's perimeter, and I imagined that it had been painted white long ago. But as it stood today, it was splintered, brown, and dilapidated. Multiple posts were missing, and the ones that still stood had been damaged by the weather or chewed on by the wildlife.

"Did you know this was here?" Lainey asked as we approached the memorial grounds.

I looked behind me as Gunner flushed out a new covey of birds, jumping at the sound, afraid I was being attacked again. I laughed along with Lainey, though it was nothing more than nervous energy. I didn't enjoy being there one bit, and Lainey only brought me a small sense of comfort. Much less than I imagined she would. "No. I knew the cemetery was out here in the woods, but I was here the other day, and I swear, it wasn't."

"You were here?" Lainey asked, her voice trailing off, as did my attention.

I looked around the grounds, my eyes following the beaten trail of thorny bushes, and without a shadow of a doubt, I knew this was exactly where I had stood. I wasn't the best with directions, I admit, but I knew this. I knew my mind was playing tricks on me.

I bit my tongue, refusing to sound like an eighteen-year-old suffering from psychosis. I might be worried about that, but I stuffed it deep down inside, where I was sure nobody would find it. The only problem was, *I* still knew it was there. I placed my hand on the first headstone I came upon and felt the rough texture under my fingertips as they trailed over the arc of the weathered stone. It was cool to the touch, and I imagined that at one time this stone had a lot of attention. At one time, there were loved ones crowded around it, mourning their loved one. "Jack Timmerman," I read.

"Adaline Stems," Lainey read.

I walked around each and every headstone, careful to step over the spaces where the bodies were buried. Many of the headstones only had a last name and the date, some with first and last names, and rarer yet, the date they were born. I didn't know what I was looking for, but I knew I hadn't found it yet. I searched for the name of the butcher, and I looked for signs of his lover. There were no indications that a famous love story had been buried here in the Baylor cemetery.

"You have to find her," Lainey mumbled, some three headstones away. I raised my head and looked over to her as she kneeled by a particularly short headstone.

"What did you say?" I asked. A pocket of cold air passed like a low-hanging cloud. The temperature dropped, and goosebumps covered my arms, sending a chill down the nape of my neck. I wasn't sure if Lainey heard me or not, but she said nothing. I watched her read the headstone as Gunner leaned into her side, tail wagging. I looked away, searching the forest for answers, but there were none to be found.

Lainey stood and moved to the next headstone. "I just love all of these purple shrubs, don't you?" she asked. I hadn't even noticed them until she said something. She was always keen on foliage. The purple popped, covering the ground. How could I have not noticed so many flowers? Then again, how could I have not seen an entire cemetery until I was upon it?

"You have to find her," she said, again, the moment my eyes wandered to the next headstone. I whipped my head back, absolutely positive this time of what I had heard.

"What?" I hissed.

"What?" she asked.

"You said something."

"Oh! I just love these purple flowers."

"No . . . after that."

"I didn't say anything after that," she said, confused. I stared at her, rolling my teeth over my bottom lip. She frowned, not liking the way I was staring at her. Like I was mad.

"You did," I said, digging my heels in.

She let out a small uncomfortable laugh and shook her head. "Kinsley, I didn't say anything!"

"I think it's time we go back," I said, feeling the chill seep into my bones. I checked back behind me, and the trees began to swirl as my head lightened. I stumbled forward, grabbing a headstone, feeling like I might faint.

"Are you okay?" Lainey and Gunner came to my side.

"Just a little dizzy," I said, gripping the top of the rotting headstone for balance.

"Kinsley, she needs your help!" Lainey said, gripping my shoulder with force.

"Why? How?" I labored with breath I didn't have to spare.

"Because she can't get out. Nobody can," she said.

"Get out of where?" I asked. The trees and the stones returned to their singular form as the spinning slowed to a crawl. Lainey's eyes only grew more concerned as the threat of me fainting dissipated.

"Get out of where?" Lainey looked at me, just as confused as I was. "What are you even talking about?" she asked.

I let go of the stone and grabbed her forearm. She steadied me as I stood to my full height. "You were talking about the girl and how I needed to help her," I said.

"Kinsley, you're starting to scare me. I haven't said *anything*. I don't know what you're talking about," she said. Crows called out from the treetops, and the sound echoed, bouncing between the pines. There was a warning in their calls. The leaves rustled in the wind with a distant static sound. As the sounds of nature became deafening, I knew it was time to go home. The forest no longer welcomed us. Lainey pulled a drink from her backpack, and I guzzled down the sweet syrupy punch. I felt the sugar tantalizing every cell in my body, and I wondered if my crazy had been a simple dip in blood sugar. By the time I handed her the half-empty bottle, I felt like my normal self.

"I'm sorry, Lainey. I didn't mean to scare you. I feel much better now. Thank you," I said, the heat from my embarrassment warming my flesh. As we walked back to the main trail, I felt lonelier than I ever had in my entire life. My best of friends didn't understand. And worst of all, I couldn't even trust myself. I didn't know who I was anymore. All the things I'd seen—the things I'd heard and felt. They were no more than a figment of my imagination. My reality was no longer real. And as I floundered in this phantom reality, I desperately needed something or someone to grasp onto. I needed to steady myself.

It was in that moment when I needed grounding that I

smelled the cologne of Walker St. James. I remembered how safe I'd felt in his flannel. The way he'd made me feel. He'd been the only one in this world who cared, in a time when my friends had abandoned me. In my most dire of times, it was Walker who'd stood by my side. It was the beautiful stranger in the canoe who'd saved my life. I didn't know what was so special about this guy that I'd only met a couple of times, but I knew I needed him now. Like a drug, he drew me to him—seeking peace when I felt the sting of instability.

# CHAPTER 13

I waited till evening before I slipped out of the cabin—unnoticed. It was an easy feat with all the commotion over Trinity still in full swing. The battle of moral obligation that took place in that cabin had no end in sight, and I couldn't take it any longer. I needed a break, but that made me feel guilty. Especially knowing that Trinity didn't have time to rest. So why should I? At least, I assumed she didn't. But I stuffed that speculation deep down, and I turned outward as I decided to take the night off from worry and despair. Like a weighted vest, I slipped it off, knowing I'd need to come back to carry the load again. But not tonight. Tonight was a break that I'd take for myself. And hopefully, by the end, I'd come away feeling renewed. Strong. Clear-minded. Sane.

I didn't know how to find Walker St. James, and I kicked myself for never getting his cell phone number. I wore his flannel tied around my waist and hoped my desire would be enough to summon him. I needed him now, and prayed that he felt it too. Call it fate or call it the stars—whatever you want—but I felt deep down that there was something between Walker and me that tied us together. A tether. Maybe it was the fact that he'd saved my life, and maybe I owed him mine in return . . . but I didn't think that it stopped there. When he'd saved my life, it had felt like the beginning.

I walked out to the end of the dock as the twilight sky continued to darken. The air was heavy with humidity. It was going to be a particularly misty night. One of those nights where the fog banks rolled in, thick and opaque. They were my favorite nights and made for the most beautiful of mornings. The loons would be calling out to one another through the poor visibility, and the whole lake would be haunted by their calls.

I paced the dock until my feet were tired and my nervous energy had finally subsided. When it did, I sat at the end of the dock with my legs crossed so that they wouldn't dangle over the dark water. I let my eyes wander in search of the guy who'd saved my life—and could possibly save me now—and they fell upon my neighbors in their back yard. I couldn't tell from where I was, but it looked as if they were gardening. I thought it was far too dark to garden, but who was I to say? I'd killed every plant I'd ever looked at. A "black thumb," my gran would say. I leaned back, my palms pressed against the wooden planks as I waited for my destiny to arrive.

*Find the boy*, I thought. *Find the boy . . . find the girl. Help the girl . . .* It all sounded so easy.

The first loon called out from the cool mist. Like a wolf, howling at the moon. I inhaled, releasing the tension I'd been carrying with me. *Help the girl.* Was she trapped? Was she stuck? Was she the girl from the ghost stories? How old would that make her? Regardless, I didn't know what I had to do with any of it. If there was one person who could help, it certainly wouldn't be me. Emma maybe, or Kai, but not me.

I closed my eyes, tipped my head to the sky, and I willed Walker to come find me. I imagined him paddling his canoe up to the dock. A smile on his face, his dimples piercing his cheeks. I imagined he'd ask for his flannel, and I'd untie it from my hips and hand it to him. Our fingertips would touch, and the exchange would send butterflies through my chest. He'd take me for a ride in his canoe, and all my worries would remain onshore as we drifted away. I needed him so I could feel sane. I wasn't sure what I was doing—if it was some kind of meditation or a simple daydream—but when I opened my eyes, Walker's canoe was tied to the end of the dock.

My back stiffened as I whipped my head back and forth, searching for him. I hadn't heard the canoe hit the dock, and I certainly hadn't heard Walker step out. I climbed to my feet and peered inside the belly of the canoe. There were no signs that it had been occupied. It was clear that he wasn't on the dock. The visibility was poor, but I could see to the end of it. I felt the urge to climb inside and paddle away. I needed to get out of here so desperately. I was losing my mind, and I felt it slipping further the longer I stayed.

I glanced back to the cabin. They'd never notice my absence. And the lake was calling me. I steadied myself with one hand on the dock post as I pulled the canoe closer. I nearly fell in the water when a figure approached me, materializing out of thin air. I gasped and whipped my head around to find Noah standing with his hands tucked deep into his pockets and a guilty sadness in his eyes. The last person I wanted to see right now was him, and yet here he stood. The only thing stopping me from running away. Slowly, begrudgingly, I let go of the canoe and stood, wiping my hands on my jeans.

"What are you doing down here?" he asked.

"I was about to ask you the same thing," I said.

"I was just out for a breather. I saw you down here all alone, and I thought maybe we should talk." Thankful for the dim sky, I rolled my eyes and immediately hoped that he hadn't seen. I crossed my arms over my chest and leaned a hip against the dock post, waiting for him to clear his conscience. "Is that okay with you?" he asked.

"If you have something to say, Noah, just say it." I

knew I had been upset with him for breaking a bond that neither of us was brave enough to secure, but I was surprised by the sharpness in my tone.

"Nothing happened between Trinity and me. I swear it."

"Okay," I said.

"You have to believe me, Kins."

"And why is that? You don't owe me anything." And that was the truth. We weren't boyfriend-girlfriend—only longtime friends who had longed for something more.

Noah bowed his head, then nodded. "That may be true, but I wanted you to know."

"You wanted me to know what, Noah? That you didn't sleep with her? Why do you care what I think?" Because, clearly, his actions proved he didn't care. So why was he pretending now?

"You know I care about you, right? We . . . We're . . ." he stuttered.

"You can't finish that sentence, can you? You know what?" I asked, pausing. Did I really want this? "I can't either, and there's a reason for that. It's because we're nothing. We're just two people who used to be neighbors. Friends along the way. And I thought that maybe there was something more between us—"

"There is!" he blurted out.

"No, there's not!" I said.

Noah took a step forward and reached for my hand. A

week ago, I would have given anything for this moment. I would have closed my eyes and leaned forward for a kiss. But as I stood here now, on a dock over evil waters, I knew I'd made a mistake when I blew out my birthday candles.

"There can be. If you wanted . . ."

I stared into his denim blue eyes and thought they looked black. His hand was clammy in mine. And I honestly didn't know what to say. I didn't know if I wanted him any longer. I knew I shouldn't. I knew I didn't in this moment. But I had no idea how I'd feel tomorrow or a week from now. I had pined after Noah for a long time. I'd known him better than I knew some of my girlfriends. I cared deeply about him, and as much as I hated it, I was attracted to him. Could I ignore the fact that I'd been hurt at Sampson's house and begin a relationship with him, hoping that maybe I'd get over it? But what if I didn't? What about Trinity? Where was she, and what if she came back? . . . What if she didn't? And . . . what about Walker? As I thought about my flannel stranger, the canoe bumped against the dock, summoning me.

"Is that what you want?" I asked in a softer tone, and I wished it hadn't come out sounding so breathy and needy. I was stronger than this.

He didn't say anything, but he nodded and took a step closer. As the gap closed between us, I instinctively took a step back. I tried not to think about what it meant, but in that moment, all I could think was one step away from

Noah was one step closer to the canoe. I wanted to get away. And Noah was one of the things I wanted to get away from. And as soon as I realized it, I couldn't keep it in any longer.

"I can't do this right now. I need some time to think. I need to go," I said, dropping his hand and turning away. It wasn't that easy though. He reached for my arm and pulled me close.

"Kinsley, come on."

My jaw dropped as I stared at him, appalled by the abrupt action. The tension between us was palpable. I waited for the electricity. For the tension to bleed into lust. But it never came. Noah's knife was still lodged in my back. His whole body slumped in sadness as I slowly pulled my arm out of his grasp. I stepped into the canoe, untied it from the dock, and never looked back.

I probably shouldn't have followed my instincts, because they hadn't been a friend of mine in recent weeks, but I picked up the paddle and began to row. I paddled through the heavy water until my arms burned. It was just beginning. I never looked back, my heart galloping as I abandoned the mess that had unraveled at the cabin.

I wondered if I was making a mistake with Noah. But I couldn't think clearly with the emotions that clouded my thoughts. The sadness was twisted inside me in tangled knots. Something was off. Something was *very* off. But I couldn't tell what. I didn't know if it was me or him . . . our relationship or this lake. But I couldn't breathe. And the farther I paddled, the more my lungs expanded. The shackles unlocked, and I was finally unbound.

The night grew cool, but I didn't need Walker's flannel to cover my shoulders. I was hot from paddling and nearly out of breath. I didn't stop until my arms grew numb, and I lacked control over their mobility. But as soon as I let my heavy limbs rest, I felt the canoe ease forward, despite the end of my paddle dragging through the thick secrets of the lake water. I took in a deep breath as the canoe propelled itself into the middle of the expansive lake. And as if the sky had been painted just for me, an array of stars glinted in the night sky. An amber Milky Way splashed the horizon, making for a brilliant view. The lake was quiet except for the water lapping at the canoe, and the sense of being exactly where I was meant to be, screaming loud and clear between my ears. I felt all the tension roll off me in sheets like hail in the eye of a storm. And as the seconds ticked by, the more I began to feel like my old self.

Maybe it was the fear of losing my mind or the guilt from wishing Trinity away the night she'd vanished, but a lump in my throat rose until tears dripped from my eyes. It wasn't until I'd put some distance between myself and that cabin that I let myself wash away all of the hurt and deceit that I had felt since coming up here for the summer. I cried and cried in the middle of the lake, under the majestic sky, until my body was spent and my mind had quieted from pure exhaustion. When I finally calmed down, I started to feel the cold. I untied Walker's flannel from my waist and slipped my arms into the sleeves, thankful for him once again.

I tipped my head back to the sky, enjoying it from a different perspective, when I heard quiet breathing behind me. I startled. Turning my head slowly, afraid of what might be in the boat with me, my heart pounded against my chest. But when I saw those dimples piercing Walker's cheeks, my heart swelled like a balloon too big for its cavity.

I wasn't even surprised that he'd appeared out of thin air—that was on par with the rest of my experience at Baylor Lake—but I *was* taken aback by the butterflies that spread throughout my belly. My feelings for this stranger were growing at an alarming rate.

I couldn't ask him how he'd come to be in the canoe or how long he'd been there without admitting my deepest, darkest fear. The fear that I no longer knew myself. The fear that perhaps something or someone else lived within me. And the fear that I could no longer trust myself or my senses.

So I started out simple. I didn't talk about the weather or the stars, but I pretended that he'd been there with me all evening. I pretended I was sane and sound, like he probably assumed I was. "Thanks again for letting me borrow your flannel," I said, turning around on the seat so that I faced him.

"It looks better on you than it ever did on me. Keep it," he said. The sound of his voice made me hunger for more. This was the feeling I was supposed to have when Noah grabbed my hand on the dock. But I had it with another guy. Not the one I had grown to love, but the one I knew nothing about.

CHAPTER 14

I couldn't keep my feet from wobbling back and forth in the belly of the canoe. My nerves were at an all-time high, and I wouldn't have had it any other way. These nerves were the *good* kind. The kind that hung on every word, doted on every movement and gesture. I listened not only to what Walker said but to what he didn't say. I did my best to fill in the blanks. Because everything inside this canoe mattered, and everything outside it meant nothing as I sat opposite of Walker St. James.

"Where are we going?" I asked, trying to see the horizon through the darkness.

"I'm taking you to a special finger of the lake. It's quite remote. Not many people know it's there," he said.

I smiled and nodded, curious to see a part of the lake I'd never known before. "I've been coming here for many years now. I thought I knew the entire lake. I don't recognize this part, though."

"I'm not sure if you've noticed it or not, but this lake can be quite mysterious," he said, his eyes settling on mine. I let myself linger there for just a moment, then redirected my attention. Every time I'd seen Walker, it had been so dark that I couldn't tell what color his eyes were. It was something I wanted to know, but I was too afraid to ask. I was becoming accustomed to the shade they were at night, and I liked the warmth that I felt behind them and their dark hue.

"It's funny you say that. I've noticed some . . . rather odd things since coming to the lake this summer. I mean, little things, like maybe I wouldn't have even noticed if you hadn't said anything . . ." I lied. Such a terrible lie. Especially since he was the one who had rescued me from the middle of the lake that mind-bending night we'd met.

"Many do. It wouldn't be uncommon."

"Really?" I leaned forward.

"Oh yeah. I told you, I come up here sometimes when I need a break from it all. And sometimes while I'm here, things get so upside down, I can't wait to get home to the mess I left. Things at Baylor can become so weird that it has a way of making you feel lucky for your past life. It's called the Baylor phenomenon. It's known well among the locals. Many people come here to run away from their day-to-day grind. But two weeks later, they're packing their bags, running back to whatever they fled from in the first place. And they do so with a smile on their faces."

"That's so weird that you just said that. I think I've been feeling that exact same thing. Although I wasn't running from anything when I came to Baylor Lake; I was just looking for a great summer." *Had* I been running from something, though? "Then again, maybe I was running from my childhood. I was so eager to move out. Move on." Most definitely, I was running from the death of my gran. From having to mourn properly. I didn't like what that realization did to my body—it was making my skin crawl. I pushed the thought away.

"Did you have a rough childhood?"

"No." I smiled. My childhood memories were filled with warm beginnings and loving ends. "But, since we've been here, things have become so twisted that I can't seem to get them right in my head. It's almost as if time is missing. Like memories are fleeting. Not specific memories —just lapses. As if I jump from one to the next and sometimes it's like . . ." I locked my jaw and shook my head. I wasn't making any sense. I couldn't possibly put this into words that he could understand. Especially if I couldn't even understand myself.

"This one time, years ago," said Walker, "I was up here with some friends. We were having the time of our lives, and out of nowhere, it ended. We were back home as if nothing had ever happened. None of us could remember when we got home or how. And to this day, some of my friends can't even remember the trip at all. I would've thought I was crazy if I didn't have the pictures to prove it. You should have seen the looks on their faces when I got the film developed. Those that didn't remember thought it was a prank. And the few that partially recall the trip still question where the rest of our time went. I don't bother with it anymore. Now I know that's just Baylor Lake."

"Huh, I should get a Polaroid camera or something. Just in case my summer becomes a trip like yours. Forgotten."

"Yes, take it from me. Document everything." His face softened into a smile, but there was a sadness that lingered.

"Do you have any more tips? I've been coming to this lake a long time, but this is the first time I've felt the phenomenon. My friends are starting to think I've lost it." Maybe that wasn't true, but *I* was starting to think so.

"I have all sorts of tips. But they're not free. Stick with me, and you'll learn a thing or two," he said, with a wink and an alluring smile that pulled me in like a moth to the flame.

I floundered there in his gaze for some time before he looked away with a shy smile. I could stay there forever, swimming in his gaze, basking in the light that he cast on me. It was in that moment that I gave up fighting my feelings for him. I threw caution to the wind, and I relished them. They were so blatantly obvious, and I had nothing left to lose. I liked the guy. And I thought I liked him a lot.

I tried not to compare, but my feelings for Noah were based on years of friendship. And what I felt for Walker was far different. It was more about a burning, yearning need for safety and sanity. And lust. I didn't only like him, but I liked how he made me feel. And it wasn't just something I wanted, but something I needed. I needed to feel understood, and if I could do it while looking into his beautiful deep eyes, then why the hell wouldn't I?

"It's like a black hole, that phenomenon. Sometimes I feel like anything is possible here," he said in a way that made me feel almost hopeful. Like maybe it wasn't a curse but a gift.

I rolled my lip between my teeth and hesitated before opening up to him. I didn't want to scare him away, but I desperately wanted to talk to him about all of it. And it seemed as if maybe he was the only person who could understand. Maybe he had the same stories to tell. Maybe I wasn't alone.

"This girl, Trinity—she's one of our friends, and she just went missing the other night. I figured she was staying with a friend or some guy that she had just met, but she never came home the next morning, and we found her phone left behind. My other friend called the cops and filed a missing person's report. We've all been pretty worried about her. And since she's gone missing, everybody in the house has been fighting. That's probably what they're all doing now, back at the cabin. I felt like I needed to get away from it all and just breathe, you know?"

"That's scary. Have you looked for her?"

"Yes, we all have. We retraced our steps from the night before. My friends and I were at a party across the lake. She wasn't there the next morning, and last she was seen was somewhere in the woods. I drove our golf cart looking for her in the forest near my cabin, but it's huge, and she could be anywhere. I'm sure the cops are waiting a certain amount of days before sending search and rescue. But it all just seems impossible. Like it can't be real." I shook my head, staring off into the distance. It couldn't be real. I'd heard of kidnappings when I was a child, but it never seemed like something that could happen to one of your friends at eighteen.

"So, you've got cops stopping by for reports and such?" he asked, brows furrowed.

"They stopped by the other night. But I was outside for most of it, trying to call Trinity's mother. She never answered." Silence stretched between us, and it was just the tip of the iceberg. I went on, diving deeper.

"I was taking the dog for a walk in the woods, and I swear I was being chased." It all tumbled out. "I don't know what it was, but it was big, and it was fast. My whole body screamed to run, and I barely made it out alive. But then when I saw my friends, they all looked at me like I was crazy. Nobody had seen the thing that was chasing me. Nobody except for me. And it was just a shift in the density of the air. Barely noticeable. Is that . . . is that the Baylor phenomenon?" I asked, squinting in fear that I had just exposed my true colors as a lunatic. But relief washed over me as soon as Walker nodded.

"Yes. That's exactly the phenomenon. Pretty much anything that would make you feel insane and send you packing. A mysterious sound, a repeating symbol, or if you have it real bad, haunting images and life-like phantoms. Sounds like you have a particularly bad case. Most don't. Most will just feel a little forgetful and have a sense of being homesick." His eyes were locked on mine, and I couldn't believe what I was hearing. I wouldn't have weeks ago.

"Huh . . ." I shuddered.

"It's almost as if your fear became a projection, which became your reality. You were out there in the woods all alone, and you felt . . . afraid? So, the thing you were worried about became a reality. It chased you because in your head you felt like prey."

I shook my head in disbelief. How could he know me so well? Walker rested the paddle on the side of the canoe, and we bumped onto the shore. I looked around at the grounds I'd never seen before. It was an entirely new shoreline. I'd scoured the perimeter of this lake before, but I'd never seen this.

"Actually, it can be a gift if you let it . . ." he said, pondering.

"Wait. You think I conjured up that animal—that thing?" I asked.

"Were you afraid *before* you were chased?" He smiled. He knew.

"Yes." I remembered the sounds of snapping twigs behind me and the goosebumps breaking out across my arms.

"Then you conjured it." I sighed as soon as the words left his lips. I should have been more afraid, but I wasn't. I felt relief. It was just silly old me. Letting my mind play tricks on me. A dark forest, a deep lake—it could scare anyone. These fears could get into anybody's head and run away with them.

"Do you think it could have hurt me? I mean, if it wasn't real," I asked, shaking my head as if I already knew the answer.

"Oh, it was *real,* all right. I'm sure that whatever was chasing you could have, in fact, taken your soul," Walker said, stepping out of the canoe and pulling it farther up on the sand.

*Taken my soul?*

And just like that, my sense of relief disappeared. Here one moment, gone the next. I stood and placed my hand in his. As I crawled out of the canoe onto the shore, I couldn't help but compare holding his hand with holding Noah's.

Walker's hand was not only dry but warm—and strong. I felt protected there in the dark with him. We let go of each other as soon as I was safely onshore.

"So that thing was deadly even though *I* made it come after me. That's . . . just . . . awesome."

"You have to be careful, for sure. Especially in those woods. It sounds like something about the trees and the water amplifies your fears. Just keep a clear mind, and you'll do just fine," Walker said, taking a seat on a large piece of driftwood. I sat next to him, enjoying the warmth that radiated from his body, and I didn't mind so much that the wood was sharp against my butt.

"It almost makes you feel crazy, doesn't it?" he asked.

"It does." I never thought I could feel understood by somebody else when I couldn't understand myself. But there he was. My other half.

"The funny thing is, all your friends in the cabin probably feel just the same way. They're probably missing memories too, and they're too afraid to say something," he said.

"Now, that would be funny, but I don't think that's the case. They seem pretty sure of themselves," I said, thinking back to how they'd made me feel so small and insecure.

"I guess the Baylor phenomenon doesn't affect everybody. Typically, it's people like you and me that it has an effect on. Just means you're special," Walker said with a wink and a piercing smile. I felt the heat spread across my cheeks, and I wanted to believe it. When I couldn't hide the smile of embarrassment, I bumped his shoulder with mine and he chuckled.

"So this may sound really weird, but I've been having dreams about my grandmother who recently passed. Do you think that maybe I'm conjuring her as well?" I asked, digging the heels of my shoes into the sand.

"That's something, isn't it? I wouldn't sweep it under the rug."

"I had a dream about her, and she told me to find this girl. She didn't tell me anything about the girl or where I'd find her. She only said that she needs my help," I said with a chuckle. Was I trying to send him running? Why was I still talking? I sounded mad. I ran my hand through my hair and peered up at him.

"A girl?" Walker asked, intrigued. His eyes narrowed on mine, and I felt embarrassed for bringing it up.

"I don't know," I said with a laugh, shaking my head. I must have sounded so stupid. "Hey speaking of, have you ever heard of the Baylor Butcher ghost story?" I asked, as if this topic was a better argument for my sanity. Why did I let myself keep talking to him?

"I have," he said, leaning in. His gaze was pensive, like every last drop of his focus was trained on me. He was intrigued, just like I had been the first time I'd heard about it.

"I don't know much about the story, other than I have

heard two entirely different sides of it. I was thinking about doing some research and learning more about it. I'm wondering if the girl in the ghost story was who my grandmother wanted me to find. Oh, my god. It sounds so ridiculous when I say it out loud," I said, laughing at myself. It wasn't funny up until now. Until I was sitting on a piece of driftwood next to a handsome stranger. The one that I was sure had been plucked from the heavens and gifted to me alone.

"The elusive Layla Barns! The girl who got away," he said, in a haunting tone. Goosebumps prickled the nape of my neck.

"Layla Barns?" I asked.

"Yeah, that was the girl the butcher fell in love with," he said. There was a pain in his voice that I could feel somewhere inside my chest. How could I be so in tune with this guy that I could already share his hurt? I searched his face, looking for answers as he stared at the water lapping against the shore.

"Do you know anything else about her?" I asked.

"Just a few things I've heard over the years as the story changes hands. I've never researched it, though, so I couldn't tell you for sure." He picked up a pebble from the sand and chucked it into the water with too much force for such a tiny object.

"Maybe it's just the memory of my gran, but I've grown really curious about their story. I think I'm going to look into it while I'm here. I've asked around a little bit, but all I've heard are tall tales."

"If you want some help, I'll look into it with you. I've been curious about what happened to Layla too. And it's not like I have much else going on. I'm just here for the summer, waiting until I have an itch to go back to my monotonous life. Air traffic control and bartending. Man, when I say it like that, I need to get a dog or something," he said with a chuckle of embarrassment.

I laughed at him. He didn't need a dog. He just needed someone special in his life. I kicked myself for thinking I could be that person.

"Let's do it. You and me. Let's crack the cold case of Layla Barns. Maybe it will bring us some peace?" I joked.

"I'm in. I'm *all* in. We should start at the library tomorrow. You won't find anything on the internet," he said, eagerly.

"Actually, you're right. I've tried." I wasn't sure what was happening between us, but we had formed some sort of alliance. A club of two. Two amateurs trying to crack a cold case like we were super sleuths. But I didn't care. I so desperately wanted something to take my mind off the weird Baylor phenomenon that made me feel unstable. And there was something that Walker was running away from, too. Maybe we could help each other.

"Well, I hate to go, but it's probably time I get you

back." Walker patted the top of my hand and I leaned into him with a sad smile.

"You're probably right."

"Always am," he said, standing. I reached for the hand that he offered and pulled myself up. This time, he didn't let go until I was inside the canoe. I watched his strong arms use the paddle to push us off the shore and begin moving us across the lake. I knew how hard it had been on my puny arms to get as far as I did, and I admired his strength as he effortlessly pulled the paddle through the heavy water.

Unfortunately, the ride back to the cabin took only a fraction of the time we'd spent getting to the secretive side of the lake. And although I wasn't surprised, I was filled with disappointment. We'd spent most of the ride stealing glances at each other and smiling when we'd get caught. I was pretty sure that whatever I was feeling was mutual.

We confirmed our plans to meet at the library before I climbed out of the canoe. And it was hard to say good night, but I held on to the plan we had to meet the following day. I'd see his eyes for the first time in the day's light. And I'd better be able to dream about him after knowing what they looked like. I snuggled into Walker's flannel as I walked down the dock toward the cabin.

I peeked over my shoulder to smile at Walker one last time before climbing the grassy knoll. But he wasn't there at all. He'd vanished. My smile faded. I searched the lake for his canoe, and I prayed that I hadn't imagined the entire night. I was hesitant to turn my back, because that would mean another night of torture inside my head. My reality clashing with some other world I didn't belong to. I hung my head and climbed the hill, wondering if I'd see him tomorrow or not. And I hated the fact that I was unsure if one of the best nights of my life had been real or not.

# CHAPTER 15

It didn't matter how many cups of coffee I had that morning, the caffeine couldn't bring me to life after the sleepless night I'd had. With a mug resting on my lips and my eyes focused in the distance, I noticed that Emma was studying me. I vaguely felt her eyes looking me over, but I couldn't pull myself into the moment. I was lost somewhere out there on the lake with Walker. I'd spent the night dreaming of him and wondering what it would be like if my days were filled with his presence. He'd be the cane that supported me. The crutch I needed so that I could stand up straight. And, no longer hobbled, we would become a pair. A perfect fit.

I weighed my options between Noah and Walker, and I imagined what it would be like to kiss his lips. I'd already spent significant time wondering what color his eyes would be in the daylight. I had been so impatient that the thought of seeing them for the first time today at the library was enough to keep me awake for most of the night. That and the fear that he wouldn't show.

It was early still, but since I had barely slept, I was up. And so was Emma. Although it was unlike her to be up so early, I welcomed her company on the back deck.

"Do you think Lainey is afraid of ghosts?" I mumbled while looking out over the foggy lake. The paint was peeling on the deck, and tiny white flakes had fallen from the railing.

"I think Lainey is afraid of a lot of things. Why do you ask?" Emma asked.

"She didn't seem interested at all when I tried to talk to her about the Baylor ghost stories. And when I talk to her about that stuff, she seems . . . I don't know. *Weird*. She just kind of shuts down. I think she might be afraid of it."

"Maybe. I love that stuff, though."

"You like ghost stories?" I asked.

"I've only read about a hundred haunted mansion books. You're not very observant." Emma chuckled, but I knew that it stung.

Emma was a big-time reader, but I'd never bothered to look at the book covers. I was dyslexic, and reading wasn't a strength of mine. I wanted it to be. I wanted to dive into stories and live in that fictional world while cuddled up on the sofa, wrapped in a throw blanket. I'd have a raging fire and a cup of hot cocoa by my side. It sounded fantastic. It just wasn't for me. The same way that being an athlete wasn't.

"I'm sorry I didn't realize that. I always figured you were reading steamy romances." I winked at her, and Emma laughed.

"Well, I read those too," she said. This time, her laugh was a little higher-pitched than normal.

"Can I tell you a secret?" I asked.

"It's a little early for secrets, but I think I can handle it. Lay it on me." Emma set her coffee down on the side table and leaned in.

"I met this guy. He's a local here. He and I are going to the library today to do some research on the Baylor ghost story. I told him I was interested in it, and he said he was too. And I'm not sure, but I kind of feel like it's a date," I said, pursing my lips and trying not to smile.

"What! I thought you liked *Noah*."

"SHHH, keep your voice down," I said, looking back into the kitchen windows. It was still early, and I didn't think anybody was up, but I couldn't be too sure. "I don't know what I think of Noah now. But I do know what I think of Walker. And he's so cute! And he's nice! And he listens to me . . ." I said, my head in the clouds.

"Walker?"

"Walker St. James . . ." I said, feeling giddy inside. I wrapped my hands in the long sleeves of my shirt and covered the ever-growing smile on my face.

"Oh my god. You've got it bad!" Emma laughed again. We talked a little more as I finished my coffee, and then I laced my shoes up for a morning hike. I was tired from not sleeping, yet I still had excess nervous energy that I needed to get rid of before I saw Walker that afternoon. Maybe I would crash later—take a little nap—but for right now, I needed to get out. I knew I liked the guy, but admitting it to Emma felt like a new level. It made it real. And that scared me, since I didn't know if our time last night had been real or not. He'd vanished as quickly as he'd appeared. I tried not to think about it.

I tightened Gunner's collar and secured the leash by wrapping it around my hand several times. I wasn't going to let him run this time. Not just because I didn't want to lose him again—I didn't—but because I needed him by my side for protection. I wasn't going off-trail this time either. The main trail in the forest was popular enough that I should be safe. And I couldn't live my summer in fear of going into the woods. As I set off, I thought about what Walker had said about manifesting my fears. I was in a different mindset now than I had been the times before, and I wondered if I'd have a different experience because of it.

The way the light filtered through the trees and danced softly on the trail was hypnotizing. Peaceful even. If I were to conjure this feeling into something outside of myself, what would it be? *Something beautiful*, I thought. I listened to the birds sing and was hyperaware of the rhythmic panting from Gunner. I concentrated on my breathing and tried to slow it down. Walker had been right about the Baylor phenomenon; it was a special force if you learned how to control it.

Was it as easy as thinking good thoughts? Pulling up good memories and seeing them unfold before you in the forest? I was sure that the shadows on the trail hadn't danced before. No, before they had jumped; they had struck out like snakes. And I hadn't heard the birds singing before—only the woodpeckers hammering the trees like a drum.

The entire experience was different, and the more I thought about how I had the power to change it, the more I felt the worry and the dark seep back into the woods. I was the last person who should be in control. I wasn't the most reliable person I knew. Not now. Not ever.

I saw a splash of color and a blur of long, dark, ominous hair disappear into the woods. *Trinity*. It had to have been her. I pulled Gunner back and stiffened, searching for the motion that I'd caught in the corner of my eye.

"Trinity?" I called out, my voice bouncing from tree to tree. It sounded as if a thousand of us were out here searching for her.

I whipped my head around, looking in every direction, but I was the only one on the trail. I began walking again. Gunner was pulling on the leash. But this time, I wasn't as sure of myself as I had been seconds prior. A morsel of fear had broken the seal, and I was sure that the small crack would widen over time. A lump formed in my throat, and I had trouble swallowing it down. *It's just a manifestation.*

I brought a shaky hand to the bridge of my nose and closed my eyes, briefly wishing they would open with a sense of confidence that I didn't possess. It was too much to ask for. I should have never asked for that much. By the time I opened my eyes, I'd been thrown into a full-blown nightmare.

Fog surrounded me—so thick, I could hardly see halfway down the leash. A red tether to god knew what. I felt Gunner pull on the other side. His presence brought me little comfort as I looked around the fog, trying to discern up from down. My heart fluttered in my chest, and my breathing quickened. I knew my panting matched Gunner's when my mouth fell open and my tongue grew dry.

I pulled on the leash, attempting to turn around. We hadn't been walking long, and I was certain I could find the clearing of Rock Creek quickly. I took a step, and twigs snapped under my feet. I froze for a moment. *It's not real.*

I took slow and steady steps forward with a hand stretched out until I slammed into something that had no place being in the middle of the trail. "Ah!" I called out, grabbing my knee. A large curved stone stood between me and my way out. A headstone. I gasped. The fog was thick and white as the dozens of headstones came into view. *It's just my fear.*

I knew I had been on the main trail when I closed my eyes, and I hadn't even taken a step before I opened them to the cemetery. It wasn't real. It couldn't be. I knew that now, after talking to Walker. I only wished the knowledge was enough to take away the fear that coursed through my veins. I tried to remain calm, but everything inside me told me to run.

*Don't run. It will only make it worse.*

I forced my legs to stay still. I didn't know how to get out of there anyway. *Don't run.* The fog was so thick I couldn't see my feet. I closed my eyes once again and tried to calm myself. *I'm conjuring all of this myself. It's just my imagination. It's only fear.*

I told myself that when I opened my eyes I'd be back on the main trail and the fog would be receding. I imagined clear skies, warm air, and Gunner wagging his tail happily at the end of the red leash. But something stronger than my will intruded on my thoughts at the last second.

I peeked through squinted eyes. At the end of the leash was a skinless, grotesque monster. With its hind legs crouched and ready to vault. Its fangs dripping with saliva, and its jowls hanging flaccid and free. I sucked in a breath, my blood curdling as my eyes sprung wide open and I fell backward. The phantom disappeared as I hit the ground.

Gunner went ballistic, growling furiously like he had

in the cabin with the ghostly intruder. I held on as tightly as I could to the leash. It dug into the palms of my hands. He was my lifeline, and I wasn't going to let him go if it was the last thing I did.

Gunner snarled, whipping his head from side to side. His hair stood up on the ridge of his back, and I began to slide on my butt as he pulled me forward. Through the fog, a figure appeared. *It very well could have taken your soul.* Walker's words streamed through my head.

Gunner was unbelievably strong, and I dug my heels into the dirt, trying to gain traction. The figure stood still, assessing the threat as I heaved all my weight into holding Gunner back. But slowly, I was being delivered to the soul eater. One inch at a time.

The figure took a step forward, and the gray shadow turned black. A face appeared—devilishly handsome and rugged. Walker St. James. A sense of relief washed over me, causing me to slacken my grip. The slight release allowed Gunner to rip the leash from my hands, burning my flesh. Gunner snarled as he ran full speed at Walker.

"No!" I screamed.

Walker did nothing to protect himself. He didn't even flinch. And Gunner barreled toward him at lightning speed. My eyes went wide with horror. I couldn't bear to see the attack, but I didn't have to. Gunner snarled as he ran mere inches past Walker, never slowing down. I could hear his growling rip through the fog as he continued to run into the distance. *What the hell was he chasing?*

My heart was pounding like a wrecking ball, swinging back and forth in my chest, breaking my bones until there was nothing but a heaping pile of dust inside me. *Why wasn't he afraid?* I pulled my eyes from Walker down to the palms of my hands, which were bloodied and burned from the leash. Stinging intensely, they trembled with pain. I scrambled to my feet, cradling my wounded hands.

I'd lost Gunner. Again.

Walker approached me slowly, with the same fear in his eyes that I'd held in mine. But something was off, and I couldn't be sure what. He came closer, stopping to place his hand on top of the headstone I'd run into. I strained to see his eyes. They surprised me. A bright luster of molten gold. He had a scar I'd never noticed before on the tail end of his right eyebrow. A jagged inch of freshly-healed skin. His hair was a dark brown and his stubble had shades of amber under the sunlight. He was even more beautiful in the sun than when he was under the stars, and all I could do was stare into his eyes.

He tapped his hand ever so slightly on the headstone, drawing my attention away from his gorgeous face. *Layla Barns.*

He'd found her. I labored to stand without the use of my hands, staggering backward to get a better view of the headstone.

"You found her!" I gasped, knowing that this stone hadn't been here before. I would have remembered this one.

"Your hands. Are you okay?" Walker asked, looking behind him for the dog.

My hands were pink and swollen, and blood dripped from one of my palms. Parts of the meaty flesh were missing, and my hands trembled, even though I tried to brace them. "I think I need to get this cleaned up."

"We should go back to the cabin. I can help," he suggested.

"Yeah, thanks." I looked down at the elusive headstone in awe one more time. "Layla Barns . . ." I whispered as I passed by.

She was dead. I'd heard that her body lay resting beside her lover's, but I think there was some part of me that had hoped she was still alive. Some part of me that had wondered if I could speak to her. How was I supposed to help her if she was lying six feet under the ground? I looked from left to right and found a headstone beside hers with no inscription. No name to go by. Just a blank stone. I looked up at Walker with disappointment, though I knew it was the butcher's.

"I was kind of hoping she'd still be alive," I said in a somber tone.

"This was long ago. She's been dead for some time now." He leaned forward, placing a hand on my shoulder, and I looked up at him with a smile. I was so thankful that he had shown up when he did. Who knows what my imagination would have done to me if he hadn't appeared.

"I couldn't sleep. I was up all night. I found out where she was buried—where she crashed—"

"Where she crashed?"

"Apparently, they were in a car crash. On the opposite side of the lake. It's a long drive, but if we leave soon, I think we could make it there and back with plenty of light. We could look around and see if there are any clues as to what else happened there. I heard there were markings on a tree and some sort of shrine. We can't miss it," Walker said.

"Okay, yeah, let's do it." I looked just beyond Walker, hoping to find Gunner before returning to the cabin. "But I should probably find the dog first. He ran right past you. I don't know what he was after," I said.

"I'm sure he'll turn up. Let's get that hand looked at, and then we can take a drive around the lake," Walker said, putting his arm around my shoulder.

I told him about how the fog had taken over and I'd appeared in the middle of the cemetery without taking a step off the trail. He assured me it was all normal practice for the Baylor phenomenon and, even though it didn't make sense, I accepted it. Because he accepted me. By the time we stepped onto the trail, we spotted both Emma and Lainey walking Gunner.

"You found him!" I called out.

"Found him?" Lainey asked. An uncomfortable silence grew between the four of us as my eyes bounced from Lainey to Emma to Walker. Only he knew that we had lost the dog, and I watched his face as he realized what was happening. I noticed the red leash in Lainey's hand, the one that had been ripped from my death grip. It didn't look like it had been dragged through miles of dirt.

The girls eyed Walker suspiciously, and I could tell immediately that they didn't like him. Lainey's brows furrowed as Gunner sniffed at his pant leg. "Hey, Kinsley. We're looking for Trinity, and I think you should come with us," she said, gesturing toward Emma.

"Yeah, you should probably help. We need all the eyes we can get," Emma agreed. I couldn't argue with that. They needed as much help as they could get, but I was pretty sure they were disingenuous in their request by the way their eyes kept flickering to Walker.

I looked up toward Walker, who was calm and collected. "Actually, Walker and I were going to take a drive around the lake. We might have better visibility there. And we could look for her on the other side of the lake, since you guys have this part covered."

"Um, the cops are coming back to the house today, and they said they need to speak with everybody. That includes you. So I really think you should join us for that. Plus, you won't have time to get to the other side of the lake and back, and it looks like you need to bandage your hand first anyway," Lainey said, fidgeting with the leash. I looked down at Gunner, who was happy as a clam. A stark difference from before.

"I guess I can't make it to the crash scene today. But we can reschedule?" I asked, turning to Walker.

He nodded, his disappointment etched in his forehead. I took in his golden eyes one last time before I left him there in the middle of the woods. I wasn't sure why Emma and Lainey were so insistent, but the tension that spread between the three of us as we walked away was palpable. I didn't like the way they were looking at one another, and I could tell that they were wary of Walker. I looked over my shoulder as the distance between us grew. He watched us walk away with his arms folded across his chest.

# CHAPTER 16

I looked over my shoulder to see Walker watching the three of us walk away. The separation between us felt like much more than a simple redirection. For some reason I couldn't yet understand, it felt like saying goodbye. An invisible string tugged my heart with every step I took in the opposite direction, and I looked at Emma and Lainey for answers. But whatever answers they had, they weren't keen on sharing. The looks exchanged between the two of them were burdened. They were hiding something from me.

"Is somebody going to tell me what's going on?" I asked.

The stuttering blame pushed off from one to the other was difficult to watch, and I became more upset with each second that ticked by. "W—well you said that you had just met this guy. And I was leery. I was leery before I did research on the butcher, but the second you left, I hopped on my computer, and I couldn't think of anything other than your safety. Out here, alone, in the woods. Meeting some man you don't even know. He's just a stranger. I mean, really, who is this guy? And how old is he? Do you even know anything about him?" Emma rambled like a freight train barreling down the rail.

"That's ridiculous, Emma. I know him. Actually, the guy saved my life when you didn't!"

"Oh, here we go . . ." Lainey said.

"What are you even talking about?" Emma asked.

I sighed, knowing I'd said too much. But it wasn't something I couldn't come back from. "I'm sorry, that's not what I meant. He's just a really nice guy. And he's not old; he's only twenty-four."

"That's six years older than us," Emma said.

"That's not that much older!" I looked between the two of them. It wasn't *that* much older. We weren't in school anymore, talking about what grade our boyfriend was in.

"And what do you mean, he saved your life?"

"It was nothing. There was an incident where I thought I was drowning. He came out of nowhere and helped me onto his canoe." I tried rubbing away the stress on my forehead with the back of my bloodied hand. It hurt. Defending my relationship with Walker was making my head hurt. They should just be happy for me. Why weren't they?

"When?" Emma asked. I glimpsed Lainey shaking her head, and I knew she thought I'd gone mad. It made me question myself.

"It was some time ago," I said, vaguely. The truth was, I wasn't entirely sure when it had happened, or if it even had. Lainey thought it was an outright lie. Maybe she thought I was trying to get attention? That was the last thing I wanted.

"Look, as soon as you left for your walk, I learned about all sorts of creepy things the butcher did to lure in women and make them fall for him. It was gaslighting at its best. He manipulated their minds, making them believe that he was the only one that made sense in a life that seemed crazy. He was a master manipulator, and I just don't want that to happen to you. You've seemed a little . . ." Emma frowned, glancing at me sideways. "A little off lately," she said gently. I tipped my head back, soaking in the truth. I knew I'd been acting crazy, but I'd hoped that nobody could see it. It was stupid to think they hadn't.

"I appreciate you looking out for me," I said. I didn't want their help, but I knew it was coming from a good place, and I had to stop and acknowledge that. Appreciate it.

We walked back to the cabin, the crunching of gravel beneath our feet filling the awkward silence between us.

Lainey halfheartedly told us about different species of bushes here and there, but mostly, we kept to ourselves. Her attempts at normalcy were unwanted and awkward. Every now and then, I would check over my shoulder, but Walker was long gone. And I was thankful he hadn't heard the conversation we'd had about him.

The house was lively when we got back. The kitchen was bustling with four guys trying to make an epic breakfast. A cure for their hangovers. Kimber was lying in Asher's lap on the sofa, and Scarlett May was wrapped in a blanket on the carpet drinking coffee. Everyone seemed to be working together this morning, and I could barely remember that one of us was still out there. Missing. I briefly thought about the night I'd met Walker. How I'd come into the cabin, and nobody had noticed I was gone. Is this what was happening now?

It was hard to think about Trinity when I felt eyes on me. I tried to pretend I hadn't noticed Noah, but the tension was searing. I went to wash my wounded hands in the sink, but as I ran my hands under the water, and the blood circled the drain, I noticed that the flesh underneath was perfectly intact. I scrubbed furiously, and then examined my perfect hands. They didn't even hurt. I felt a wave of dizziness and went to grab a glass from the cabinet to pour myself some orange juice, when Noah reached for the cabinet at the same time. We both pulled back, allowing the other to go first. And then both reached at the same time again, our hands barely bumping into each other.

We both obviously felt the awkwardness after our conversation on the dock. I'd left him wondering, and our relationship had been hanging in the balance ever since. But somewhere in the night, while Walker paddled and I gazed out at the night sky, I'd realized I had feelings for him, and they unequivocally trumped my feelings for Noah.

I tried not to look at him directly, but it was unavoidable. When our eyes caught, I knew that my feelings for Noah had died. There was something in the way he held himself that told me he knew where I stood. His shoulders slackened, and the corners of his mouth drew downward. The light from his eyes was gone. I poured my orange juice, feeling guilty for the pain that I'd caused him. And even though the exchange had gone unspoken, I knew I'd have to say it aloud at some point in the near future. It wasn't a conversation I was looking forward to having.

Ironically, I bumped into Ethan on my way out of the kitchen, spilling my orange juice all over my chest. I deserved it. I deserved a lot more than a spill for making these two feel inadequate in any way, shape, or form. I wasn't good enough for either of them, and I *definitely* wasn't good enough for Walker. The thought of making them feel small made me feel sick to my stomach. And now, Ethan felt bad about my shirt, too. I assured him it was okay and rushed out of the kitchen, not because the stain was about to set, but because I couldn't wait to get away from the claws of compunction that were threatening to tear me apart.

Emma and Lainey followed me upstairs, and they closed the door behind us when we reached the master bedroom. "What was all that?" Lainey asked.

"Oh, I didn't tell you? Noah asked if we could have a relationship last night, and I told him I didn't know what I wanted." I pulled my shirt over my head and tossed it into the sink. Lainey and Emma sat on the edge of the bed while I dug through the dresser for another T-shirt.

"No!" Emma said.

"Wait, I thought you liked him?" Lainey asked.

"I did. Until . . ."

"Until Walker," Emma mumbled. Lainey and I looked at her, and when their eyes fell back on me, I nodded, confirming. The air in the room shifted and became uncomfortable.

"Yeah, I don't know when it happened, but I really like this guy. I've been thinking about him constantly." I pulled on an old but comfortable T-shirt.

"I wanted to show you an article I found. Will you at least read it?" Emma asked. She turned her laptop toward me, and I sighed.

"Well, that's my cue. I'll leave you guys to it," Lainey said, standing up.

"You don't like the ghost stories, do you?" I asked.

"I just prefer to think none of it ever happened. The thought of murder makes my skin crawl. Why would I ever want to dive into that world? Why do *you*? It just makes little sense. Why you guys are interested in this is beyond me. I just can't." Lainey spun toward the door and paused. "You do remember I had to have an emotional support dog accompany me here, right? This whole thing about Trinity . . . and now a ghost story—it's too much." Lainey waved her hand through the air dismissively. She closed the door behind her, and neither Emma nor I found the words to reply to her.

"I guess it's just us then," I said to Emma. I felt terrible that Lainey had been upset about all of this. We all were, but she was the most fragile of the group.

"Guess so."

"Thanks for helping me do research. I know it's kind of weird and all, but I appreciate it. I haven't gotten too far on my own, yet," I said.

"Just read this, and we can start from there. But I wanted you to at least be aware of this killer's tactics." Emma pushed the laptop toward me, urging me to read. I sat on the edge of the bed, placed her laptop in front of me, and glanced over the document. The words blurred together, and I felt the anxiety boil in my chest. The font seemed too tiny, and the concentration needed too vast. I shut down before even trying.

"Just tell me what it says," I said, shrugging, pushing the laptop across the bedsheets.

"Just read it!"

"I can't! I don't want to!" I felt my voice hitch in my throat.

"Why are you being so weird?" Emma asked.

"I'm dyslexic, Emma. You know that!" I hated repeating it. Like admitting I'd done something wrong. It was like wearing a scarlet letter across my chest. I'd told her before in passing, but I guess it never really sank in.

Emma stared at me blankly, and I felt my face heat with frustration. "I know that. But you *can* read . . ." she said.

"Yeah, I can. It's just frustrating as hell. Do you know what I see when I look at that screen? I see the white space between the letters and words. I search for patterns that aren't there. I see a lot of little marks that tend to blur together. I see an uphill battle. And I'm exhausted just by looking at it. If you want me to read this article, I'm going to need full concentration and dedication. And I just don't have that in me right now."

I wasn't going to pretend to read it either. I did that sometimes. When the stakes were high and somebody was waiting for me to read a meme or a funny joke. They'd hold their phone up to my face, and I'd just freeze up, worried I wouldn't finish reading in time, and it would get weird. They would wonder what was taking so long, and I'd choke. So, I'd just gaze at the passage, try to pick what a normal speed would be, and then smile at the end, hoping it was the reaction they were looking for.

It's not that I didn't read. I did. But it had to be on my own terms. It had to be interesting, and it had to be quiet. No distractions. And I'd use my finger to help keep my eyes from jumping from line to line. It was the little words that tripped me up the most. They could be here or there and then back again. Nobody understood because they were all good at reading. And there is a real segregation in the younger years when reading is cool and you still struggle.

*Dumb.* It was one of my first identity markers. I had cool light-up shoes. I had friends. But I was dumb. And that stuck with me. The trends came and went. Hell, the friends did too. Most of them. But it was stupidity that stuck with me. It burrowed its way into my subconscious, and I believed it.

"So, if you could just tell me the key parts of this article that you want me to know, then we can move past this fairly quickly." The tightness in my chest wasn't from the explanation I needed to give to one of my best friends but the tension I felt from just looking at the screen. And the expectation that I'd read it. The disappointment that would follow when I wouldn't.

I hated admitting that I had dyslexia or that I needed help. It was like telling somebody that you had been faking your whole life. Like you pretended to be somebody you weren't. An intellect. Sure, I got good grades. And none were the wiser. But what they hadn't seen was that I had spent countless hours every single night at my parents' dining table with tears in my eyes as I tried to wade through the homework and studying. I had never read a full book before, but that didn't stop me from finding the answers I needed. Call it cheating, call it making do, but I had the grit that kept me in the game.

I'd gotten by, but it was only by the skin of my teeth. I had barely hung on in every single class, but I was the only one to ever know how much I struggled. Even my parents weren't fully aware. I should have just been a terrible student. It would have been so much easier. But for some reason, getting good grades meant a lot to me. And at some point along the way, I'd come to realize that effort was just as important as intellect. There were many kids that never had to study and could get A's on all their tests. And then there were kids like me, who studied for hours upon hours to only grasp the lower end of the B.

"Okay. Sorry." Emma shrugged. I sat down on the bed, avoiding eye contact as she filled me in on the twisted ways of the Butcher of Baylor. It wasn't anything I hadn't figured out myself. A murderer must have done some pretty awful things if he was killing in the first place. But the part that concerned me the most was that Emma related these nefarious acts to Walker. I didn't understand how he had anything to do with this or why she felt like my life may be in danger when I was alone with him.

"How did this remind you of Walker?" I asked. I watched Emma flounder and immediately concluded that her argument was unfounded. Dogmatic.

"Well, it doesn't sound very safe for you to be gallivanting around the lake with some guy we never met before. He could be dangerous," she said in a motherly tone.

"He could be. And Noah could be Trinity's killer!" I said, regretting it the moment it came out of my mouth. Emma stared at me in shock. "I didn't mean that."

"You think Trinity is dead?" Emma stammered.

"No . . ." I shook my head.

"And you think Noah did it?" Emma said beneath her breath.

"No," I said, as I considered the possibility. "No, I didn't say that. That's not what I meant."

"But that's what you said."

"I know. I'm just under a lot of stress. I think we all are. I don't know why that came out, but it's not what I meant. I swear." I turned away from her and looked out the window.

"Then what did you mean by it?" she asked. I spun around to face her. She was a little paler, now that she'd been considering that one of our own did something to Trinity.

"I mean, I really like Walker. And I don't think he's dangerous. He's a really nice guy. And just because I don't know him as well as I know Noah, I don't think we should judge him because one of our friends went missing. I mean, we shouldn't judge Noah because he was the last to see Trinity, right? Why does this have to be so complicated? This was supposed to be the best summer of our lives, and now Trinity is missing! And I'm falling for a complete stranger who my friends think is a murderer!" I threw myself backward onto the bed, draping an arm over my eyes. I listened to Emma sigh.

"He *is* pretty cute," she said. A small smile crept across my face as I glanced at her from beneath my arm. She tried to hide her blush behind her hair, but I could still see it.

"Emma Olsen! Did you just say that he was, and I quote, *pretty cute?*"

Emma was fairly introverted as it was, but when it came to guys, she was incredibly shy. She never talked about them, and even though I knew she liked Levi, I'd never spoken to her about it.

"I mean, for you. He's cute for you. You guys are cute together—"

I laughed in the face of her lie. And I was glad that we had finally broken the ice.

We stayed in the master bedroom for most of the day,

pulling up articles on the twenty-year-old accident and scouring the local high school's old yearbooks. Most of them had been scanned and uploaded to the internet, and we had a good laugh about the past styles that were now long gone. We researched Layla Barns until we were confident we had found everything the internet had to offer. I had a pretty good idea of where the accident had occurred, but that wasn't very exciting, because Walker had already gathered that information. It seemed both sides of the ghost story had some truth to them. And at the end of the day, I hadn't learned anything new other than where she had gone to school and that she was a local here. Born and raised.

It wasn't until the air shifted in the bedroom—Emma had frozen rigid and the blood had drained from her face— that I considered our research to have uncovered anything meaningful. I knew we were on the verge of something big when she looked like she had seen a ghost. I waited for her to speak, but it was clear she was unable. I grew impatient, my breath catching in my throat. Emma's eyes flickered toward mine and then back again to her laptop. Her back was as straight as a board, and her fingertips hovered over the keys.

"What'd you find?" I asked, unable to keep it in any longer. I figured it was some sort of grotesque picture of a victim pulled from the lake, so I didn't try to look at her screen. I didn't need to see that.

"Read it," she said. But when I glared at her, she nodded and pulled her computer back to her lap. "Right. Sorry. I'll read it. It says, 'The accident that took the life of two haunts Baylor Lake until we can uncover answers as to what caused this terrible wreckage. Residents gather on the side of the road with candles in honor of the two young lives lost. The car carrying Barns and boyfriend—'" Emma paused, her eyes slowly tracking back to mine.

The anticipation was killing me.

"'Boyfriend . . . St. James, skidded down the embankment, crashing into multiple trees and landing upside down by the water's edge. Police are still investigating, as there were no witnesses.'"

"St. James? What a coincidence . . ."

Emma's forehead creased with worry, and she continued to read. "'High school best friend, Chelsea Sims, says, *I know they're together again, and that their love will last an eternity.*'" Emma continued to read, but I stopped listening.

My eyes trailed off into the distance, finding the glow of the window. As I tried to place the generations of potential St. James, I wondered why he had mentioned nothing to me before—other than the fact that he, too, was interested in the story. Of course, he was interested in the story. He was related to the deceased. His family probably had questions of their own.

"How many St. James do you think live in Baylor?" I asked.

But there was no answer from Emma. She sat still and cold as a rock, and I wondered where her emotion had gone. She wasn't giving me anything to go on. Her face was as blank as if she were sleeping with her eyes open, and I feared for just a moment she really *had* seen a ghost. Was it behind me? I whipped my head around to find nobody at all. Though the room *was* oddly frigid. In the silence, I could hear the TV on downstairs, and I listened to the rumbling of the voices. I looked back at Emma, who finally formulated an answer for me.

"One . . ."

# CHAPTER 17

I tried to fall asleep several times that night. None of them were successful. My head pounded with stress, and I had dry eyes from staring at the ceiling. I couldn't understand how the one person who'd made me feel safe this summer carried the same name as the Baylor Butcher. I didn't know his relationship, but it was obvious that he was tied to the story somehow, some way. Talk about family drama . . .

He was either tangled in the web of the greatest love story ever told or the most heinous killing spree Baylor has ever seen. And based on the feelings I had for Walker St. James, I had to imagine that it was the former. Maybe, just maybe, I was the next love story. I pondered how the best love stories always ended in tragedy. Anxiety settled in my stomach like bricks; heavy, with sharp corners. Maybe I didn't want to have an epic love story after all. On the other hand, mediocrity was pretty terrible too. I got out of bed and flipped on the lights, unable to sleep.

My grandparents had had a beautiful love story. The only tragic part was that my grandpa now had to live without his best friend. But knowing what pain that would cause him in the end, he'd still go all in. Their love was worth every sharp edge that came with watching her wither away. My parents had a good relationship, too. They had fun together. Even my great uncle Tanner and his new wife Brooklyn proved it was never too late for love. If true love was genetic, I was destined for greatness.

I opened my laptop, and seeing that it was nearly out of battery, I dug out the charger and plugged it in. I wasn't as good as Emma with research; I didn't read the articles the way she did, scouring every word. But I was able to get the gist of it. I pulled out keywords here and there. Usually, the words that were longer or in bold at the top of the pages. Sometimes, I'd scan with my finger until a certain word or phrase would jump out at me. Often, there would be too much jumping and too little comprehending. But Walker St. James stuck out like a sore thumb against the black text. His high school wasn't difficult to find, and before I knew it, I was looking at a high school photo in the online yearbooks.

My breath quickened when I finally spied Walker's

picture. He was a handsome teenager. My cheeks tightened into a smile. I stared at the thumbnail picture until the pixels slowly came to life before me. The eyes shifting ever so slightly to look directly into mine. *What the hell?* I slammed the laptop shut, feeling like I had just gotten caught snooping. My heart pounded as I sat frozen, one hand on top of the laptop, just in case it sprang to life. None of it made sense. But that was normal for around here.

I needed to talk to Walker, but a part of me was afraid. Afraid of what I might find out. What if Emma and Lainey were right? What if Walker was dangerous? I couldn't stop the thought from creeping in; what if *Noah* was dangerous? I tried not to compare the two, but it was proving to be more difficult than I would have imagined. Until recently, I'd been all-in on one of my best friends. But my feelings for Noah had changed when he'd chosen Trinity on the night he thought I'd never see. Had I run straight into the hands of a cold-blooded killer? If one thing was clear through all of this, it was that I couldn't trust my judgment.

It was already night, and my eyes were burning like they'd been set on fire, and my head hung heavy as I fought the sleep I needed. Suddenly a small *tick-tick-tick* sound came from outside the window. The first time was easily dismissed, but by the second and third times, I could no longer ignore it. I listened for the TV downstairs, but it was quiet. Everyone in the house must have been asleep, as they often were when I needed them most. A spatter of stones hit my window, and I ripped the sheets off my bare legs and crawled out of bed. In nothing more than a large T-shirt and a pair of underwear, I padded to the bedroom window. My heart raced as I placed my hands on the cold glass and slowly slid the window open. The cold air rushed in and awakened my senses. I peered out the window to see a dark figure down below.

"Is that you Wilde?" a man's voice called out in a raspy whisper.

"Who is that?" I asked, straining my tired eyes.

"It's me. Walker. We need to talk," he said. My stomach dropped both in fear and excitement. The stakes were sky-high. I would either live out the ultimate love story . . . or die trying.

I shouldn't have gone to him. But I was drawn to him like a moth to a flame. He was my friend, at the least, and he was on my back porch calling for me. Was I supposed to shut my window and go to sleep? That wasn't possible. And the truth was, I wanted to see him. I liked the guy. Regardless of the confusion stirred up by the articles.

"One second," I said, closing the window and rushing to slip on a pair of pajama shorts. I bounded down the stairs quickly and quietly. The last thing I wanted to do was wake up anybody in the house—especially Noah. But as I passed through the living room, it was clear that I wasn't the only one awake. Quiet whispers escaped a lump underneath the large comforter on the floor where the peak of the blanket had flattened and stilled. I only briefly wondered who I was interrupting, and I was thankful that I no longer felt the sickening twist in my stomach when I walked up to something I wasn't supposed to see in the cabin. There was nobody here for me any longer, and if Noah was under that blanket with somebody else, it wasn't any of my business.

I unlocked the back door and crouched with the clicking of the lock sliding open. My eyes wandered around the room and a sleeping bag stirred. I was pretty sure it was Ethan's sleeping bag. He was another one that I particularly didn't want to wake up. Although I could have used his help back in the grocery store, I didn't want his protective presence looming over my conversation with Walker now.

I opened the door slowly and slipped out, careful to close it quietly behind me. The back porch light turned on as I stepped out. Immediately, I fell for his deep dimples under the scruff of his face. His eyes were hidden under the shadow of a ball cap, making him only more mysterious and drawing me in for a deeper stare. He stepped closer, reaching out for a quick hug. And I should have run, but I did no such thing. I wrapped my arms around his waist and indulged myself. A guilty pleasure. His core was strong, and I clung to it like a child would their favorite blanket. A blanket that brought comfort throughout the dark, lonely nights. It pained me to let go, my heart was like a butterfly trying to escape its cage, but I couldn't hang onto him forever.

"What are you doing here?" I asked, suddenly embarrassed at the thought that he could tell I was stalking him over the internet.

"I had to see you," he said, adjusting the bill on his hat. His eyes twinkled, but I caught a glimpse of something dark around his brows. "You left in such a hurry, and it had me worried. I know you said that you've had trouble sleeping lately, and I have too. I figured you'd be awake." Walker shrugged, hiding his hands deep in his pockets.

"Are you . . . bleeding?" I asked, pointing to his brow. I leaned in closer.

"Oh! That's nothing," he said, pulling the bill of his hat down again.

"What's wrong?" I asked, reaching for his hat. He took a step back, flinching away from my grasp.

"It's nothing."

It was hard for me to let it go, but he obviously didn't want to talk about it. I wondered if he had come to me for help, and I looked for clues to tell me as much. "Well, you were right. I haven't been able to sleep. And I'm sorry about earlier. Something came up, and my friends needed me." A partial truth.

"Did the cops come?"

"No. They never showed," I said. He shifted from one foot to the other.

"Are you sure I can't get you anything? Like a bandage?" I asked. "I can clean that up for you?"

Walker shook his head but ultimately caved with a little pressing on my end. "It's just a scab, but if you want to bandage me up, I guess that would be all right." I nodded, looking back to the quiet cabin.

"Everyone is sleeping, so we have to be quiet. There's a first aid kit in the downstairs bathroom. Just follow me," I said, leading the way. I opened the door as my gaze fell on Ethan's sleeping bag. I pretended not to notice when he lifted his head to see me sneaking a stranger in. And while I wanted privacy, I couldn't help but notice a small part of me that felt relief to have watchful eyes.

Somewhere deep inside, there must have been a hint of doubt. Falling for a guy felt like a lot of things. A racing heart. Butterflies tickling your stomach. Nervous energy. It sounded a whole lot like fear. A pounding heart. A churning stomach. Adrenaline. It was very possible that I was afraid of Walker, even as his rugged good looks and intoxicating smell drew me in. But I had no reason to doubt Walker other than the stupid article Emma had read to me earlier that day. I wished I had never seen it. Because now, I couldn't unsee it.

Walker followed me into the tiny bathroom, and I closed the door behind us. Trapping us inside together made my heart sing and the hairs on my neck stand on end. I couldn't tell if I was falling in love or fearing for my life, but whatever it was, it was more intense than anything else I'd felt before.

Walker lifted his hat from his head, and his dark hair flopped to the side. His brow was cut open, and the gash looked fairly deep. Blood had dripped and dried near the corner of his golden eye. My breath hitched in my throat at our close proximity as I met his direct stare. "Oh," I muttered. "What happened?"

"It's nothing. Just a little scrape." But it was more than a scrape. He probably needed stitches. His scar had been ripped right open, and the surrounding flesh was puffy and tinted blue. Whatever he had done, he was going to get a giant black eye. I looked under the cabinet for our first aid kit. I pulled out the red tin and placed it on the countertop with a clatter, only vaguely concerned about the noise I was making.

"It's more than just a scrape. I'll do my best to clean it, but you probably need to get checked out at the doctor," I said, my back turned to him.

"I don't need to go to the doctor," he said, his breath warming the back of my neck. The warmth ran down into the depths of my stomach, and I turned around, only to drop the peroxide bottle on the floor.

"Shit!" I hissed, kneeling down to pick it up. I looked to the door, listening for the sound of anyone stirring at the noise, but all I could hear was the beating of my own heart. I set the bottle upright and yanked a towel down to soak up the mess. I rose again with the bottle and a swab. My hands shook as I dampened the cotton. "This might sting a little." I reached up to Walker's eye and lightly dabbed the wound.

He winced, and I felt his pain as if it were my own. "Sorry!"

He smiled. One dimple kissing the side of his cheek, his eyes never leaving mine as I slowly continued to dab his brow. I didn't know if it was our proximity to one another, the small bathroom with the closed door, or taking care of him when he was in need, but there was something in the moment that felt extremely intimate. Our shared breath was intoxicating, and I wanted to lift onto my tippy-toes and taste his lips. My hand trembled on the side of his face as I steadied my palm against his cheek. I couldn't keep my eyes on the dried blood any longer. His lips were slightly parted, and my heart was about to leap out of my chest. Pure instinct took over, and I lifted to kiss him.

Walker placed his hands on my shoulders, bracing me from coming any closer, our lips a mere inch from meeting. I felt the burn of rejection in my eyes first. Then it spread to my throat. Rejection felt a lot like dying inside. Like ice crystallizing in my veins until everything was frozen solid. I wanted to die right there. Shrink until I no longer existed. I looked to him for answers as I lowered onto my heels.

"I'm sorry," he whispered.

"No—"

"I can't," he said. I shook my head, trying to brush off the humiliation. I spun around, reaching for another cotton ball to drench, and he caught my wrist. Dropping the bloodied cotton swab down the sink, I refused to look at him. "It's . . . It's not you," he said.

I sucked in an uneven breath. It was almost worse than not hearing anything at all.

"Do you want to tell me what's really going on here?" I asked.

"What are you talking about?"

"I read your name in an article tied to Layla Barns." My eyes scanned the contents of the first aid kit as I waited for answers. Answers I didn't want to come.

"I wanted to tell you. I was going to. I was only waiting for the right time. I didn't want you to find out this way," he said.

I spun around and continued to clean his brow like nothing had ever happened between us. "Tell me now then," I said, devoid of emotion. I dabbed aggressively, even though Walker winced. I was now numb to his pain.

"I . . . It's a long family history that I don't want to get into. A tragic death that everyone knew about. I was given this name out of love—for he who couldn't pass it on himself," Walker said, pain dripping off every word.

And this I felt. I paused, pulling the swab back. Then who was the butcher? A relative?

"It's a curse. Passed down from generation to generation. A love that cannot be." Walker leaned against the sink, his head hanging in sorrow. Was that why he wouldn't kiss me? Because he thought our fate was cursed?

"But that's not going to happen to you," I assured him.

He lifted his gaze to meet mine. His eyes were like spun honey when he said, "It already did."

I didn't understand. I was right here. And nothing was standing in our way. "I don't understand, I—"

"I have a girlfriend," he said.

My face fell. *Girlfriend?* How had I misread this?

"*Had* a girlfriend," he corrected himself.

"Had?" I asked.

"She passed away."

"Oh," I whispered. I knew what that felt like. To lose somebody.

I could see the longing behind every fiber of his being, and even though it hurt to know he felt like this for another, I wanted to take away his pain. I didn't want him to feel this way. I knew all too well what it felt like. Having Walker express his heartache for another girl was like dropping my heart, then watching it shatter into a million tiny pieces.

Wasn't this ironic? I'd put all my eggs in this basket— this handsome basket—and all the while it had a hole in it.

A discrete hole at the bottom, one I could never have seen coming. I felt like the one who was cursed, not Walker. I wondered if there was ever a chance for us somewhere down the road. A chance for him to turn his fate around and fall for me instead. Was I crazy? I already knew the answer.

# CHAPTER 18

The next morning, Ethan made several attempts to get a word with me. I avoided the first few, but there was only so much I could do. He cornered me on the stairs. "Are we going to talk about what happened last night?" he asked with worry in his eyes.

"I don't think there's anything we need to talk about, Ethan," I said, shaking my head, one hand still on the banister. I took a step up the stairs, but he willed me to stop and talk.

"Who was that guy?"

"That was just a friend of mine. You don't need to worry about it. I won't be seeing him again," I said, only a part of me hoping it was true. The better part. The part that knew what was good for me. It was a part that was becoming more and more unfamiliar to me by the day.

"Did he hurt you?" he asked. He took another step toward me, and I leaned back on my heels.

"What? No. Why?"

Ethan scowled. "Because you ran out of the bathroom after the crash, holding your head and wincing."

"What? No, I didn't," I said, just as confused as he was. "No, he didn't hurt me. We were just . . . he was just hurt. He hurt himself, and I was fixing him up."

Ethan obviously didn't buy it. He looked at me sideways and pressed on. "He hurt himself? How?"

I opened my mouth and then closed it again when I realized I had no idea what he had done to himself. I didn't know how he'd split his brow open, and he'd been very vague about it. Perhaps for good reason. "He slipped. No big deal."

"Okay. Then why were you guys fighting? Then why did you storm off? And why did I have to fight him off last night?" he asked. Ethan's patience was running thin, and I could tell by the way his elevens had deepened between his eyes.

"I don't know what argument you're talking about, Ethan."

"Who are you?" he said, using air quotes. "No . . . Kinsley, you have to listen to me," Ethan continued. It was a conversation that had never happened. I wasn't the only one losing my mind.

"Look, I don't need you looming over me all the time. I

don't need to be saved!" I said, my hands in the air. But it was a lie. I needed somebody to save me. I hated that I was so weak and mentally inept. I needed to try harder. Be better.

I spun around, grabbing the banister and pulling myself up the stairs and away from Ethan. Away from the *truth*. That I was incapable of taking care of myself. I knew I wasn't the best self-advocate, but Ethan's words solidified that. A part of me wondered if I should run back home to my mom and dad where I could be looked after like the child I was.

The day crawled on as everybody prepared for an epic party. It was the last thing on my mind, and I stayed under the covers of my bed, wallowing in self-pity. Both Emma and Lainey came to talk to me, but I didn't speak a single word. They already didn't like Walker, and I didn't need to give them another reason. Plus, I didn't want to know what they thought of me now. I was two for two. I was the girl who would give her heart to anyone . . . just as long as they promised to break it.

A storm rolled in that evening that matched my bleak, edgy mood. While the rain fell and the music blared, I took a drink from Kimber and nursed it cautiously. I needed the fruity cocktail to knock back my woes, but I couldn't tolerate any more mental dysfunction beyond what I had already experienced. I needed my senses intact. Because I was on the edge. I'd been battling the idea of going home all day. And as I looked around the room at all my friends and their carefree, self-absorbed entertainment, I inched ever closer toward the idea of packing my bags.

I looked down into my pink drink and swirled the ice cubes around with my finger. I should leave now. The thought came on repeat.

"I think Mason is about to do something stupid again!" Emma slurred.

"Oh no! Like what?" I looked around the room for the first naked guy I could find. And I swore to myself, if he took his clothes off and ran through the cabin one more time, I'd march upstairs and grab my things.

I was already on the verge of giving up on the best summer ever. Trinity was gone. Simply gone. Things were happening in the woods that I couldn't explain, and there was a real danger in that water. I didn't want to hang around watching everyone pretend that life was good. Normal. Because it wasn't. There was something seriously off about this place.

"I don't know, but he's unscrewing all the light bulbs in the den. Must be up to something, huh?" Emma asked.

"Jesus . . . I can't deal with him right now." I sighed, burying my forehead in the heel of my palm.

Sampson chose that minute to come through the front door with a gaggle of girls and a few of his buddies from the bonfire. Scarlett May ran to greet him at the door. They were all wet, tracking mud through the house as the storm raged on. I didn't want to look at the footprints that littered the carpet, so I drowned myself in my pink drink instead. It wasn't long before Kimber brought me another, and if it had been stronger than the first, I never would have known. My head was swimming.

I was squished between Kai and Noah on the sofa when I thought I saw somebody tall, dark, and handsome in the crowd. A navy-blue flannel, dark hair, and a baseball cap disappeared into the sea of people. I straightened my back as I watched for a reappearance. Noah continued to babble in my ear about second chances when I stood up mid-sentence and followed the apparition.

I rested my hand on the bare shoulder of a girl wearing a tube top. Her shoulder was still wet from the rain as I lightly moved her out of my way. She stumbled forward with a giggle. I moved through the crowd, peering into each and every room of the cabin. But the handsome mirage was nowhere to be found. I walked into the den, peering into the shadows. I felt the presence of somebody or something else breathing. A dark figure emerged from the corner.

I backed up against the wall and fumbled for the light switch. My fingers frantically scrabbled across the wall to turn the light on, but when I found the switch and flipped it, the room remained pitch black. "Dammit, Mason!" I hissed.

"It's me," Walker said.

"What are you doing here?" I asked.

"We need to talk. There are a lot of things you don't understand."

I smelled his warm beachy cologne before my eyes adjusted to the dark. I might as well get the closure before saying goodbye. "What about this curse?" I asked. But I didn't want to know about his ex. I only wanted to know if the door was truly closed between us.

"I come from a long string of epic love stories. All of them tragic. I loved her then, and I love her now. She has my heart and always will." Walker's golden eyes burned with bottomless desire and longing. But all I could hear was one word. *Always.*

"Always?" I asked, my voice hitching. Walker winced, and I tried to take a step back. His heart had been claimed, and there wasn't a chance for him and me. Ever. And every minute I spent falling for him was another minute I let my heartache grow deeper.

I had just lost my gran. I had come to the lake in hopes that my friends and a fun summer would take my mind off that pain. But all I did was chase after guys who were unavailable. I traded one pain for another. I couldn't keep digging this hole. I needed to love myself more than that.

"So, are you related to the butcher then?" I asked, looking for reasons to leave. Because my own heartache wasn't enough to keep me from him.

Suddenly, my headache came back with a vengeance. I reached up, grabbing the side of my head, but I never once took my eyes off of him. I watched as his eyes shifted from sorrow to something else. Something I feared. Uncertainty swirled inside my chest.

I blinked once. That's all it took, and we were back in the bathroom. The lights hurt my eyes, and I squinted through the pain of my migraine. Walker's brow was bleeding, and I was helping him clean it. I'd gone back exactly twenty-four hours to the night before. Walker never broke character.

"Who are you?" I asked, not wanting to know the answer. I took a step backward, but my back hit the towel rack against the wall. Suddenly, I didn't want to be trapped in a tiny bathroom with him. What had once felt intimate felt dangerous now.

"Wilde, you have to listen to me," he said, taking a step forward.

"No!" I snapped.

"Wilde," he said, reaching out. I dropped the bottle of peroxide and shrieked. The door burst open, and Ethan barged in between us. I ran out of the bathroom, leaving the two of them together, and I heard Ethan and Walker get into it as I ran up the stairs.

"I'm not here to hurt you, Wilde," Walker said.

I gasped. The room was dark, and my back was up against the wall of the den. I was back. The party was raging in the cabin. The storm was raging outside.

What had just happened? The bathroom. It was like a

flash. A moment in time that had slipped through the cracks. Glitched in and out of the present. Had Ethan had a premonition about the fight? Or had I simply forgotten about it? It didn't feel like a memory. I could have sworn it was real. It felt more like an alternate ending. Like I could have chosen how the night had ended with Walker in the bathroom. My first alternate ending was the reason for my sadness. Walker was in love, just not with me. And the second ending, the one I'd just seen, was the reason for my chilling fear. The darkness in his eyes. A fear I could feel, but not remember why I'd ever felt it. I was afraid now, my hands trembled.

He stared deep into my eyes, and I knew I had fallen for the wrong guy. Not just any guy, but a direct descendent of the Baylor Butcher.

"I'm feeling misunderstood by you. There are some things you need to know before you draw your conclusions about me. I'm not a monster," he said, and I didn't need the light to see the pain in his eyes because I could hear it dripping from his voice.

"What just happened?" I asked, breathless. I looked out into the dark den, wondering where the bathroom had come from, and where it had gone now.

"Ignore that. Focus, Kinsley." Walker placed his hands on either side of my face, and our eyes locked. Our souls intertwined. I hated myself for feeling empathy toward him.

"Have you killed people? Did you throw their bodies in the lake?" I asked, my voice breaking.

"What!?" He flinched backward.

"You heard me. Answer me! If you didn't do it, who did? And did you help them? Were you an accomplice? How many St. Jameses are there?" I shook with anger, not about his past but my own present. How'd I ever let myself get here? I was falling for somebody who had killer written in their DNA. Somebody I wanted to be close to but was equally afraid of. If he wasn't directly guilty, he was guilty by association. I ripped his hands off me.

"Of course not! What are you talking about? You think I am the killer? The Baylor Butcher? That's nothing but an old wives' tale. Are you serious?"

My heart thudded. Slow and strong.

"Yes, I'm serious. I've heard two stories now about the Baylor Butcher. One is a love story, and one is a horror story. So, which one is it? Which one are you?" I asked, trembling with fear.

"Don't forget who saved you from that lake." He reached out to touch my arm, and I jerked it away from him. "Wilde . . . I'm not a murderer. I would never hurt anybody. At least, not on purpose. This place is messing with you. You have to believe me?" he pled. And I couldn't help but hear Emma's voice ring through my head, *Essentially, he gaslights girls into thinking they're crazy.*

"There's a lot more to this story than I can tell you

right now, right here, in this dark den. And if I answer these questions in their simplest form . . . I'd never see you again. And that's not a chance I'm willing to take." He spoke hastily until it came in a whisper. "I need you, Wilde. I need your help. I'm begging," he whispered, sounding like a tortured soul. A victim himself. Regardless of his past, he was just as afraid as I was.

I couldn't grasp why he needed me. Why would anybody need me? My sanity was nonexistent. I was a complete and utter wreck. I had no control over my life, and some days I lacked the will to try. And on the darkest days, I wondered if I should have drowned in that lake. Maybe it had been my time. And maybe I'd escaped but shouldn't have.

I looked up to the dark figure before me, and with all my fears, insecurities, and inadequacies, I did what I did best—I ran from what I couldn't understand. I felt his fingertips slide off my waist as I escaped the den. I vaguely noticed Mason chewing something with blood running down his chin and a small crowd gathered around him in the living room. Cheering him on like he was about to crush a world record. I was pretty sure the only thing he was crushing was the lightbulb from the den.

I ran up the stairs and locked myself in the master bedroom, but Walker was close on my heels. As soon as I took my first breath behind the locked door, he knocked on the other side. "Kinsley, let me in?" he asked softly.

"Go away, Walker!" I yelled.

"Who's Walker?" the voice asked.

I froze; my ears perked.

"It's Noah. Can I come in?" I felt a rush of disappointment. My shoulders dropped, and I was done. I pulled out my suitcase.

"Wilde, let me in!" I perked up. Freezing in the silence. I was sure it was Walker this time.

"Who are you, man?"

"Who are *you*?"

I rolled my eyes and sat on the edge of my bed. I picked up the old telephone on the nightstand and called my mom, ignoring everything on the other side of that door. The phone rang three times, and I thought she would never answer. But when I heard her voice on the other end, all the other voices from the party seemed to fade away.

"Mom?" I asked.

"Kinsley, is that you?" Her voice sounded weary on the other end of the line.

"Yeah, Mom, it's me. How are you?" I asked.

"I'm doing well. How are you?"

"I'm doing all right, I guess. I've been better. Actually, I'm thinking of sending everybody home and coming back early."

"What? Why? Is everything all right?" she asked.

"I didn't know how to say this earlier, but we sort of . . . *lost* . . . Trinity." I bit the corner of my lip. The knocking on the door continued, and it stole my attention for a moment before my mom could answer.

"What do you mean, *lost?*"

"Well, we were at a party, and she sort of disappeared. We haven't seen her since. It's been about a week, and nobody has heard from her. I tried to call her mom, but she didn't answer."

"Did you call the cops?" she asked.

"Of course, we called the cops! It was the first thing we did! They barely opened up a missing person case. They haven't been doing squat!" I said, thinking back to the one time they'd shown up and asked a few questions, jotting down the answers on a notepad.

"I'm going to call Trinity's mom," she said.

"Wait! Mom? I'm worried. What if something happened to her?" I asked, sitting on the edge of the bed and staring at the open suitcase.

"You *should* be worried! It wouldn't be the first time..." She stopped, and I could hear her breath hitch at the other end of the line.

"What do you mean, it wouldn't be the first time?" I asked, a knot forming in the depths of my stomach.

"Dear, I've gotta go now. I've already said too much."

I frowned. How could she have possibly said too much? If anything, she'd said way too little. What was she talking about? "Wait! Mom?" But her response never came. "Mom!?" The dial tone hummed through the receiver. An icy shiver ran down my back. Something was going on—something strange. But one thing I would never have guessed was that my own mother would be in on it.

A thump at my bedroom door told me that somebody was still waiting for me on the other side. But if I hadn't known who I could trust before, I certainly didn't know now.

It was when the knocking stopped that I noticed the party had fallen silent, too. I finished stuffing my laptop into my backpack and crossed the room quietly. I placed my ear against the door and listened for signs of life. There was a rumbling downstairs, and I could hear sounds coming from outside by the lake rather than inside the house. I couldn't wrap my head around why everyone would be outside in the storm.

At first, I was glad. Happy to have the party leave for another spot. I'd have some peace and quiet so I could pack alone and not be bombarded by boy problems and, worse yet, phantom problems. But my curiosity was piqued. It was like a buzzing in my ears that continued to grow louder, and I couldn't ignore it. I looked outside my window, and what I saw was more concerning than anything from before. A large group of partygoers stood by the water's edge in a small circle looking at something.

I gripped the doorknob, confident that neither of the guys were waiting on the other side, but I still opened it cautiously. I poked my head into the hall and was greeted by silence. A part of me screamed, *trap*, but a larger part of me couldn't help but wonder what was so fascinating to these people. What could pull them away from free booze, free food, and shelter?

A fight? A fight would pull them away. I wasn't sure why, and I'd never understood it, but people loved to see a fight. I imagined two of our friends rolling around and bloodying the shallow waters. I imagined punches thrown and broken noses. The crowd surrounding them, taking pictures and videos to share with their friends. Seconds crawled by as I wondered who it was. And I just knew. I just knew that it was Walker. My stomach twisted. But who would fight him? And why? Was it Ethan? Ethan was jealous all right, but he wasn't the fighting type. He was a follower at best. Was it Noah? Would Noah fight Walker because of me? Or had this not been about me at all? I liked that thought, but deep down, I had a sick feeling about Walker, and I was worried.

I made my way downstairs and out the back, passing not a single soul. There were no stragglers making out on the sofa, and nobody was passed out on the living room floor. No stoned friends loitering in front of the open refrigerator, and no line for the restroom. The house was eerily quiet, and I hated every second of it. The anticipation was deafening, and I feared what I was about to find. I knew in the moment I crossed the kitchen and saw nothing but empty cups that tonight's party wouldn't be like any other. Tonight's party was going to be a night to remember. The way fire burns the skin, leaving a mark to last a lifetime.

When I stepped off the back porch, I could feel the tension thicken in the damp air. Gasps bounced from one end of the crowd to the next, and whispers carried through the air like the storm's wind. The rain was just a mist now, but it clung to my cheeks as I hurried down the grassy knoll to the water's edge. I threw my arms in the air, nearly slipping on the slick blades of grass. Several flashes went off through the crowd as various people took pictures of whatever lay in the center of the group.

I wondered where the ruckus had gone. There was no yelling, no grunting, and no commotion of people trying to break up a fight. Everyone was oddly quiet, and they were suspiciously still. I had no idea what I was getting myself into when I penetrated that crowd, but I fought tooth and nail to find out, pushing and squeezing my way into the center.

When I'd cleared the thick crowd of hungry eyes, I found not a fight but a body—a dead body. It had washed up on shore and lay mangled in the sand with water lapping at the legs.

The skin was a cool gray, which told me that there was no longer any blood pumping through the veins and probably hadn't been for quite some time. It was face down, with long exposed legs and bare feet. It was a girl. Tattered clothes covered bits of her body, but she needed far more to be considered decent. Long, dark, ominous hair lay matted across her face. Her mouth was partially open. My stomach wrenched as the bile rose in my throat.

I had never seen a dead body like this before. I'd seen my grandmother recently. But she'd been covered in makeup and dressed in her best, tucked away in a casket with folded hands. She hadn't looked like herself, but it was a peaceful illusion. Everyone said that it would help with the mourning process. I didn't believe that to be true. Maybe if it had been my grandmother that lay in that casket—but it wasn't. It was no more than a shell of a person I used to know. The part that I loved so dearly was gone. And that was the part I longed to see one last time. This . . . this, on the other hand, was anything but peaceful. This was a girl who had struggled. A girl who had fought for her last breath and lost. This was a tragedy. A nightmare.

I scanned the crowd as they all watched the body lying on the sandy shore, the water pushing and pulling at the dingy remnants of clothing. Everyone's eyes were glued to the girl except for one pair. Walker stood on the opposite side of the small clearing, his eyes fixed on mine. My breath hitched in my throat as I caught his gaze. I didn't know what it meant, but for that short period of time, I felt relieved that it wasn't him lying in the center of the crowd. My eyes watered as they lowered from Walker's, back to the girl whose soul had left her some time ago.

Walker was safe.

Asher crouched down next to the girl and lifted the scraggly hair off her face with a stick. I recognized her instantly. It was Trinity. Her eyes were fixed open with a vacant stare. They were no longer the alluring, hazel snake eyes, but a foggy, opalescent blue that swallowed her whole. Her face was frozen in an expression of fear like a time capsule of her last breath.

Asher dropped the stick and lurched backward, falling onto his butt and causing a small ripple of fumbling throughout the crowd. Kimber screamed a wretched cry, and strangers took her into their arms. With wide eyes, I searched the crowd for answers. All these people and no answers.

Everyone was watching and waiting for an authoritative figure to take action. It wasn't any of us. Nobody knew what to do. We were only eighteen. Most of us anyway. And while eighteen had seemed like an adult just a few weeks ago, when we were graduating from high school, now it seemed like we were no more than children.

None of us knew how to handle the death of a friend. And none of us had ever dealt with a murder. The killer still lurking in the woods.

Were they out there now? I looked into the faces that surrounded me. Was it him, or him? Or maybe that girl who showed no empathy while Trinity lay lifeless at our feet? Was it Noah or Kai who had seen her last? There was something in my chest that told me it wasn't Walker, and I had to believe that.

As of late, my mind had been playing tricks on me. My grasp on reality was dwindling, so when my gut told me something, I knew it was an unreliable source. For all I knew, *I* had been the one to kill Trinity. I still had questions for Walker, and I still wondered if he was dangerous—though I believed he wasn't a threat to me— but as I looked down at the cold, gray body lying face down before us, I was positive that she hadn't died by the hands of Walker St. James.

I didn't know who the killer was, and judging by the speculative stares dripping with paranoia all around me, it was clear that nobody else did either. But that wasn't my focus now, though maybe it should have been. Right now, there was only one question racing through my head: *who would be next?*

I'd never thought anybody would die. But if I had to guess who'd be the first, I would have said Trinity. Or maybe Scarlett May. They were the kind of girls who'd get themselves into trouble. The kind to make secret enemies. But as I looked around the crowd now, if I had to guess who was next, I'd guess . . .

My stomach dropped, and my mouth ran dry. It was *me*. My guess would be me.

I couldn't pry my eyes off her dead body, and I wasn't the only one. All of us stood, staring silently. A few were crying, but most of us were paralyzed. I didn't know who had done it, how it had happened, or who was next, and I imagined that the same string of questions was going through everyone's head at the same moment. These were the questions I saw in the faces of not only my friends but Sampson's group of locals, too.

Movement in a far-off corner caught my eye, and I arched my back to see who it was. It had been Noah who'd pulled away from the group. I watched him walk away, wondering what he was up to, until I saw him lurch forward and puke into the bushes. A few people dispersed, and I wondered where they would go and what they would do next. Were they all going home? Was the party over now that a life had been stolen?

I heard an authoritative voice call out to me over the crowd. "Kinsley, what's your address?" Lainey asked, her phone pressed to her ear.

I made my way to her as she gave my address to the police. The crowd started to back up, presumably not wanting to be associated with the incident. It was clear that the police were on their way as Lainey's voice cut through the silence. It was enough to send three-quarters of the party home. All of our friends stayed, and some of Sampson's close buddies did, too. But most went home.

*Home.* My home was calling me too. I felt deep inside that this wasn't the place for me any longer. I'd made a terrible mistake in coming to Baylor this summer. I needed to get out of here, and I needed to do it now. If I wanted to survive this summer, I needed to go home. I thought about my backpack half-stuffed upstairs on the bed, and I slipped out of the crowd to go grab it and make my silent departure.

From the corner of my eye, I glimpsed a baseball cap, flannel, and dark jeans disappear into the woods, and to my surprising sorrow, I was pretty sure I'd never see Walker again. I knew it was for the best, but there was a part of my heart that ached for him. He'd tried to talk to me earlier, and at this point in the night, he'd given up. Gone home with the rest of them. I didn't blame him. Sometimes, I gave up on myself too.

Still, there was a tightness in my chest, knowing I had made the decision to run. Because staying and fighting wasn't an option for me. I wanted to live. And I was in over my head. I couldn't even find a missing girl, and the more I looked, the more trouble I wound up in. I couldn't stay now that I knew this threat was real. Now that Trinity was gone. Really gone.

I snuck upstairs to grab a few of my most precious belongings. Cell phone. Laptop. Keys. All the rest could stay in the cabin for me to grab at another time. A safer time. A time when I wasn't being hunted by a cold-blooded killer. A mist in the night. I slung my backpack over my shoulder and grabbed a baseball cap on the way out the door.

I wasn't going to tell anybody of my plan to flee, but when I bumped into Emma on my way out, I couldn't not say goodbye. "Where are you going?" Emma asked. I looked around the room, thankful nobody was watching us.

"I've gotta get out of here. I'm going home."

"What?" Her head cocked to the side, and her voice hitched.

"Look, weird things have been happening, and I'd be lying if I said that Trinity was the worst of it," I whispered, pulling her away from a few stragglers entering the cabin.

"What are you talking about? What else is going on? Is this about the ghost story? You're going to leave because of a damn ghost story?" Her voice was growing rough.

"No. There are a lot of things that have happened since we came to the lake that I can't talk about right now." I looked over my shoulder to see who was watching. I didn't see anybody, but I felt their eyes nonetheless. "I'm not safe here! And honestly, neither are you. Come with me." She closed her eyes and dropped her head.

"Kinsley, we're here for the summer. The entire

summer. I'm going away to college, and I won't see you for —I don't know—years. Are you really going to leave when we all need you? We need to stick together. That's how we're going to survive this. I mean, Trinity is gone. You can't leave too." Emma's eyes begged me to stay, and while she had a point that we should all stick together, there was urgency boiling inside of me that screamed that I should flee.

"I can't. I can't do it. I have to go. I'm so sorry." I hugged her quickly, pinning her arms to her sides. She was stiff as a board. "I love you. Be safe," I said hastily as I ran out the door into the rain.

"Kinsley, wait! You can't go!" she called out behind me, but I never looked back.

I ran up the driveway and onto the main road. I ran past my neighbors' house. The curtains pulled back as they peeked out, and a warm yellow glow was cast into the night. The police cars came into sight down the street. The red and blue lights illuminated the pines like searchlights as they drove in. I vaguely wondered if my fleeing the scene would make me a suspect. But I'd rather be a suspect than a victim.

And I believed that. I believed that if I stayed just one more night, I'd be next. Death would find me one way or another. At the hands of the killer or by way of nightmare. I knew I wouldn't last through the night. So, I ran from my fear. I ran into the woods and down the stormy street. I ran until I had to stop to catch my breath.

I found myself a couple of miles down the road, my shoes rain-soaked and my lungs burning. I realized then that I hadn't really thought this through. I couldn't walk in the rain all the way to the airport. It was a good hour and a half away, and I needed a plan. I needed more than a plan. I needed tickets. One thing at a time. First and foremost, I needed a ride. I needed to get out of this rain. I pulled out my phone to call a cab.

I wasn't sure if it was the thick forest cover or the summer storm, but I had not an ounce of service to call for a ride. For the first time, I looked behind me. It was nothing but blackness and the sound of rain hitting the pavement. The night was chilly, and my feet were blistered, but I felt none of that. The will to survive took precedence over comfort.

I continued to walk forward because there was no chance that I was going back. I wasn't afraid of the animals lurking out in the woods. But I was afraid of the killer. I was afraid of the evil that lived inside that lake. And I was afraid of *myself*. Something I couldn't run from.

It was my mind that I feared. Walker had said the Baylor phenomenon fed on my imagination. He said that I had a particularly bad case compared to others. And I worried I had put myself in a compromised position being alone in the woods at night. A state of mind where I could be killed by my own shadow. And if the killer didn't find me here, the Baylor phenomenon would.

I wished Emma had come with me. I tightened my arms around my waist. And as a branch cracked in the woods, I even wished that Ethan was by my side, there to protect me once more. Another branch cracked . . . this time closer. I quickened my pace. It was my fear that I needed to control the most. Otherwise, things would get out of hand. I braced myself as I tried to be strong and brave. I forced myself to slow down. I tried to imagine a protective bubble all the way around me—a bubble filled with light and strength. And I wasn't sure whether it was my conjuring or just a coincidence, but just then, the forest lit up with the warm headlights of a big rig.

As the headlights approached, I felt it was fate drawing the truck in. I'd never hitchhiked before, but at this moment, on this particular night, where I was sure my life was on the line, I took my chances. I stepped out into the street, my arm outstretched and my thumb up. The truck plowed through the storm, coming closer and closer. I didn't think it was going to slow down. But my luck had turned around, and the big rig slammed on its brakes, screeching to a halt.

My heart pounded as the large white cab pulled up alongside me. The heat from the engine radiated in the frosty night air, giving me temporary warmth and filling my lungs with gasoline fumes. I bit my lip, questioning my decision as I read the words on the side of the truck. Decker Transports. I wasn't sure what I was getting myself into, and I wasn't sure what they were transporting, but I had to imagine that anything was safer than staying at the cabin for one more night. Believing that the threat was behind me, I took a step forward, accepting my ride. My fate.

# CHAPTER 20

With no other options, I slipped my hand around the door handle and pulled it open. I didn't look at the driver as I crawled into the cab. There was a heavy stench permeating the air. The smell of cigarettes and something else. Beef jerky? Pork rinds? I shut the door behind me and secured my seatbelt. Then, and only then, I let my eyes wander. The open beer can in the cup holder was my first warning sign, but I feared that whatever was out there in the woods was far worse. Through the glow of the radio, I could see the grime that had built up on the console—most likely over years. I placed my hands on my lap and forced a smile. "Thanks for the ride."

"Pretty little girl like yourself shouldn't be out here in the woods all alone at night," he said. His voice was a low grumble. A warning or a threat, I didn't know.

I lifted my eyes to the driver. He was large and gruff. A scraggly beard hung down to the middle of his chest, and a putrid smell escaped his mouth when he spoke. He was wearing a red plaid flannel, but unlike those that Walker wore, it wasn't attractive. Far from it.

"I didn't have service to call for a ride," I said.

"What's your name?" he asked. I looked around, wondering why we weren't driving. Why were we just sitting in the middle of the road? And why did he want to know my name?

"K—Kansas . . ." I lied. As if it would do anything to protect me. But I had seen too many shows, and my mom had warned me too many times not to let a stranger know your name. Because they would weaponize it against you. Although I couldn't see how in this particular situation. I was already in the man's truck in the middle of the forest.

"Well, Kansas, you're all wet." I didn't like the way he articulated the word. I shifted in my seat. I peered down at my lap, my hair dripping all over the seat.

"I'm sorry. I—"

"That's all right." I felt his eyes trailing down my body, and a sick feeling came over me. I looked at the door handle and questioned whether I should get out and run straight into the night. But as soon as the thought entered my mind, he put his foot on the gas and the truck lurched forward. *It's too late now.*

"I, um, I'm going to the airport. Are you headed in that

direction?" I rubbed my forearm, wishing I had spoken with more conviction.

"Sure . . ." His jaw was tense, eyes unblinking.

Sure? Generally, it was a yes or no question. But he made it sound like he'd go anywhere—or more like he would *say* he would go anywhere—that I wanted. I pinched the bridge of my nose and closed my eyes. I took in a deep breath of old cigarette smoke, and it did nothing to calm my nerves. I didn't know how I'd ended up in this situation, and now that I was in the cab of a locked truck, driving down the windy, wet roads of the forest with this gruff stranger, I wondered if I had made the wrong decision. Possibly a decision that would cost me my life. But there wasn't time for that now. I was moving forward with the plan either way. The wheels were turning and the pines passing by. I tapped my finger on my thigh as I accepted my fate, looking out the foggy window.

The trees blurred together as we picked up speed, turning into one dark brush stroke. And it was in that stroke of trees that I saw something that didn't belong. Something that stuck out—not like a sore thumb—but like an ethereal glowing light upon a dark stormy background. It was there on the side of the road that we passed my gran. Her full-body apparition stood just a few feet into the woods, watching me pass by in the Freightliner's window. I straightened and craned my neck, trying to watch her as long as I could. She disappeared by the next bend in the road.

My stomach was queasy. It could have been the powerful stench of jerky or knowing that my time was coming to an end, but I thought it was more likely from seeing my dead grandmother on the side of the road. She'd come to me frequently in my dreams, but never once had I seen her when I was awake. I thought she'd been near a time or two. That eerie feeling of somebody watching you from a distance was hard to miss . . . and I'd always figured that it was her. But this time . . . this time, I knew. I *saw* her with my own two eyes.

What did it mean? Had she come back because I found myself barreling down the wrong path? Was I not supposed to come to the lake with all my friends? Maybe if I hadn't, Trinity would still be alive. Although there was a part of me that believed in fate, and that part believed that when it was somebody's time to go, how they went didn't really matter. Their time would find them one way or another. Was my gran telling me it was *my* time? I peeked at the gruff driver beside me, and hot acid boiled up my throat and splashed into my mouth, sending a shiver down my spine.

I sat rigid in the deflated seat. I must have sunk a foot deep, as the padding had been worn thin. The dashboard reminded me of the cockpit of a plane with all of its buttons and levers. It looked nothing like being in the front seat of a normal truck. Old-school rock played softly in the background, but it wasn't enough to deafen the silence between us or cut through the tension.

"Where are you heading?" I asked.

"Oh, don't you worry about that, pretty little thing. I'm heading where you're heading," he said. I held my breath. His comment dripped with disturbing thoughts.

"You're headed to the airport, too?" I asked. He didn't answer, and he didn't need to. All he needed to say was in the smirk hidden beneath his beard. He wasn't going to the airport. *And neither was I.*

"So, what's your boyfriend think about you walking out here all by your lonesome?" he asked, peering at me from the side of his eye. I looked behind me and was shocked to see two twin-size bunk beds. No sheets, no pillowcases— only a pair of ratty old mattresses. It looked like there was a sleeping bag shoved in the corner, and a large black trash bag was draped over the bottom bunk. I didn't want to know what was on the top bunk. I swallowed the lump in my throat and spun a lie.

"My boyfriend is meeting me at the airport. My whole family is meeting me there. They're all waiting for me. I was supposed to get a ride, but the storm was too thick with cloud cover and I couldn't get a callout. I didn't want to be late and miss my plane, so I started walking. It was a stupid idea, but I figured I could at least get somewhere. I have service now. I could probably just call a cab so that you don't have to drive me," I said, looking at my phone, which had no service.

"No! No, I'm going that way anyhow. I'll drive you," he said, forcing a carefree tone, but it sounded foreign in his mouth. I sucked in a broken breath and nodded.

"Well, if it's not too much of a hassle, I suppose it helps me out. Thank you." Kindness. It wasn't a weapon by any means, but it was all I had. My backpack only had a laptop, my wallet, and a worthless cell phone. I was sure that if I dug to the bottom I could find a pen or two, but would it be enough? I looked at his large meaty hands and dismissed the idea that a pen could save me. It was utterly stupid.

I directed my gaze out the window and once again saw the familiar glowing figure amid the dark blur of the forest. We plowed by, giving me a close-up of my gran's face. It was stolid and still as stone. Her hair lay motionless in the passing wind of the Freightliner, and she was dry in the midst of the storm. I couldn't believe my eyes. She looked right at me.

"I don't get passengers often. So it's a treat for me. I get someone to talk to. Someone to—look at . . ." he said in a gravelly tone. And I hoped he wasn't looking at me then, because he would've seen the disturbance that had been pulsing through my veins and was surely written all over my face.

We drove into town, and I was thankful the moment I saw streetlights again. We passed a gas station, and I told him I could get out there, but he refused to drop me off. When the service returned on my phone, I got a text message to Emma detailing my whereabouts. I told her what Freightliner had picked me up and described the scruffy man sitting next to me.

It didn't bring me any comfort knowing that he had a better chance of being found if I didn't survive this trip because I'd still die. And then, would I even care what happened to him? Probably not. I'd be more interested in haunting him the way my gran did me. I imagined the ways I would do it. I'd probably make him think he was going crazy one day at a time—a slow burn, the way I had suffered through my summer thus far. I couldn't think of anything worse.

But on the fifth time I asked to hop out of the cab early, he let me, and I had a renewed faith that I might just survive the night. When I stepped out of the truck and slammed the door behind me, my knees nearly buckled beneath me, and I let out a long, heavy breath. I watched the Freightliner disappear into the storm. I had a second chance. And I couldn't help but think my gran had something to do with it.

I stood under the roof of the gas station, shivering in the rain as I called a cab. I texted Emma my update and refused to read the long string of texts that she had written me back in response. It wasn't a time to be lectured. I was well aware of all the things I had done wrong. I was just lucky I had survived to learn the lesson. When my cab arrived to take me the rest of the way, I melted into the back seat. My body was like Jell-O after being rigid for so long.

Some thirty minutes later, I finally arrived at the airport. I slung my backpack over my shoulder and stepped into the rain, running to the grand entry overhang. Large glass sliding doors opened, and the bright neon lights welcomed me in from the storm outside. I couldn't be more thankful to be surrounded by all these people. I was safe now, and I'd be home in no time.

I couldn't wait to see my mom and dad. To sleep in my own bed. Did I feel guilty for leaving my friends to fend for themselves? Yes. I did. But what was stopping them from leaving? Why hadn't any of them gone home the second Trinity went missing? Were they all taking this adult thing so seriously that they wouldn't run back to the safety of their parents' homes? I didn't care if it made me immature. I'd be a coward by night if it meant survival.

"Hello. I'm looking for the next flight out to Decord City," I said, tapping my fingers rhythmically on the high counter.

A pretty uniformed woman with a tight, slick bun typed away on her computer. She cocked her head to the side. "I have a flight leaving in forty-five minutes," she said, her eyebrows raised questioningly.

"Really?"

She looked at me and, with a warm smile, typed a little more. "And there is an open seat in first class with your name on it! I'd be happy to upgrade you for free," she said. Her voice was like a bell. It was the best thing I'd heard all night.

I must have looked pretty distressed for her to bend over backward for me. "Oh my god! Thank you so much! I've never sat in first class," I said, tugging on the bottom of my jacket and brushing the hair out of my eyes.

"My pleasure. You'll have to hurry, though. The security line has quite the wait right now."

"I'll run!" I said, pulling out my wallet.

The sound of her laughter brought a genuine smile to my face. My luck was finally turning around. Maybe that Baylor phenomenon had lifted since we were out of town? She handed me the ticket and stilled as she looked into my eyes.

"Get home safe," she said in a hushed tone. I couldn't pull my gaze from her cool chocolate eyes. Her comment pulsed like a warning. Had I told her I was going home? I hadn't. The intensity broke as she welcomed the next customer. Chipper yet again.

The man's oversized duffle bag bumped into me, and I stumbled backward. Perhaps she knew I was going home because of my ID. Of course. I was only being paranoid. I had to shake it off. I was safe now. I hurried to the security line, and it was backed up, just like she'd said. I stood impatiently at the back of the line, checking the time on my phone. With my luck, I'd probably miss my flight. The only flight I'd ever have a first-class seat in.

Security walked by, taking a special interest in me. I probably looked guilty of something. It was the same look that had gotten me a first-class upgrade that was going to get me a full-body pat-down. If I looked like I'd just seen a ghost, there was nothing I could do about it now.

"Hello, Miss. What flight are you on tonight?" the security guard asked. His brown eyes shone warm against his dark skin.

"I'm heading to Decord City on flight 351," I said.

"351? That leaves in half an hour. You're never going to make it in this line!" he said, stepping back and looking the line over.

I clenched my jaw. It was the very thing I'd feared. "I know . . . How long do you think it will take to get through the line?" I asked, my eyes scanning the crowd.

The woman in front of me turned around and chimed in. "I swear, I've been in this line for twenty minutes and I've only taken two steps forward," she said, her face like stone and brows pinched.

"Oh, no." I'd miss my flight for sure. I was going to have to sleep in the airport until the next flight out.

"Tell you what—follow me," said the guard, lifting the yellow barrier for me to pass. I hesitated only for a second.

"What about me?" the woman asked, throwing up her hand.

"Sorry. Only for flight 351," he replied.

"I'm flight 351!" someone called out from the middle of the line, but the security guard paid no attention. My cheeks heated as I hurried to keep up with his long, quick strides. He lifted the barrier in the front of the line and waved me forward. I blushed as I ducked under his arm.

"Sorry," I said with a wince, stepping in front of a family. The mother groaned, and the father shook his head. The little girl clasped her book of fairy tales to her chest, and she glared at me too. Thankfully, I was called forward quickly. I placed my backpack on the conveyer belt and walked through the metal detector. No pat-down.

"Is this a laptop, hun?" a lady asked as she pointed to the x-ray of my backpack.

"Oh, shoot. Sorry, I forgot to take it out."

"It's okay. No need to re-scan it. Have you found the girl yet?" she asked, staring at the screen.

"What?" My stomach dropped.

"I said, have a safe flight! Next!" she called out, waving the family forward.

I stood frozen, searching for answers in her expression. But, just like at the cemetery, the woman had no idea what she had said. It was much more likely that I was the one hearing things. The little girl's book bumped into my backpack, and her pink roller suitcase nearly plowed over it. I snapped back to the present and took my belongings from the conveyer belt.

I found a seat by my gate with time to spare, and I watched the people pass by in the airport. Such an eclectic crowd. I watched wholesome families pass by. Religious groups. Teens dressed in black from head to toe. The best part was they were all under one roof. Everyone had at least one thing in common, no matter what they looked like. They were headed somewhere. On an adventure, a much-needed vacation, a work opportunity. Some of them might be off to spread the ashes of a loved one. No matter where they were headed, they were waiting, and like me, probably filled with anticipation.

# CHAPTER 21

I shivered now and then, my clothes still wet from my trek in the storm. The air conditioning pumped throughout the airport, and I wished I had packed a change of clothes in a small bag to take with me. It wasn't long before someone over the speaker called flight 351. And as a first-class ticket holder, I was able to board first. I slung my backpack over my shoulder and hurried to the end of the short line.

I heard a familiar little voice behind me, and I didn't need to look back to know it was the girl that I cut in front of in the security line. She wasn't angry with me now, though, as she chatted with her little brother about how excited she was to ride on a plane for the first time. I listened to her shrill voice, and I remembered a time when soaring high in the sky seemed like a dream come true. Now I would snap my fingers and be home if I could.

"Do you think we're going to see all the people that live in the clouds? All the people with their unicorns? I get the window seat," the little girl babbled.

"No, I get the window seat!" her brother said.

"No! Remember, I gave you half my cookie last night, and you gave me the window seat."

"Mom!" he yelled out. I smiled, remembering that time too. The time when everything turned into a fight and all could be settled with a cookie. I took a step forward as the line moved swiftly.

"Your sister gets the window because she has a very special job to do. She has to find the girl. And she'll be looking out the window for her . . ."

My jaw clenched. I couldn't help but turn around and look at her, and when I did, it was clear that she found my glare intrusive. What girl was she talking about? A girl with a unicorn that lived in the clouds? *I must be losing my mind.*

I stepped forward. My turn was next. I slapped my plane ticket across the palm of my hand as nervous energy sprang to life in my hands. When it was my turn, I stepped up to the lady in uniform, who reached for my ticket.

"Did you find the girl?" she asked absentmindedly.

"What?" I barked, and she snatched the ticket out of my hand, her eyes bulging momentarily before blinking rapidly.

"I said good evening," she muttered, scanning my ticket.

"Oh, I'm sorry I just—"

"Seat A6," she said hastily, eager to move me along. She handed me my ticket, and I trudged down the corridor, checking over my shoulder often. Things were becoming weirder and weirder by the minute, and I couldn't wait to get into the air and leave it all behind me.

When I reached the plane, there was a small gap where the corridor met the plane, and I could see the tarmac below. The cold air rushed in through the gap, and somehow, taking the step over that gaping hole felt like a much larger step than it was. I felt like I was making a decision, choosing a path where there had been a fork in the road.

"Good evening. Your seat is A6 to the left." The flight attendant waved me on to my seat.

The moment I saw my seat, I all but forgot about the fork in the road. The decision I'd made to run. Leave my friends behind. Leave Walker behind. I'd never sat in such luxury on a plane before. The seat was wide and plush. I wondered what kinds of goodies they'd give me for being in first class. All I really wanted was one of those little blankets they hand out during long overnight flights. I reached above my head and twisted the air conditioning nozzle closed.

The family filed in after me and surprisingly took up

the first-class seating to my left. I vaguely wondered what the parents did to make enough money to buy such expensive tickets. The boy and girl fought over the window again, and I turned my head and looked out at the workers below. They were hustling and bustling despite the stormy weather. I knew how cold it was outside, but at least these workers were properly dressed.

I took out my cell phone to switch it to airplane mode and was surprised by the numerous text messages I'd received. Not just from Emma, but Noah too. I looked around at all the people filing in and slouched in my seat to read the texts. I opened Emma's long messages and skimmed through them. They started off mad. Angry that I would leave her at such a desperate time. Then it continued to build. She was angry with me for my brash decision to leave. She even went so far as to accuse me of having a death wish myself. I knew that getting in the stranger's truck had been a stupid idea—especially after we knew a killer was on the loose—but I didn't need to hear it from Emma.

It was pure instinct. Something was seriously off at that cabin. Call it the Baylor phenomenon, call it pure evil, but I didn't want to stick around to see just how far it would go. I'd already been dragged underwater by the claws of some malevolent monster, and I didn't want to know what would happen when I met that monster face to face the way Trinity had. I didn't want to be the next girl to wash up on shore. And I refused to feel guilty about that.

Emma had asked several questions about the guy driving, and when I hadn't answered, she'd threatened to tell the cops, who were currently at the cabin writing up reports and collecting the body. She talked about how they questioned everybody who had stayed behind, which hadn't been many. She also mentioned that Kai had had some sort of breakdown, but she didn't know why. And that Kimber had been throwing up in the bathroom for nearly an hour.

It was these texts that made me feel like my instinct to survive had triumphed over the loyalty that I had—should have—given my friends.

Guilt started to spread throughout my chest. Not just about Emma, but Kimber and Kai too. I'd left them in a time of need, and for what? So I could feel safe and toasty in my childhood bed? So my mother could tuck me in at night? I knew the reason I'd fled the cabin was based on fear. But at what cost? I'd already lost one friend. Had I just lost the other ten? Had I given them all a reason to lose trust in me? I wasn't the kind of friend they needed by their side when times turned rough. I was a coward.

I was just about the worst friend anybody could have. And I hadn't even gotten to Noah's texts yet. With some of Emma's messages left unread—I couldn't bear to know what else she had thought about me or what else had happened in the cabin after I'd left—I texted her one last time that I was on the plane and was safe. Then I switched my phone to airplane mode. I couldn't read anymore. The decision had been made. And I'd have to live with myself for that. I tucked my phone away in my damp backpack, and I closed my eyes, leaning my head against the window.

I drifted off to a familiar place, the plane's engine thrumming in my ears and lulling me to sleep. It was the void again. A roaring fire that cast no warmth. A rocking chair that rocked ever so slowly, even though nobody occupied it. I could still hear the kids arguing beside me and briefly thought about how my mind was in two places at once—split between my world and one beyond. I couldn't tell if I was awake or asleep as I explored the empty space.

"Gran?" I called out. Was she here? Or was she still in the woods where I had last seen her? The fire crackled, and the air shifted like it had made space for another soul. Gran sat in the rocking chair like she'd been there the whole time. A book of fairy tales was open in front of her face, a tall stone tower with a small window on the front cover. Long, yellow locks that bound down to the ground. It sparked a memory that I couldn't quite grasp.

"Gran?" I asked, and she lowered the book.

"Oh, dear. What are you doing here?" she asked. Her eyes grew as she took me in. I ran forward, kneeling beside her and grabbing her hands.

"Oh, Gran!" I gripped her hands so tight, surprised that I could feel the flesh of her feeble bony hands in mine. The tears welled in my eyes, as she had never been more real to me since her passing. I looked up into her cloudy eyes, and even through the cataracts, I could see the empathy she held for me.

"Dear. You're not supposed to be here," she said. The book folded closed and lay across her lap.

"I know, Gran! I know! I think I made a mistake. I think I was supposed to stay at the lake. But I was afraid. I don't want to find the girl. I want to go home!" My voice cracked while I pled with her as if she were my gatekeeper.

Gran pried a hand from my grasp and stroked my head gently. Her hands didn't tremble a bit; they hadn't been that way in years. She'd passed just three days before my eighteenth birthday, but it seemed like forever since she'd last run her shaky hands down the back of my head. With everything going on at the cabin, I'd forgotten just how much I missed her. And I knew that, somewhere along the way, that had been my plan. To forget. I thought if I could just put it behind me, the pain of losing her would subside. It didn't though. It only manifested in different ways. Sleepless nights. An emptiness inside. And now guilt for trying to forget.

I vowed to myself that I wouldn't sweep her memory away any longer. That I'd let it come, and that I'd welcome it. I'd share it. And maybe that way, the pain of losing her wouldn't be a secret burden that only I knew I carried. Even though I couldn't feel the warmth from the fire, I could smell her perfume, and it did weird things to my chest. A tightness spread across my throat as I gripped her hand. I knew our time was running short. I couldn't break down now, though. I didn't want her to see me like that.

"I know you're scared, dear. So am I. But you have to help the girl. It's the only way." Gran's features softened as she held my gaze steadily. Her mouth wasn't moving now, but somehow, I still received the message crystal clear.

"Layla Barns? Is she the girl?" I asked.

"The girl." Gran nodded with encouragement.

I didn't know what she was talking about. She never gave me any details—only this one demand. Was I supposed to know how to do this myself? I knew from looking into her eyes that she'd believed in me when I hadn't believed in myself. And if she needed me to do this one thing, then I must do it for her. I must find a way. Essentially, it was my gran's dying wish. One so very important that she had come back from the dead for it. I wanted to ask why, and how, but the most important thing to me in that moment was that she knew she could count on me.

"Okay, Gran. I'm going to do it. I'm going to find her. I want to make you proud. I promise. I promise I'll do it." I said it hastily, but I meant it. I was going to be brave. I was going to face my fears—the thing that had killed Trinity, and the mind-bending phenomenon of the lake that threatened my sanity—and I was going to find that damn girl and help her get home if it was the last thing I did. I stood up, holding onto Gran's hands as long as I could.

"Oh, dear, there's just one more thing. Go easy on that dear boy . . ." Gran's head tilted as she looked up at me.

"Noah?" I asked. My head flinched backward.

"Not that one, dear. The other one." Gran winked a cloudy eye as she became fuzzy and distant.

"Walker? Are you talking about Walker?" I asked. But it was her time to go, and there was nothing I could do to stop it.

I watched her disintegrate into thin air, and all that was left were little particles that shimmered before turning to dust. The fire fizzled out, and the smoke rose into the air, taking the chair and children's book with it. The last to go was a thirteen-day calendar on her wall. A wall that didn't exist. It hung on nothing but thin air, and one day was crossed off in red. Watching the last bit of the red-marked calendar flutter away was like watching my heart leave me. I was hollow without it. And I knew that I had a long road ahead of me if I wanted to get it back.

I lurched when the flight attendant's voice came over the loudspeaker. My eyes opened to the bright cabin and the whining kids. My heart galloped in my chest as I felt the air thin around me. I gasped, hungry for oxygen as I grabbed the seat in front of me. I lowered my forehead to rest on the hard tray folded up before me, and I closed my eyes. That thirteen-day calendar was something I'd seen before. And I couldn't help but think that there were only twelve of us in that cabin. Thirteen if you counted Gunner. That was before Trinity died. It was only after she went missing that the first day had been crossed off. A sickening pit formed in my stomach as I concluded that all my friends in that cabin had a mark on their back. Me included.

I knew how fate worked. I knew how it would bend and twist but never break. Fate was inescapable. It was impervious to change. And people who had escaped their own fate had a funny way of falling back to where they belonged, sooner or later. And oftentimes in a worse situation than they should have been in. No, you couldn't outrun your destiny. And only the desperate tried. If I had a mark on my back, it was going to follow me whether I was home under my parents' roof or in that cold, haunted cabin. And if I was going to die either way, I'd rather not do it being a rotten friend. I had to get back there. *Now*.

I had to get off the plane, and I had to go back to Baylor Lake. Abruptly, I jumped out of my seat, startling even myself. My legs had a mind of their own, and they strode right up to the flight attendant as she was delivering the safety instructions to the passengers over the loudspeaker. I interrupted without a second thought, and I pled fiercely.

She held her microphone down to her chest and glared at me with a slackened jaw.

"I'm sorry. I'm so sorry. I have to get off the plane. I have to get off!" I said hastily, my eyes darting around, looking for signs in her face. I could hear my pleas echo over the loudspeaker from the bits and pieces getting picked up on the microphone. My eyes burned as I tried to hold back tears of regret. I'd made a terrible mistake, and if she could be so kind to let me off the plane and make it right, I'd be forever in her debt.

"Ma'am. Ma'am, you have to sit down. You can't be up here." She patted my shoulder forcefully, trying to calm me and put some distance between us; but there was no stopping me now. I stepped closer, and her eyes filled with alarm.

"I'm sorry. I have to get off. You have to open the door!"

"Ma'am, you need to sit down. We can't open the doors after they've been shut. You can't get off the plane." Her tone was direct and growing louder.

I tried to push past her and get to the door myself, but another flight attendant blocked the way. I was vaguely aware that I was making a scene, but my instincts took over, much like they had when I'd fled the cabin.

"Something's wrong! I've got to go!" I said louder. After hearing my own voice that sounded nothing like me over the loudspeaker, and the several gasps and stirring of chatter that erupted from the passengers, I suddenly realized what I had just done.

"Something's wrong? What's wrong?" a man yelled from a few seats back.

"What's wrong?" somebody echoed from farther still.

A male flight attendant grabbed me firmly across the shoulders and shoved me back to my seat. He forced me down, and I popped back up, relentless. This time, he used more of his strength and I found myself at a crossroads. I was either going to fight this man, probably unsuccessfully, or I was going to comply. I gritted my teeth. It took everything inside me to comply. I would have to get off in Decord City and turn around and fly back. It would take me all night long or longer, and I wasn't sure how long my friends had before their marks would catch up to them. A whole night seemed like an eternity.

Many passengers watched as I settled back down. The little girl beside me was one of them. I glared back at her as she was trying to pull her fairytale book away from her little brother. I couldn't help but notice the cover. It stuck out like a red flag. A tall stone tower with locks of gold flowing down to the bottom. It was the same book my gran had been reading, and I couldn't help but notice that it looked similar to the tower I'd seen in the forest.

It was then that I remembered something. Déjà vu swirled in my head. It had seemed so insignificant at the time. Lainey had pointed out the rapunzel plant. The little purple flowers that covered all the shrubs. It had been right there before me the whole time. The tower. It was everywhere. Even my gran had been showing me the clues along the way. I had tried to find that tower for a second time, and it had disappeared. But somehow, I knew that if I went back into that forest, knowing what I knew now, I'd find it. And when I did? I'd find Layla right along with it.

I still wasn't sure how I could help her. I wasn't worried about it, though. As long as I found the girl, the task would be complete. My mission. Maybe then my friends would be saved, and no more marks would be made. It was a heavy burden to carry, and I wasn't sure I'd be able to do it alone. But I had to try.

The plane's engines got louder, and I could feel the rumble beneath my seat. The flight attendant walked by and handed me a couple of shots of alcohol. It was clear by the look she gave me that she knew I was underage, but she didn't want any trouble, and neither did I. I nodded apologetically and took the two glass bottles from her hand. One of the perks of being in first class, I supposed.

The plane started to roll down the tarmac, and I fixed my eyes on the tiny people waving their lights in their glowing vests down below. The rain was lit by the lights on the plane's wing. I told myself I'd be back that very night. I tried not to fret over the things I couldn't control, but as the plane took off, throwing me back into my seat, I knew I was in for a ride.

CHAPTER 22

There wasn't enough oxygen. And what little there was, it was much too thin. Tiny gray spots floated at the rim of my vision, and my head was light as air. I reached for the white bag before me. I wasn't going to throw up, but I was on the verge of hyperventilating. I shouldn't have run. My friends were back there now, and they needed me. I put the bag up to my mouth and took deep breaths as I cowered in the corner of my seat. I didn't want anyone to see me. I already had a target on my back from the stunt I'd pulled with the flight attendant, so I didn't need to draw any more attention to myself than I already had. But as I breathed in the recycled air, hating the way the bag crinkled so loudly, I thought about how I'd let Walker down most of all.

I was ashamed that I'd had to fight my feelings for Walker, even after finding out that he was in love with someone else. As if that was the worst part. As if I hadn't accused him of being the Butcher of Baylor Lake.

The fact that I could still long for the moments we'd spent locked in the bathroom together in the middle of the night . . . the proximity of his breath on my neck . . . it worried me. It worried me because I wasn't thinking clearly. Baylor was like a black hole, stealing my wits and leaving me utterly defenseless.

But what did the curse upon his family even mean? That Walker had had the greatest love story of all time? Did it mean he had no room in his heart for me? Ever? His love story was all dried up?

It was hard to wrap my head around the fact that the one person who made me feel safe, normal, and sane was the one person who I couldn't keep by my side. And what did that mean for me? I thought of the weird things that had been happening to me that made me question my reality, and I placed Walker at the end of a growing list of abnormalities.

Walker had been nothing but kind to me, though. He'd been there for me in a time of need. A lonesome stranger who was looking for a friend. I shouldn't have turned my back on him the way I had. He didn't owe me anything, and just because his heart was spoken for didn't mean I couldn't be loyal to him. He'd saved my life, after all. And it's not that I owed him anything; I *wanted* to be there for him. And I'd let him down.

His golden eyes seemed to shimmer in the sunlight. His dimples hidden beneath his scruff. I even adored the scar through his eyebrow. I thought about it for a second. Hadn't the scar been there before he'd injured himself? I recalled seeing him for the first time in daylight. I'd noticed the scar on his eyebrow then. It must have been a freak accident to have reopened it sometime later. I could have thought all night about Walker's face—every inch of detail —but the turbulence was doing nothing to calm my anxiety. I gave up on the hyperventilation bag and stuffed it in the pocket of the seat in front of me.

I was going to turn around the second this plane landed, and I was going to tell Walker that I was sorry for the way I had acted. And everything I'd accused him of. Did I have to tell him the truth? The truth that I was afraid? Jealous? No, I didn't have to tell him I had feelings for him. I only had to show up. Be there. Loyalty wasn't about being honest a hundred percent of the time; it was about not turning your back on someone in their time of need. Which was exactly what I'd done. I hung my head.

If I hadn't been such a coward, maybe I could have been a good friend. But I was never going to be anything other than a work in progress. I was never going to be anything but the scaredy-cat, the loner, the invisible, the illiterate. I would never get a guy like Walker. Even with his mangled past. Hell, I couldn't even attract Noah until my competition literally dropped dead. And he had been my friend and neighbor since I was a kid. You'd think I would have had time to grow on him. I shook my head and looked out the window, wondering what was wrong with me.

It was black outside, and had it not been for the flashing lights on the wing of the plane, I'd never have known that it was still raining. When the lights flashed, I saw just how torrential the storm had become. I saw the wings flexing under the fierce wind, and I felt the blood drain from my face. Like all these passengers here, I was at the mercy of the storm. A plastic bag caught in the wind. Turbulence shook the plane, and I grabbed my armrests tight, my knuckles turning white as I reminded myself just how safe planes really were. I looked over at the little kids beside me, and they were oblivious. Too young to know a thing about reality. The plane dipped, and I lost my stomach. A shudder from a few rows back. And then I flinched when a woman stole the open seat next to me. She buckled up quickly.

She was rough-looking, kind of like she belonged in the mountains. Which wasn't unusual, since we were flying out of Baylor. But it didn't look like she belonged in first class. Then again, neither did I. I was still wet from the storm and lacking dry clothes. The woman squeezed her eyes shut. Her face was sweaty and flushed. She pulled the seatbelt strap tight against her belly. "Hope you don't mind! I sure would like a seat in first class, and after seeing you flip out earlier, I thought you could use a companion during the rough patches. You think the turbulence is bad now, just wait," she said, her eyes fixed ahead.

I looked the woman over from head to toe. She had auburn hair flecked with gray. I couldn't tell if the creases in her forehead were from time itself or a life full of stress, but I would have guessed she was in her forties. I didn't know a thing about her, but it felt like she was running from something. I looked back to the coach seating and none were the wiser.

"I don't mind." The thought of having someone next to me was a welcome distraction. I only wished that her panic was odorless.

"Oh, good. Because I'm not going back there," she said, hooking a thumb over her shoulder.

"Have you ever been in first class before?" I asked.

"It's my first time."

"Well, then it looks like we have something in common." I offered a small smile and closed my eyes as the plane shook vigorously.

"What's your name?" she asked.

"My name's Kinsley," I said, holding my hand out.

"Name's Mary," she said, taking my hand. "So, you want to tell me why you wanted to get off the plane? You're not some psychic, are you? We're not gonna crash, right?" she said with a breathy chuckle.

"Sorry! No. I'm not a psychic. Far from it. I can't even

tell what's going on in the present, let alone predict the future," I said, mimicking her laughter. But it was nervous laughter. I was still uneasy about being in the wrong place at the wrong time. About my poor decisions and lack of foresight. The cabin lights flickered on and off, and I looked around at all the worried faces. I turned to my window for answers, but Mary drew me back in.

"That's normal." Mary's lips were pursed into a thin, straight line.

"Right. I know. I'm just a little jumpy, I guess."

"Are you afraid of flying?" she asked.

"Not particularly. But I've never flown in a storm. And it looks to be a bad one," I said, peeking out the window one more time. Lightning lit the sky, and the wings flexed up and down.

"We're safe up here in the air. These planes are built to withstand a lot. Now, why did you want to get off the plane?"

I cocked my head. It was a lot to unpack. But I guess I had time, being that I was stuck on a wrong way flight. "I only wanted to get off because I made a mistake by coming. I ran from something I shouldn't have. And now, I think I'm ready to face it head-on. Only, they wouldn't let me off the plane."

"So, just to be clear, no predictions of the future?" Mary's eyes seemed to burrow into me, and I laughed, looking down at my lap.

"No. Why? Do *you* have a prediction?" I asked, more curious than ever.

"Me? No! But, I'd have to imagine a girl such as yourself, pleading to get off the plane before it lifts into the air, is a bad omen. Do you believe in bad omens?" The deep crevices of her forehead deepened. My eyes wandered around the cabin as I pondered her question.

"I guess I do."

And then, like a bad omen itself, the plane dropped. Several screams were unleashed throughout the cabin, and for a brief moment, the lights went out. As quickly as it happened, it was over, but the adrenaline remained, coursing through my veins. I was sure my face was as white as a ghost, but Mary looked worse. A sheen of sweat beaded her upper lip. I looked out the window, and as the lights flashed, I could see several panels on the wing were now missing in the severity of the storm.

"See, the thing about bad omens is . . . they precede a terrible event."

Something sickening churned in my chest as I looked at Mary for answers. I wasn't psychic, but it seemed like maybe she had some opinions about the future that she was holding back. And I didn't like where this was heading. Originally, I thought Mary had sat next to me to calm my anxiety. Maybe even for the upgraded seat. But now, I questioned why she was really here.

"You see, I've been watching that storm out there. It's

been ebbing and flowing alongside your anxiety. It was pretty bad when you tried to get off the plane, but we were safe on the tarmac. And it seemed to have calmed when I sat down. But when I spoke of bad omens, it took a turn for the worse. You didn't like that, did you? So, why don't you tell me what you really are?" Mary said in a deep secretive tone. What I really was? I wanted to know who *she* really was. She seemed to know more about what was going on than I did.

"I don't know what you're talking about," I said, shaking my head. But just then, the plane dipped again, and the same voices from before called out in fear. I tightened my grip on the armrest, my fingernails bending against the plastic.

"See! You're doing that, aren't you?" She leaned in, her face jutting toward mine.

"No! I'm not doing anything!" I said. Mary's distraction was no longer welcome, and I couldn't get away as I was trapped in my seat, pressed against the window.

The flight attendant's voice came over the loudspeaker as Mary and I were locked in an uncomfortable stare. "Please remain seated with your seatbelts securely fastened. There is turbulence now, and we expect it to get worse before it gets better. We're going to climb in altitude to look for smoother patches of air. Please bear with us."

I pried my eyes from Mary's and pulled on my seatbelt strap. It was already tight against my hips.

"You better make sure we climb to smoother air," Mary said, pressing the back of her head against her headrest and closing her eyes. The plane rumbled, and my head bobbed up and down, but my gaze never left her face.

"Stop that!" she hissed under her breath. Her eyes remained closed, and a bead of sweat dripped down her temple.

The plane dove, and several more people screamed. My heart lurched in my chest as I stared at Mary, questioning if she had foreseen this bad omen.

"I said *stop that*! Control it!" she hissed through her grinding teeth. Perhaps *she* was the bad omen. Perhaps *she* was the one responsible for all of this. And then I remembered the Baylor phenomenon. The manifestation of fear itself. But surely not; we weren't in Baylor any longer. Mary's eyes watered with panic and were flanked red with fear. I wasn't afraid of flying, but clearly, she was. She'd sought me out because she couldn't stop thinking about a crash. She thought I had the answers when I tried to get off the plane. But she was crazy. And she was sitting right next to me, her negative energy radiating off her in waves and filling the cabin.

"I'm not doing anything!" I snapped at her. The plane shook, along with my anger.

"Stop it! Make it stop!" she seethed. The storm was angry, both inside and outside of the cabin.

"I'm not doing it!" I yelled, snapping as the anger

boiled inside me, clashing with the fear and anxiety to make for one giant force.

"I. Said. St—"

Mary pulsed. And just as the threat reached the back of my throat, an explosion ignited the tension that had been building inside me all summer long. A lightning bolt flashed outside the window, and the cabin plunged vertically.

The flight attendant in the aisle lifted into the air, her back slamming against the ceiling of the plane and then plummeting to the floor with a thud. The screams sounded distant with the whoosh of blood hammering through my ears. The turbulence was so violent my head shook wildly, making my vision no more than a blur. I whipped my head from side to side, looking out my window. It wasn't until another lightning bolt lit the air that my eyes beheld the blurry truth. The wing was glowing red and missing the last three-quarters.

I stopped breathing the moment I saw the wreckage. My stomach was in a perpetual state of free-fall. I was frozen in fear as my mind raced to understand. Was this it? Was I dying now? The turbulence was bad. Terrible. But we couldn't survive with only one wing. I was going to die a disloyal friend. It had been my latest fear, and it was coming true. I knew my time was limited.

A hand gripped mine, the strength bone-crushing. It was just enough to grab my attention. But when I looked over expecting to see Mary blazing with rage, I saw my gran sitting in the seat instead. I wasn't sure if she'd possessed Mary, or if Mary had simply vanished. But it was my gran sitting next to me, her hand on mine. My heart kicked as my eyes took her in.

One last comfort. Like an angel here to collect me. She was as real as anything could be. She was blood and flesh, and she was right next to me. In that moment of bewilderment and wonder, I forgot my life was ending. I guess that's how it was meant to be. Your mind conjures up something so unimaginable that it protects you from the tragedy at hand. I remembered the stunning Ferris wheel glowing in the dark waters the night I'd almost drowned.

"Gran?" My breath left me as the lights flickered on and off. Gran was the only vision I had that was clear and unwavering. The screams were never-ending, but they had faded further in the distance.

"Why are you doing this?" she asked, her voice not her own but Mary's deep threatening tone. Her forehead was creased and pulled tight.

*Why am I doing this?* I wasn't doing anything. I'd already told Mary that. I couldn't control this any more than I could control the storm outside.

"Gran?" I asked, not knowing if it was crazy Mary or my late grandmother. My eyes searched the cabin frantically, and my stomach was reaching its upper limit of motion sickness. It swirled up to my chest and was approaching my throat. I didn't know where the flight attendant who had hit the ceiling had gone, but there were several empty seats now. Missing passengers. Was I doing this? Was *I* the bad omen? Was it the mark of fate that I had brought onto this plane?

I looked at the kids beside me, and the dread on their little faces made me even sicker. I wanted to help them. I wanted to save them. And if I thought for just one minute that this was my fault? I'd surely die from a broken heart. I didn't deserve to live if this was my doing. I felt my face turn cold with mortification as the plane spun in circles, spiraling down toward the ground. I sucked in a deep broken breath.

"Gran? Help! Help!"

"You can do this," Gran said, her sweet voice encouraging as it broke through Mary's rage.

"No! No—" I pled. I couldn't do it. I couldn't do anything. I could barely get into college. What made her think I could save a one-winged plane from crashing?

"*Wake. Up!*" Gran pled, her pale green eyes glistening. There one second and gone the next.

"You did this!" screeched Mary, her voice crude and vile. She was back with a vengeance. Gran's face bled into the auburn hair with its gray flecks. "You did this!" She crushed my hand, and pain shot up my arm. My gran was long gone.

I took a blow to the face. It was a dull pain that sank

into my cheek and spread beneath my eye. The lights flickered, and I saw the children's book with the tower and the long blonde locks that flowed to the ground sprawled across my lap. Only, this time, it wasn't a cartoon drawing but the exact haunted tower I'd seen in the woods.

Something sparked in my mind, and I knew what I had to do. But did I have enough time? The lights went out and didn't come back on. Through the darkness, I saw the city lights outside my window fast approaching—a blur of undeniable speed.

We were going to crash all right. I wasn't sure if it was the free fall or the spinning, but my head felt light . . . as if I were flying. I had the urge to run. Flee. But I was so disoriented, I didn't know up from down. It didn't stop me though. It couldn't stop me from wanting to survive. Nothing could. The instinct I had to save my life was pure and raw, and it took hold of me now.

I unbuckled myself and was immediately lifted into the air. Mary's grip on my hand was painful but grounding. I felt my sweaty hand pull out of hers, and I slammed into a seat, my shoulder smashing into a corner, my arm bending until it broke like a twig, and my legs plunging into passengers on my way to the back of the plane.

My head slammed against the back wall. The pain was intense. Like submerging my head in ice-cold water. It trickled down to my neck and out through my shoulder blades. I didn't know if it was blood, and I didn't care.

I was pressed against several bodies that were no longer living—the lucky ones—and a few that were. Those that were broken and battered still felt the crippling fear of the last few seconds before the plane crashed.

I wished the blow had taken me out, but I had survived to watch the end. It was unlike anything I had ever seen.

It happened in slow motion. The city lights lit the cabin from the outside in. The nose of the plane impacted the ground, and suddenly there were flames everywhere. The stark bright light of the explosion illuminated every single soul as it took their lives.

The family up front, Mary, the newlyweds, the elderly, the kids, the pregnant, the men, the women. I saw it all. I saw every last breath. And I couldn't help the guilt that spread throughout my body, from my fingertips to my toes, knowing that I was the one who had created it all. That it was my mark that had taken their lives. I deserved to watch every face suffer.

Moments after the light reached me, I felt the wave of heat. The plunge of ice around my head and neck immediately turned to a furious blazing fire. White flames heated my insides by the time they had barreled halfway up the plane. It was like being burned at the stake—only I hadn't committed this crime by choice. I'd never wanted this. I'd never wanted anybody to get hurt. And then I was dead.

# CHAPTER 23

I died. Every damn cell in my body died as my body ignited in flames. Obliterated. I got every ounce of what I deserved. It was my raw emotion that had brought that plane down, drawing it into the vortex of my fear. I sucked in a deep, shuddering breath before lurching forward. My eyes sprung open and I took in my afterlife. The odd thing was, it was identical to the life I'd had before. I was in bed at the cabin. Drenched in a cold sweat. My heart galloping as I struggled to slow my breathing.

My head pounded as if I really had crashed and burned. But hadn't I? I brought my hands to my face. My fingertips searched for marks. Evidence of the crash. But there was nothing. Nothing external anyway. My insides were clearly marked. Traumatized. I was still sick to my stomach, and my head . . . my head felt like it was torn in two and bleeding profusely. I reached up to my hairline, but there was no such sign. The whole thing had been a nightmare. A ruse. I couldn't wrap my head around it. I threw off the covers and jumped to my feet, my head pounding excruciatingly as I rose. I grabbed at my temples as the pain nearly took me to my knees. Tears pricked my eyes, and a low whimper shuddered from my throat. I closed my eyes, trying to breathe through the stabbing pain, and then slowly, ever so slowly, I stood upright.

If the plane crash had only been a nightmare, then the guilt could subside. I hadn't killed all those people, and I didn't deserve this pain. I told myself that over and over. *I didn't deserve this pain.* But there it was, persisting. Etched in stone, branded upon me for life.

I licked my lips and wondered what I would find downstairs. I couldn't be sure of anything. I lifted my hands before my eyes and scrutinized them. As far as I could tell, they were mine. The same old hands I'd always had. The weird-shaped fingers, the bulbous knuckles. My mom used to call them piano fingers. I just thought they were freakishly long. I went to the bathroom in search of a mirror. But as I stood in front of it, I couldn't bring my eyes to meet my reflection. I didn't know who would stare back at me.

I watched my hands trail around the rim of the porcelain sink, making slow circles, until I was ready to face myself. I lifted my gaze and stared deep into her eyes. She was a shell of the girl I once knew. Something was missing, too. Something I couldn't quite put my finger on. It was the thing that kept me from identifying with her. The reflection scowled back at me, and I cowered, pulling my gaze away from her intense stare. I grabbed my toothbrush and vigorously brushed my teeth, looking anywhere but directly at the girl in the mirror. I didn't know her, and I didn't want to. I remembered Walker. And I remembered my promise to help him.

I had to find him to tell him everything I knew. And together, we needed to find that damn girl. But I didn't know how to find him, and I was pretty sure that he'd never want to see me again. I recalled the look in his eyes as he'd stood over Trinity's dead body. I hadn't been able to read that look then, but now, I imagined his eyes had been filled with sorrow. I was the only person he felt like he could relate to, and in a world where he felt as alone as I did, I'd left him. Worse yet, I'd accused him of murder. He probably never wanted to see me again. But that wasn't going to stop me from trying. I had to finish what I'd started. Not because I was a badass, but because I had no other choice. I couldn't leave Baylor if I wanted to. The crash had proven that much.

I tiptoed downstairs, afraid of what I might find around the corner. Afraid of all the angry, judging eyes. I knew I'd left them to handle the investigation by themselves, and I'd have to beg for their forgiveness. I'd do it, though; I was prepared. I could live with that mistake. I could live with anything, as long as I hadn't killed off a plane full of people.

Scarlett May rambled, the sound of her light and airy voice meeting me on the stairs. I listened while making my slow descent. "I just don't know what I'm gonna wear. Because on one hand, I want to look cute, which would mean the heels, but on the other hand, it's like, how can I *not* wear the cowgirl boots?" It was a good sign that she had nothing more pressing to worry about than her clothing.

"Well, I think you have to wear the cowgirl boots. I mean, they're classics. And the Water's Edge Concert is country anyway. I was thinking of wearing a plaid flannel. Asher has this one that I like, blue and gray. It's oversized, so I can just wrap it around my waist. That'd be cute, right?" Kimber said.

I stared at them from the stairs. I wasn't sure how this conversation fit in the morning after finding Trinity's body, but I was about to find out. The next step I took, the stairs creaked, and both girls looked in my direction.

"What? What are you gonna wear?" Kimber asked. Their empty eyes waited for an answer. It was so simplistic that it hurt. I continued down the stairs, slowly trailing my hand down the wooden banister.

"Um, I'm not sure."

"You might want to figure it out soon. The concert's tonight. We're thinking of going country. We all should," Scarlett May said.

"Yeah, maybe," I said under my breath as I passed through the living room.

The girls continued to chatter as I walked into the kitchen. Everything was the same. Just as normal as could be. Nobody seemed shaken from seeing Trinity last night or being questioned by the cops. Nobody looked at me with judging eyes. It was as if it had never happened. Ethan looked at me and smiled, holding up a coffee cup. I looked at the blue ceramic mug and then back to him. It was as if he was almost . . . pleasant. Was that possible?

"Kinsley? Are you all right?" he asked when I failed to respond.

"Yes. Yes. I'm all right. Just a little tired. Coffee would be great, thank you."

He then poured me a cup of coffee, and I sipped it, assessing everybody one by one. There wasn't an ounce of guilt wafting through the air. No grief. No tension. It was almost as if I was living in a parallel universe. Was that possible? Had the plane really crashed? Could this truly be my afterlife? Somewhat the same but better in certain little ways? The caffeine did wonders to help me, and I almost felt myself succumbing to the positive vibe in the cabin. *Almost.* But no matter how much I wanted to stay and enjoy myself with my friends, I had a nagging voice in the back of my head telling me to get to that tower.

Mason sat in his boxers, debating with Kai who the opening artist would be at the concert. Noah sat alongside the other guys, but he paid them little attention. His eyes were trained on me. He, too, was in a good mood, a flirty one. He smiled out of the corner of his mouth and winked at me while I tried to put the pieces together. I couldn't get over how weird it was to see everybody happy.

It was as if it were the first day we arrived at the cabin with the best summer of our lives still ahead of us. I looked around the kitchen, scratching my head. Something else was off. There wasn't one single sign of the raging party we had thrown last night. No plastic cups. No hangovers. No muddy footprints tracked in from the storm. It was perfect. I almost expected Trinity to walk around the corner. Had she even died at all?

Kai turned up the volume on the TV. "One hundred forty-seven people died Thursday night on flight 351 to Decord City. Caught in the storm, the plane came crashing down in the middle of Grand and Fifth, demolishing the historical bank here in Charlee City."

My gut sank. The TV showed the wreckage of the plane crash. The crash I'd caused. The crash I'd *died* on.

"Wow, check it out. A plane crashed!" Mason said, pointing to the TV.

I nearly spilled my coffee and quickly put the mug down on the counter. I had to get out of here. Finding this girl couldn't wait one more second. I pulled the back door open and grabbed my shoes. I laced them up, ignoring the fact that, even though they'd been left out in the rain all night, they were bone dry.

At this point, nothing in my life made sense . . . but that could change. It could, if I found the girl. I was convinced of that. She could right this wrong. I'd do my part in finding her, and she'd do hers. She'd give me my life back. My sanity. I set out on the trail, and I didn't look back at the cabin as I disappeared into the woods. My sights were set on Walker and the tower.

Time flew by. The entire day passed as I searched for the tower. It wasn't where I'd left it—not at the clearing. But I'd stay out all night searching if I had to. And when I got cold, tired, and hungry, I'd just remember the faces illuminated by the explosion of the plane. I'd remember my gran sitting next to me when I'd visited her in the void. When I told her that I'd do everything in my power to find this girl for her. For me. And for my friend, Walker. Because he was a tortured soul, just like the one I'd become.

My legs were weak, and I was dehydrated, but I kept going. And when I felt the eyes of the forest watching me, I had enough grit to ignore it. *Let them watch me.* It wasn't going to consume me the way it had before. I was different now. I was on a mission. But the new me only lasted for so long. There were only so many twigs snapping that I could endure before my heart picked up speed, and I was utterly crushed to realize that I was the same old girl. A girl who was afraid of her own shadow. A girl who'd run away.

Whispers swirled in the wind, and a light mist rolled in from the west. A hand grabbed my shoulder, and I spun around to find Walker's golden eyes. I all but lunged into his arms. He laughed, happy to see me too.

"Walker! I'm so glad to see you! I'm so sorry I left. But I'm here now. I'm here now." I said. He pulled away and looked at me with an arched brow. The gash had healed into a bloodied scab. The scar would be worse than it had been before.

"I'm happy you came back. But I didn't know you left," he said with a shrug. The weight of a dozen bricks lifted from my shoulders. I never wanted him to feel abandoned by me, especially since that's what his ex had done to him.

"Yeah, I don't think anybody did. Hey, question—was there a storm last night?" I asked. Walker looked at me questioningly, and I hated the way it made me feel. Like I was crazy. Like he *knew* I was crazy.

"You're asking me if there was a storm last night? I mean, you were there, right? Do you not remember?" he asked.

"No, I know I was there. I just . . . can you just, answer the question?" My eyes dropped to the ground, unable to face him.

"Yes. There was a storm," he said.

"Okay. Did we happen to find anything down by the

lake? Anything . . . abnormal?" I asked, my eyes still searching the ground.

"Well, if you consider Trinity's body abnormal, then yes. We found something," he said.

"Oh, thank god!" I blurted, giving him another hug. Relief washed over me, and I *knew* I wasn't crazy. Walker made me feel normal. It was always him. Only him.

"Don't sound too excited now," he said, his eyes wide.

"No! I didn't mean it like that! I just meant . . ."

"I'm just messing with you, Wilde. I know what you meant."

I reluctantly pulled my arms off his neck and took a step back. "You do?" I asked.

"Let me guess, nobody seems to care this morning?" he asked, his golden eyes boring into mine as he tilted his head.

"How? How did you know that?"

"Remember? It's that Baylor phenomenon. Everybody makes you feel crazy here. It's just the way it is." Walker shrugged and began to walk down the trail. I followed quickly behind him without a thought.

"I think I know where Layla Barns is." I had to say it. If I didn't say it then, I was afraid I never would. Walker wanted to know more about what happened to Layla. It was tangled in his family history, and he sought answers. I couldn't blame him. And for whatever reason, my gran had sent me to help him get those answers. Furthermore, I needed to help the girl. For all I knew, Walker had been summoned to help her too. She wasn't dead like everyone had thought; she was hiding. Hiding in the stone tower like in the fairy tale. I was convinced of that.

"Where she *is*?" he asked.

"She's alive . . ." I said, grabbing his shoulders.

"Really? What makes you think so?" he asked.

I tried not to let the excitement in his voice distract me from telling him all I knew. But there was that small nagging voice that said, *He's too excited. He'll leave you the second you tell him what he is looking for.* I ignored it. Walker and I were friends, he wouldn't leave me.

"Yes. It just clicked. All the signs. Layla isn't buried in the cemetery with her lover, she's hiding. And I think she needs our help getting home. Have you ever seen a tower out here in the woods?" I asked.

"No. What kind of tower?"

"It's this really beautiful old stone tower. There's no door at the base, but there is a window at the very top. I saw it one time when I was looking for the graveyard. I've been looking for it all day, but it seems to be moving on me. I can't find it." I lifted my hand in the air, then let it fall.

"Ah, that happens here, too. Things go missing. They get turned around and spit back out in a different location. But that's okay. We can still find it. Just takes a little work." Walker was optimistic, and it was infectious. I nodded.

"Okay. And how are we going to do that?"

"Stop right there. And close your eyes," he said, placing his hands upon my shoulders. I gazed into his eyes before I closed my own. Completely at his mercy, I breathed deeply, feeling his warm hands on me and wishing they would travel. "Remember the Baylor phenomenon?"

"Yes," I said, with my eyes closed.

"It doesn't just work against us. It runs both ways. We can make it work for us too."

"Like magic?" I asked, scowling.

"Shhh. Now just *be*. Listen to my breath, inhale and exhale." He took in a deep audible breath and let it out. "Match yours to mine."

I listened, tuning out all the sounds from the forest. The little branches cracking, the birds chirping, and the subtle wind rustling through the leaves. It was harder to tune out his touch, but eventually, I shut that down too. I focused all my energy on his breathing. Matching my breaths to his was easy; not completely falling for him was another story.

"Now imagine the tower," he said. I didn't want to. I wanted to imagine his hands slipping down to the small of my back. I wanted to imagine his breath on my neck. I frowned. Why did I do this to myself? Why did I like a guy who would never like me back? And why was I pretending to summon a stone tower? It would never work.

"You're not focusing. You need to focus for this to

work," he said. I felt my cheeks warm, and I started over, drowning out the sounds of the forest and listening to his breathing. Then I imagined the tower as I had seen it before.

I could see the stone wall up to the window. I could see every single crack in the mortar, but more than seeing it, I could *feel* it. I could feel the cold, damp stone beneath my hands, and I could smell the moss on the stone.

"Now, imagine where it is," Walker said softly.

I didn't even have to think about it. I lifted my hand and pointed. It wasn't far. And it also wasn't where I had seen it last. My eyes shot open and narrowed on my pointed finger. There was no path before me, and I immediately doubted my telepathic skills. I cocked my head to the side and smiled at Walker, embarrassed for trying to be something I wasn't.

"Guess that didn't work," I said, wanting to shrink.

"What are you talking about? Of course it worked." Walker grabbed my hand and tugged me forward into the bushes where there had been no path before.

"Are you serious?" I asked, not paying attention to anything other than his hand holding mine. They fit together so perfectly. If I hadn't known any better, I would say we were meant for one another.

The bushes nipped at my legs as I tried to take large steps and tiny hops over them. "How far do you think it is?" he asked.

"Well, I mean, I don't think it was far, but that wasn't anything. I didn't *do* anything. We can't trust what just came up in my mind out of nowhere! This is ludicrous!" I said doubtfully. Somebody had to say it. Walker stopped and dropped my hand. Disappointed, I looked to the ground. My feet were hidden beneath the rapunzel bushes.

"Tell me this, Wilde . . . if I had closed my eyes and told you I had a gut feeling, would you think a thing of following it?" I imagined Walker telling me he had a gut feeling. Good lord, I'd follow his gut feeling anywhere. But I wasn't going to tell him that.

"But that's different—"

"How?"

It was a good question. I trusted him. I shrugged.

"Exactly. It's not different at all. You have to learn to trust yourself, Wilde. There are going to be times in your life when you can't trust anyone, and it's going to fall on you to take care of yourself. You need to show up for yourself." It was as if he was reading my thoughts. Could he do that? I looked up at him. And there was so much warmth behind his eyes in that moment, I almost *did* believe in myself. I nodded, and we trudged on through the thick bushes.

"Do you see all these purple flowers?" I asked, watching my feet disappear beneath the shrubs.

"The rampion? They're also known as rover bellflower."

"And rapunzel," I said before lifting my head to behold the stone tower. I stopped, and Walker looked back at me before lifting his gaze. He also seemed surprised to see it standing before us.

We both stood still, taking it in. It was a beautiful sight. Not the one I had seen before in the middle of the clearing. No, this time the tower was planted in the rocks at the water's edge. I had never seen it while out boating, but I wished I had. It was breathtaking. Walker looked back at me excitedly, and I felt like we had a small win. I smiled, the warmth of his eyes filling my chest. It was pride like I hadn't felt in a long time.

"Just like magic . . ." I whispered.

"See! I told you! You just have to believe in yourself!" he said, striding forward. I smiled to myself as I hopped over the bushes behind him. I guess I could do *something* right. This one small thing . . .

As we reached the tower, I was so overjoyed that I didn't realize at first that there was an actual door. But when Walker opened it and peeked his head inside, my brief pride was replaced with something pungent and cold. It was the familiar sorcery of insecurity. It felt like I was about to lose the only solid thing I had in my life. Because once we climbed those stairs, something bad was going to happen, and I was going to lose him.

Losing Walker wasn't the only thing I was afraid of. What happened when I found the girl? Layla. How was I supposed to help her? What was I to do? Was I really the chosen one for this particular mission? Or was I going to let my gran down? Somehow, I knew it was the latter. I couldn't do this. And if I could, it wouldn't be done right.

Walker urged me to hurry and join him. We climbed the steps, and I stayed close behind him. The tower was dark and cold. It must have dropped twenty degrees the moment we stepped inside. I reached out and touched Walker's back, and he grabbed my hand, holding it warmly and securely, giving me the strength to continue. We took the rest of the stairs together, and I never wanted it to end. Sure, my life had been hell since arriving at the cabin, but Walker made it right. Whatever was waiting for me at the top of the tower could wait a little longer because, in that moment, my hand in his, I finally felt whole, and I didn't want to let go of that.

# CHAPTER 24

The tower was cool and musty. We were losing daylight. It wasn't quite dark outside yet, but inside the stone walls, there was almost no light. With only one window at the very top, the spiral staircase was pitch black and ominous. I took the steps one at a time, slower than Walker would have liked. But, while he was eager to find answers, I didn't want this to end. Not just because I was afraid of failing, but because I was equally afraid of succeeding. Neither outcome worked in my favor.

Walker tightened his grip on my hand and gently urged me forward. I felt comfort knowing that he was right in front of me. I felt ahead with my foot, feeling for each step before I took it. My eyes were wide as I searched for light. The tension in the air loosened as we came up the last rung of the stairs and light from the sunset sky came through the single window. Pink and orange lit up the landing, and had the stakes not been so high, it would have been romantic.

Timidly, I walked to the middle of the open floor, slipping my hands into my back pockets and allowing my eyes to sweep the tower. There were no signs of the girl. Boards were piled up in the shadows, knickknacks stashed here and there. Trash and other belongings from transients that had sought shelter at one time or another. I wondered if we would run into the person who'd been sleeping here when my eyes landed on the burgundy leather jacket crumpled on the floor. *Trinity's jacket.*

"Whoa, what's that?" said Walker, grabbing my arm. I whipped my head around and followed his gaze up the tower wall. It was hard to see in the shadows, but I could make out numbers written in red paint across the rock. I took several steps forward, scrutinizing the sloppy numbers. It hit me like a ton of bricks. It was one through thirteen. The number one was crossed out in dripping red paint. At least, I hoped it was paint.

"What do you think it means?" he asked. He ran his fingers across the paint and then drew his hand back, examining the red chalky powder on his hand. I glanced back at Trinity's jacket.

"I've been seeing this in my dreams. I'm not sure what it means, but I have a theory."

"And what's that?"

"Well, it's always thirteen. And including myself and the dog, there's thirteen of us in the cabin. I never related it to people until one of the numbers was crossed off. It was only after Trinity went missing that a slash went through the number one. After that, I just had a feeling." More like a deep, sinking sense of doom in the pit of my stomach.

"I think it's kind of like a hit list of sorts. I think we all have a mark on our backs. It's stupid, and I have no proof. It's just a thought. A worry." I turned away from the red-painted numbers and looked out the window. In contrast, it was a beautiful view of the lake. I could see the crowd in the far distance waiting for the band to play at the Water's Edge Concert.

"You've seen this in your dreams?" Walker asked. Before I could answer him, a loud thump sounded from the base of the tower and echoed up the spiral stairwell, sending chills down my spine.

"What was that?" I whispered.

Walker made his way to me. At first, I assumed that it had been the wind slamming the door shut, or even an animal, but as the seconds ticked by, it became clear that what we heard were footsteps climbing the stairs. Not just any footsteps, but heavy, nefarious stomping that grew closer and closer. Much too heavy to be the Layla Barns I'd pictured in my head.

With each step, my heart pounded harder and my breath quickened. Walker slowly moved in front of me, spreading his arms in a protective stance. He had saved my life once before, and I didn't doubt he would try his best to do it again if necessary.

I craned my neck to look over his shoulder at the stairwell opening. A dark figure approached, and he was gigantic, both wide and tall. He grumbled to himself like a vicious animal—nothing intelligible. Just feral. There was a moment when he froze upon the landing and the three of us sized each other up. But this one man was bigger than the both of us combined. And once he realized it, he trudged forward. Walker took a step back, and I did too. And as he stepped into the sunset's rays, I recognized him from the grocery store. It was Big Jimmy.

He'd been unkempt the day I'd met him and looked even worse now. He didn't need to come any closer for me to know that he had gone off the rails. And even through the dimming pink light, I could see the ill intent in his eyes. I didn't dare look away. He looked toward his stash of belongings. The empty liquor bottles, broken wood pallets, and Trinity's jacket. I remembered the stories around the campfire at Sampson's house. They'd said he was crazy. They'd said he'd hurt people. A liability, they'd called him. And now, we were in his hideout, and we had seen too much.

Jimmy pulled something from his belt buckle, and a switchblade flipped, catching the light from the window. I failed to swallow the lump rising in my throat. Jimmy held it out as if he were ready to strike, stab, and rip from top to bloody bottom.

"Jimmy! Jimmy, it's me. We met one time at the grocery store. Do you remember me?" I asked, trying to think of something to snap him from the trance he seemed to be in. Like a dog on point, he took another step forward, slow and stealthy. If he was the dog, we were the flock he was targeting.

"You gone and done it now, didn't you?" His voice was deep and gravelly.

"Did what?" I asked, taking another step back in unison with Walker.

"You went a-looking, didn't you?" He tossed the blade in the air and caught it again, his eyes never leaving us.

"Looking for what, Jimmy?" I asked, grabbing the backs of Walker's arms.

"You're looking for her. The girl!" he yelled, and a deep red flesh colored his neck and into his face.

"We're not looking for anybody! We just found this tower, and we were curious, but we'll be on our way now."

I took a step from behind Walker, but Jimmy called my bluff and lunged. I let out a yelp and jumped backward. But there was no more room, and my back slammed against the stone wall. Jimmy continued and Walker jumped in front of me, tackling him.

There was no fight—not even a chance. Jimmy threw Walker to the ground and continued coming for me. But

Walker kicked out and snagged his leg, and Jimmy went down with a thud.

I tried to run, but Jimmy kicked his giant foot and caught me in the stomach. All the air went out of my lungs, and I dropped to my knees.

I was only vaguely aware of the scuffle that was taking place feet away from me; my focus was on taking my next breath. My arms were wrapped tightly around my stomach, my mouth open and hungry for air.

"I told you! I told you! The butcher will come back!" Jimmy yelled as Walker did everything in his power to keep him from me. "I told you! And now you're gonna pay!"

I had just gotten a foot underneath me to stand as Jimmy ran at me with the knife. And as I began to get up, Walker slammed into Jimmy's back. The three hundred-plus pounds of Big Jim tripped over me as I rose, and the force of his weight couldn't be stopped as he tumbled forward. He bashed into the wall and out the window of the tower. I was smashed to the floor, trampled by his momentum. What once was a tiny window that had barely let the light of the sunset slip into the shadows was now a gaping hole in the side of the tower.

Having been kicked again in the ribs, I lay across the floor of the tower gasping for air. The pain was muted by shock. I knew the threat was gone by the lifting of tension in the air, but I didn't quite realize what had happened until I looked at Walker. His hands were on top of his knees, and he was drawing in quick, shallow breaths. His forehead was creased, and his eyes were large with surprise. I looked out the window, the only viable exit, and I saw the multitude of missing stones. I scrambled to my feet, placing one hand around my waist and one on the cold rock wall, and peered out the gaping window.

Big Jimmy lay sprawled across the rocks below, the gentle water lapping at his limbs.

I sucked in a breath and whipped my head around toward Walker. "We killed him!"

I said it. I said it out loud. But just because it was true, didn't mean I was ready to accept it. Hearing myself say it was like an accusation. And even though it was self-defense, I knew my life would never be the same. Because I had killed a man.

"Wilde!" Walker whispered, his eyes not on the body below, but on the wall of the tower. I followed his gaze to the red-stained numbers upon the stone. Ever so slowly, a red slash etched its way through the number two, sending an electric tingle inching down my spine.

Neither one of us had any words. We stared in disbelief, panting. When the red paint had stopped dripping down the wall, the music began across the lake at the Water's Edge Concert.

"Thirteen people? Thirteen people have a mark on their back?" Walker asked.

I pressed my back against the stone wall and my knees trembled under the limp weight of my body. I slumped down to the floor, wrapping my arms around my knees and starting to tremble. At least . . . at least it wasn't only the people in my cabin that had the mark. Perhaps it was thirteen Baylor residents or visitors. Maybe it was at random.

"Wilde? Are you okay?" he asked. I nodded curtly. But I *wasn't* okay. Nothing was okay. I'd killed a man. I had crashed a plane. And now eleven more people were going to die—and for what? I raised my eyes to see Walker's concern in the fine lines around his eyes. He didn't seem to be rattled by what had happened here this evening, and that should've concerned me more . . . but I sought comfort in his warm eyes. His face softened with a smile and I sucked in a deep, refreshing breath.

"I'm sorry we didn't find what we were looking for here. I don't know what I was thinking. This girl, Layla. I kind of imagined her with the long locks of blonde hair flowing from this broken window down to the base of the tower, but it was nothing more than a fairy tale." I shook my head, my eyes wandering around the small landing.

"Don't apologize. It's not your fault we didn't find the girl. Maybe she doesn't exist anymore. Who knows? But if it's okay with you, I'd like to keep looking for her, with your help. I've gotten closer in the last few days with you than I ever have before. And I've been following this case for a long time." His eyes stared unfixed into the distance and his face fell with disappointment.

"Why is that? Why do you care so much? You have to give me some answers here." I said, looking up at him. He took a seat next to me and propped his forearms on top of his knees, interlacing his fingers.

"I . . ." Walker stammered, his gaze pensive and sad.

It felt like I'd asked the wrong questions. I knew there were secrets between us, but I never knew when something I said would draw out his pain. The tower was silent except for the country music echoing across the lake. I knew he didn't want to talk about it, but I needed to know who the butcher was, and why he was so invested. I'd promised my gran I would help him, and Layla, but I didn't even know what I was supposed to help them with. My eyes fell on the pile of stashed goods that were hidden within the shadows as I thought of how I'd failed to keep my promise to my gran.

"Long ago, I made a promise to help the girl, too. You're not the only one getting messages to bring her home," Walker said in a defeated tone.

"Really? Why didn't you say so?" I asked.

"I was afraid you wouldn't help if you knew the truth," he said.

"Why? What truth?" I couldn't imagine a reason to not help Walker look for Layla, especially after he had saved my life. I owed him so much.

Walker frowned. He tried to speak, but nothing came out.

"Who are you getting messages from?"

His brows creased and he dropped his head in his hands.

"Are they dreams, like mine?" I asked. But he didn't move, and he didn't speak. Why was he keeping secrets from me? Why wouldn't he just talk to me? I sighed. I couldn't go on like this. And I wouldn't leave this tower until my questions were answered.

Something stole my attention away from Walker's silence. I squinted into the darkness. "What's that?" I asked, nodding to the pile of Jimmy's stolen possessions. Something was lying in the shadows. Another personal item. But this one wasn't Trinity's. Walker jumped to his feet and picked it up. It was a purse. He turned it over in his hands, and I watched him intently.

"That's Trinity's jacket," I said. Walker looked back at me and swallowed, turning his gaze back to the bag. He didn't say anything. "But that's not her purse. I've never seen that before."

He stood there, rigid. After a long moment of silence, he came to sit by my side again. He handed me the purse and looked away, running a hand through his disheveled hair.

I pulled the zipper across the top of the bag and peered inside. I pulled out a small silver compact, tickets to the

Summerfield State Fair, and a wallet. But something seemed off. The *tickets* were off. I scoured the fine print.

"These tickets are twenty years old! I can't believe this has been sitting up here for that long," I said, opening the wallet. Walker had no interest in looking at the compact or the ancient tickets. I didn't know if he was upset that we hadn't found Layla or that we had just murdered a guy, but either were feasible options. I continued to examine the wallet. I pulled out the ID of a beautiful girl. Luxurious long brunette hair and ruby red lips. But there was one thing even more striking than her looks, and that was her name. *Layla Barns.*

"Oh my god!" I said in a whisper. Walker turned even farther away.

It was all coming true. All my hard work, my premonitions, Gran's hints. I was meant to find this, and I'd been drawn straight to her belongings. I hadn't found the girl, but I had found a clue, and that was something. It was the first tangible clue. A step closer to understanding what all this was about.

"Oh my god! Walker! We found it. It's Layla's!" I said, holding out her ID. But for reasons I couldn't understand, he didn't want to look at it. I shook his arm, but he didn't budge. He hid his face in the depths of the shadows. I tried to read him, but I could only see the dim outline of his jaw. A tear caught the last of the light, sparkling at the top of his cheek, and ran down into the scruff where his dimples lay dormant. It wasn't the time for more of my questions, though I had them piling up by the dozens. It hurt me to see him like this, and it hurt to know that there was nothing I could do to help.

Slowly, I turned my attention back to the identification and flipped it back to reveal a personal photo of Layla and her boyfriend. Only this wasn't a boyfriend from twenty years ago, this was Walker St. James. *Now.*

My stomach dropped. Sucking in a sharp breath of air, I felt woozy and confused.

Walker wiped the tear from his cheek. "I wanted to tell you. I just . . . I didn't know how," he said. A million thoughts ran through my head, and I was unable to settle on any one in particular.

"I love her . . ." It was the only thing he could say, and it was full of nothing but honest pain.

I tried to pull the few things I understood together, but like a puzzle, pieces were missing. "I knew you had a girlfriend. Not right away, but eventually. And I knew you wanted to find Layla Barns. Probably as much as I did," I stated the facts, not for him, but for me to hear out loud. "But for the life of me, Walker, I just can't figure out how these two things go together." A tremble racked my body like an aftershock. I looked at him, but he was still shying away.

"Now, you just told me that you love her, and I'm trying to understand how you're in this twenty-year-old photo. Because when I look at you and I look at this photo, you're exactly the same."

"Isn't it obvious?" Walker asked, looking at me for the first time since we found the purse. The red in his eyes matched the dying sunset.

A nervous chuckle escaped me, "No! Not unless you're a ghost!" I blurted, half-joking half not. But when Walker's dimples failed to make an appearance and his gaze ran cold, an unsettled feeling seized my chest, holding it captive. Because I knew that this was no joking matter.

"You're . . . You're?" I clambered to my feet, the tiny hairs on the back of my neck rising. *Impossible . . .*

I stuck my head through the broken wall in search of fresh air to help clear my mind. A light breeze lifted a loose strand of hair and tickled my neck. My heart galloped in my chest as Walker slowly climbed to his feet, careful not to spook me any further. He rested his elbows on the edge of the stone and gazed out into the darkening sky.

I don't know how long we stayed like that, silently staring into the distance, but the shock wasn't wearing off. The sunlight had fully dissipated, and the artificial concert lights were glowing just beyond the lake. There were too many questions in my head. Was it possible that they canceled each other out? An odd calmness blanketed my mind. *He was a ghost . . .* There was a gnawing feeling inside me, and I was shocked that it wasn't dripping with fear, but curiosity. How? When?

This strange soul beside me—the one that had captured my heart—was not only taken but . . . but he wasn't even alive. He was a spirit. He was a phantom. I turned to him and let my eyes wander over his hair, his lips, his jawline that met the collar of his flannel. Unafraid, I reached out, grabbing his bicep, and when he looked at me with that longing, it hurt to know that he wasn't aching for me but for her. Maybe even his past life.

"How is this possible? You're real. You're solid. I can feel you. You saved me—" I could have gone on forever, but thankfully, he didn't let me.

"How did you not know, Wilde? There were so many signs. I kept waiting for you to notice, but you never did," he said, tears pricked his eyes.

"Signs? What signs?" I asked.

"You see your gran, and she's no longer here. That should have been your first sign." His voice was soft, sympathetic. This hurt him as much as it did me.

My eyes widened. I really *had* lost my wits. This was it. This was my new reality. I, Kinsley Wilde, was some sort of clairvoyant. I saw dead people, and I conjured fears.

"Yes. That probably should have been a clue. I . . . I guess I can see beyond the veil."

Walker ran his hand through his hair, shaking his head and sighing heavily. My eyes trailed back out to the concert, though I could barely hear the music over my shock.

I thought back to Layla's headstone resting in the forest. I guess she was dead after all. I felt the disappointment wash over me for failing my gran. How was I supposed to find her now? How could I help her if she had already crossed over? I thought back to Walker and how he'd plucked me from the lake the night we'd met. I supposed Layla would find me, now that I was a magnet for the paranormal.

I thought back to the day I'd looked beside Layla's grave and knew her lover was resting next to her. But how had I known that? An extension of the memory surfaced. One I'd forgotten, possibly on purpose. I wafted the heavy blanket of fog with my hands to uncover the name, Walker St. James, etched on the headstone next to hers. I felt sick to my stomach. Light in the head. Woozy. Like I was about to pass out. How had I forgotten that? It was so extremely important, how had I forgotten it? Or more importantly, why had I hid it from myself?

I rested my forearms on the window next to Walker's, trying to steady my breathing and strengthen my weak knees. "So, if you are Layla's love, then you *are* the butcher?" I asked.

"No. I told you, that's just an old wives' tale that followed a tragic love story. *My* love story," he said.

"If the butcher isn't real, then who killed Trinity?" I asked. Walker's eyes dipped down to the ground.

"Oh." I glanced down at Jimmy's remains and

swallowed a lump in my throat and nodded. There was no real butcher of Baylor Lake, but there was a killer. It was justice. A life for a life. I hadn't done that to him; he'd done it to himself.

Shoulder to shoulder, we watched the concert from the best view in town. My thoughts were lost in space, beyond my grasp. I paid no attention to the body below, and I caught myself thinking that it was romantic. It felt that way. It felt like it could be. And it was far better than acknowledging the truth. The truth that I could somehow see beyond the veil. See the dead. And perhaps even fall for one of these special souls.

I had just tripped a man who had then fallen to his death. He lay dead on the rocks in the shallow water below. I had fallen for a guy who wasn't even alive. And I could tell that, somewhere inside of me, there was evil waiting to seep out. And with it came a great power, one I had yet to fully understand. I didn't know myself as well as I thought I did.

"Hey, Wilde?" Walker asked. I looked at him, and his eyes reached deep inside me, seeming to clench my heart. I wasn't afraid, only saddened that this extraordinary soul was no longer a part of my reality—and that one day, he would have to leave me behind. The day that I helped him find Layla would be the day he'd rest in peace. And the last day I'd have the honor of knowing him.

"Yes?" I asked, my tone breathy and laced with a desire

that was impossible to fulfill. My heart was a bottomless well next to his.

"You know . . ." Walker winced as if it pained him to say.

"Just say it."

"You know you're dead too, right?"

# THANK YOU

Thank you for taking the time to read Phantom Reality.

**Please take a moment to write a review. It's _so_ important for a book to have social proof, and I'd love your help getting this series out there.**

Want to find out what happens next? Read Dark Reflections.

For more information, subscribe here:
https://www.subscribepage.com/redenbooks

Xoxo,
Laura

# ABOUT THE AUTHOR

Laura C. Reden is an emerging paranormal and fantasy author.

Overcoming the struggles of dyslexia, Laura found that creative passion and hard work triumphs over her disadvantage.

Laura is a Southern Californian native, wife, and mother of two daughters. Her pastimes include video production, pottery, and horseback riding. While she received an education in social and behavioral science, she currently works as the chief financial officer for her family-owned law firm in San Diego.

If you are interested in staying updated on new releases, subscribe to my monthly email list. It's short and sweet with opportunities to help name characters, get advanced review copies, and even have your pet featured in upcoming scenes.

https://www.subscribepage.com/redenbooks

Xoxo,

Laura


BB bookbub.com/authors/laura-c-reden

a amazon.com/kindle-dbs/entity/author/B08L1KH3LM

# ALSO BY

YOU'VE HEARD THE TERM «OLD SOUL» BEFORE,
BUT WHAT IF SOME SOULS NEVER REALLY DIE?

# THE TETHERED SOUL SERIES

FOLLOW THE TRAGIC TALE OF A DYING GIRL,
AND BOY WITH AN IMMORTAL SOUL.

# LAURA C. REDEN

DREAMS ARE FICKLE, EMOTIONS ARE BOLD.

# THE
# PHANTOM SERIES

CAUGHT BETWEEN WORLDS,
KINSLEY WILDE CAN SEE THE DEAD,
MANIFEST HER DREAMS, AND CONJURE HER FEARS.

# NOTES FOR BOOK CLUB:

# NOTES FOR BOOK CLUB:

www.ingramcontent.com/pod-product-compliance
Lightning Source LLC
Chambersburg PA
CBHW061044190726
48286CB00006B/1600